ALEXANDER GRIGORENKO

MEBET

ИНСТИТУТ ПЕРЕВОДА

AD VERBUM

PUBLISHED WITH THE SUPPORT
OF THE INSTITUTE FOR LITERARY TRANSLATION, RUSSIA

MEBET

by Alexander Grigorenko

Translated from the Russian by Christopher Culver

Proofreading by Maria Badanova

Publishers Maxim Hodak & Max Mendor

Book cover and interior design by Max Mendor

Published with the support
of the Institute for Literary Translation, Russia

© 2020, Alexander Grigorenko
Agreement by www.nibbe-wiedling.com

© 2020, Glagoslav Publications

www.glagoslav.com

ISBN: 978-1-912894-90-1
ISBN: 978-1-912894-91-8

First published in English
by Glagoslav Publications on November 16, 2020

A catalogue record for this book is available from the British Library.

This book is in copyright. No part of this publication may be reproduced, stored in a retrieval system or transmitted in any form or by any means without the prior permission in writing of the publisher, nor be otherwise circulated in any form of binding or cover other than that in which it is published without a similar condition, including this condition, being imposed on the subsequent purchaser.

ALEXANDER GRIGORENKO

MEBET

Translated from the Russian by Christopher Culver

GLAGOSLAV PUBLICATIONS

CONTENTS

PREFACE 7

THE FAVORITE OF THE GODS WHO IS A LAW UNTO HIMSELF . . . 9

THE BLIZZARD MAN 14

THE BETROTHAL 18

THE REVENGE OF THE PYAK CLAN 21

THE ONE-EYED WITCH 26

MEBET'S TOKENS OF APPRECIATION 31

THE BLIZZARD WOMAN 38

THE WAR REINDEER 41

FORKED ARROW 49

MEBET'S GLORY 59

HADKO'S WEDDING 63

SEVSER IS BORN 79

HADKO'S DEATH 86

THE SHADOW DANCE 89

THE SANCTUARY 94

THE MOTHER 97

MEBET'S BIRTH 98

THE PATH OF THUNDER 106

THE FIRST CHUM: THE KOY 108

THE SECOND CHUM: THE REKKEN 111

THE THIRD CHUM: THE SPIRITS OF RESENTMENT	113
THE THREE LARGE CHUMS	117
THE SEVENTH CHUM: THE DEAD ARMY	124
THE GODS INTERFERE	131
THE LAST BATTLE	139
THE WOMEN'S CHUM	143
THE LAST CHUM: YEZANGA	148
THE VISION	164
MEBET'S MORNING	167
AFTERWORD BY SEVSER	170

PREFACE

The taiga has no history. It does have a memory, however, which persists in half-fantastical legends and tales. Even the stories which claim to be accounts from those who personally participated in great events or witnessed them firsthand – such as the migration of the ancestors of the Yakuts from Lake Baikal to the Lena River – rather resemble folktales. The white man has sought for centuries now to painstakingly sift these fantastical stories for useful material, to melt them down into hard historical facts, perhaps not of a great quantity but at least an acceptable one. Thanks to the white man for this. Nevertheless, deep inside he understands that there is a good share of absurdity to his efforts. Europeans' reason goes astray, dies among the legends handed down in the taiga. It cannot survive in this boundless space, made sacred by blood, which does not obey numbers and figures. The peoples of this ocean of green live in such a way that yesterday and events of a century ago can stand side by side. The Red Army marches into the Mansi villages immediately in the wake of the Vikings. An old Evenki man waits for an appointed meeting not with the aid of a clock or calendar, but by the crackling of a wedge driven into an old pine log. The inhabitants of this world include spirits and deities just as much as forest animals and people. The poor Nanai man Dersu, who killed a tiger in his youth, saw no difference between a man and an animal, and therefore his conscience tormented him for the rest of his life.

Scholars have scrupulously recorded a great many of the countless remarkable things here, and explained their import and their sources, but they remain exotica, something that one can marvel at, even sympathize with, but nevertheless something that one cannot really grasp.

Yet in human history the taiga has played its role, an invisible one that has not been subject to description. For millennia this ocean of green has absorbed bits of the clashes that have raged in the civilized worlds of Europe and Asia, and yet it has given nothing in exchange, it has cast nothing ashore – it has turned everything into a mystery, an enigma, an undecipherable text. It may be that this is why the taiga remains the only expanse on the earth where human strivings have yet to be explained, and here a person can look forward to the most remarkable and crucial encounter of all: coming face to face with himself.

Alexander Grigorenko

THE FAVORITE OF THE GODS WHO IS A LAW UNTO HIMSELF

Mebet, of the Vela clan, won glory from an early age through his strength and bravery.

No one could best him in games, in fighting, in racing, in the hunt, or in battle. At the bear feast, he could leap over a hundred sleds, and when he was invited to participate in feats of strength, none were willing to vie with him. Never was anyone able to defeat Mebet, whose very name meant "The Strong One."

He was orphaned early on, but he did not go to live with his kin. He remained on his parents' hunting grounds and dwelt there alone. Mebet did not invite companions for the hunt, he did not need anyone's help – he chased elk on his own, and he walked alone in pursuit of the bear. He caught a great many birds. Whenever he was in need, fortune shone on him like a sun that never set beyond the horizon to rise up again. He was a carefree sort, like one who knows that his strength is stronger even than fate.

It happened that Mebet slew an animal in a patch of the taiga that belonged to others, where the Ivsha and Pyaki hunted, and he took his catch into the tundra, into the lands of the Yaptik, Vaynot, and Okotetta clans. When they came to him and reproached him for violating the laws of hunting, Mebet smiled and replied that the beast was free to run wherever it pleased, and Mebet was not to blame for that. His smile came from a position of strength and could make other men ashamed of their own weakness, and this time no one thought to raise his weapon.

But it happened that one day, five men from the Ivsha clan set out against Mebet. In their territory they had found blood on the snow and they followed it in order to catch the thief and hold him to justice. When they had reached the hunter, they saw that it was Mebet, hauling a slain deer on his light sled.

The Ivsha men raised their bows and shouted to him, "Leave the deer, it is ours. You killed it on our land."

Mebet turned and said to them, "Let us reach an agreement, kinsmen. You leave me my quarry, and I will let you keep your lives."

"What kinsman are you to us?" one of the men said, without even waiting for an answer. "You deign to walk through others' land as if it were your own."

Then one of the Ivsha, still quite a young lad who had just started to hunt with his elders and so now swelled with a silly, childish pride, shouted out, "He is making fun of us. There are five of us and he is alone. What are you waiting for?"

The youngling was first to let his arrow fly, seeking to hit the hated thief directly in his face. But Mebet shrugged at death like shooing a horsefly away, with the same gesture. The arrow bounced off a tree and into the snow. He caught the second arrow in its flight and broke it in two, and the third arrow missed him entirely – the shooter's hands were clearly shaking. Two of the Ivsha men stood frozen with their weapons raised, still unable to fire off a shot.

Amid the silence, Mebet's bowstring twanged its brief and terrible song. In a very short instant, as short as the cracking of a twig, he had let three arrows fly and now three of the Ivsha men dropped down into the snow, howling with pain in their struck legs.

"Maybe we should reach an agreement," Mebet proposed again. "You give me the deer and I let you keep your lives."

The Ivsha men said nothing in reply.

Mebet picked up the strap of his sled, turned to them, and said:

"I was sure that you would agree. I wish you good hunting, kinsmen."

Then he walked away without a backward glance.

The Ivsha men kept quiet about this episode to the other clans; it was embarrassing that the five of them were unable to overcome a single man. However, just as time passed, so did their shame. Soon among the people of the taiga and of the tundra, there was no one who had not heard of Mebet, who could catch arrows in mid-flight and was therefore a law unto himself.

Thus he lived his life, young and contented. Even the gods would not unleash their wrath upon such a fortunate fellow. He could get away with everything: the gods had played a sort of game, granting to one mortal man the right to not submit to what all others had to submit to. With Mebet's impeccable luck the gods were toying with mankind, and it pained people to look at his unprecedented way of living. The distrust and envy of other people led them to dub this man of the clan of Vela "The Gods' Favorite" and he bore this moniker until the end of his days. But the most astonishing thing of all is that Mebet gave no more honor to the spirits than to his fellow mortal men, though he never outright blasphemed against the gods, as often happens among simple people when they are hounded by failure.

The Gods' Favorite occasionally came to the great feasts when large numbers of people came together. The girls and young women hid from him, afraid of being punished by their fathers or husbands for the brazen look that would appear on their faces, unwillingly, when they caught sight of Mebet. He exceeded all others in height by a head, he was stout with firm limbs, his hair and eyes shone, and he had slender, nearly imperceptible cheekbones.

But the old women said that no woman, impressed though she might be by this handsome man of the Vela clan, would readily agree to enter his dwelling, for so different was Mebet from the other men whom the women of the taiga (and their mothers, and their mothers' mothers) had known. If people did not still remember Mebet's mother and father, they would probably have considered him a foundling child left by some mysterious foreign race. There was a time, the elders said, when many outsiders came passing through the taiga, but that had happened so long ago that no one among the living still remembered those peoples or even their names.

There were rumors that Mebet's mother had been seduced by one of the gods, and to stop her husband from killing her when this deception was found out, the spirits drove him into the swamp where he drowned. This happened when Mebet's mother was carrying him and complaining to her kinsfolk about how unbearably heavy her belly was. Mebet knew about these stories and said nothing to dispute them. He thought little of success and glory, for these things came to him of their own accord and therefore were valued nothing. He mostly preferred to think about himself, and with time this became one of his chief pleasures.

Once, people sought to rebuke the Gods' Favorite:

"If you are so strong, then why don't you have wealth and a lofty title? You could become a great leader, the greatest who has even lived or will ever live."

Mebet thanked them for these words of praise but said nothing in reply.

This made the people upset:

"You look down on us, and you fail to show respect even to the most esteemed among us."

"Do those most esteemed so lack in appreciation from the many that the disrespect of one man offends them?" he asked them.

Then the people began to seethe with anger and indignation:

"You slay animals in the territory of others. You take what does not belong to you. You are a thief."

After these words were spoken, the smile vanished from Mebet's face, but he answered them in the same calm voice:

"A person takes as much as his strength and mind allow. A baby cannot pursue a beast day after day, it has only enough strength to reach for its mother's breast. A strong man will not stoop to catch the mice that scurry in the earth around his feet, for that would not be worthy of his strength. And what is not worthy of his strength, lessens his strength. Any tribe or people won their territory through their own strength, for those who know how to hunt and show bravery in war will never receive less than they deserve. Therefore, I have taken nothing of other people's things, but only my own."

The people had nothing to answer to that.

In the year when Mebet turned twenty, there was a large bear feast. Mebet alone, without anyone to help him, caught a bear and feasted within the circle of the elders. It even seemed as if Mebet's company was an honor for the elders and not the other way around. Mebet ate little and did not contribute to the conversation. He stood up before the others did and, taking leave of them with a slight bow, he went to watch the people wrestling in the snow and measuring their strength against one another. The smile did not disappear from his face, a face that was magnificent like a vision from another world.

The more kindly disposed said that Mebet's pride was due to his youth. Many suspected that that pride would simply fade along with his youth.

As the Gods' Favorite was walking around, he heard a voice behind him say, "Hey, little one, come here."

Mebet turned and saw an old man lying on his side on a skin spread out next to a big sled. The old man clearly wanted to stand up, but he was unable to.

"Help me get onto my sled. My legs don't work."

Mebet picked the old man up and gently set him on the sled.

The old man stared at Mebet for a long time, as if he could not take in enough of this unfamiliar young man's healthy appearance. Then, his eyes still on Mebet, he suddenly said:

"You're a fool, young one."

"Why is that, sir?" Mebet asked him in a genial tone.

"You aren't even aware that your heart is being broken. One can find all things on earth and in heaven, except for a heart which never breaks."

The Gods' Favorite laughed and walked away.

Another thirty years of his life passed, and his heart had never broken. In his life he had experienced many things that would make a man tremble and faint. Yet Mebet never trembled, never fainted, and he often thought back to the old man and his empty prophecy. As the years went by, the Gods' Favorite never lost his strength: he could still catch arrows in mid-flight and he needed no companions on the hunt.

THE BLIZZARD MAN

Two months after that feast, Mebet married. He abducted the bride, for he thought that abducted girls serve as a sign of a man's strength, and therefore they were better than wives married according to convention. He had often assisted his peers in such abductions, not out of friendship as much as for the simple amusement, and eventually people came to think that every instance of bridal abduction was Mebet's work.

The girl whom he chose was a beautiful one. But her father had capriciously given her a man's name: Yadne (which means the One Who Goes by Foot), and this had frightened all ordinary suitors away from his daughter. Young men feared that along with this unladylike name, they would bring into their homes an unfeminine and uncanny power. Mebet scoffed at such superstitions, and it was Yadne whom he came to favor.

Only when it came to children did he prove unlucky. Each year his wife would bear a girl, but these daughters died one after another, either still in infancy or at an early age. Mebet wanted to send this wife away and take another, but before he made a final decision to do so, Yadne again fell pregnant and bore him a son.

In the month of winds, when it becomes impossible to tell the earth and sky apart due to the all-encompassing snow, Mebet stepped into the chum, though the tent-like dwelling was considered unclean now that a woman had given birth within, and he picked up the little baby's wet and wailing body. He held it for a brief moment, handed the child back to his wife, and then left without saying a word.

Hadko, or the Blizzard Man, was the name that the Gods' Favorite chose for this son and heir.

As he grew, he proved a good son. At the age of twelve he brought a wolf home, and at seventeen he caught an elk. True, he was unable to hide his catch in the proper way, and so the meat was plundered by some forest animal. Still, Mebet was pleased, and only one thing troubled his heart: Hadko had not inherited his father's magnificent features. He was strong and stately, but he had prominent cheekbones and dark eyes like his mother. Worse yet, he heeded the laws of other men: he would stop pursuing an animal when it ran into the territory of other clans, he would not fish in rivers belonging to others, he respected the shaman and, whenever he was among a multitude of people, he would bow deeply to his elders. It brought the Gods' Favorite no pleasure to see this, but he did not reproach his son.

Whether Mebet's mother had lain with one of the gods or not remained only a rumor, though it was close to the truth. But no one had any doubt that Hadko was born to an ordinary man. Soon Mebet was convinced that his son feared violating human customs more than he feared any beast – whenever Hadko went hunting, he was calm and composed, and he proved successful more often than not.

At a feast the Blizzard Man caught sight of a lovely girl from the Pyak clan. He started to ask his father to visit her parents and speak with them about arranging a betrothal and the paying of the bride-price.

"Do you really like this girl?" Mebet asked him.

"Yes, father, I really do."

"You love her?"

"Yes, I love her."

"Are you prepared to make her your wife, so that she would bear you children, and are you prepared to sustain her and protect her?"

"I would do anything for her. I will not let any spirit or beast get close to her."

The Gods' Favorite kept his blue eyes on the dark, shining eyes of his son, as if he was seeking to find there any common traits. His son however sought in his father's eyes only an answer, and he prayed to the heavens that the answer would be yes.

After a long silence Mebet said:

"If you love this girl and you are prepared to protect her all her life from spirits and beasts, is that not the bride-price? Isn't your desire to be with her greater than two or three dozen reindeer that are spread over the taiga or tundra for the benefit of whoever can catch them? Beasts wear their hides so that you can take them whenever you have the desire to do so. So why should you need to pay any bride-price, then? Merely to please old man Pyak, who is greedy like everyone else?"

Hadko's gaze dimmed and became dull like the water from melted snow.

"Father, give me a small portion of your herd," he asked quietly, almost in a whisper.

Mebet refused. "Do you want me to take this woman for a wife?"

Hadko thought that he had understood what his father wished, but he had been wrong.

"No," Mebet said. "I am not opposed to your marrying her. She really is beautiful, I can see that. Go and take her, and bring her to our camp. I will accept her as if she were my own bride and I will treat her kindly. Just do not ask me for any deer, let alone any beads, or hides, or copper pots. You know that I would readily pay the price for anything, just not for the weakness of my own son."

"What should I do?"

"Do whatever you want. I have said my piece, but I will not get in your way. You have long since taken seven steps from your father, so why do you need my counsel?"

Thus they parted. For several days Hadko did not say a word, he dedicated himself feverishly to all the work that was assigned to him. His mother would ask what had happened between him and his father, but she did not expect to hear an answer. Yadne herself was afraid of bringing the subject up with her husband: the Gods' Favorite never raised his voice at his wife, but he never spoke with her unless it was about something urgent.

However, over these days, as Mebet looked at his glum son, he felt a burden lifted from his heart, for he could tell that a young and taut anger was ripening within Hadko.

One day his son went off into the taiga without telling anyone. When he vanished, so did a new spear, three dozen arrows, a reindeer, a sled, and Mebet's best dog. Hadko had set off on a long campaign and though several days had passed and it was now the new moon, he had not returned. His mother was tormented by the thought that he would never come back. At night Yadne would weep. Mebet kept silent, but when he had finally had enough of his wife's lamentations, he grabbed her by the chin and told her quietly:

"Do you think that you can draw him out of the taiga with your howling, like people lure birds out of the marsh by playing a flute?"

Then, after a pause, he added in a condescendingly gentle air:

"He has some of my blood within him. That is enough to get him back home safely. Don't cry, you will only do him something ill."

Hadko returned when the cold in the taiga began giving way to wind and snow. His skin was blackened by the frozen air and from fatigue, and he drove a sled that was heaped with catch: elk meat, fox and marten skins. His mother came rushing to meet him, but her son walked blindly past her outstretched arms and stumbled into the chum. He slept for two whole days.

When he finally awoke, he greedily downed a great deal of food, accepting all that his mother offered him. Yadne sat opposite him and wept almost inaudibly.

Mebet did not greet Hadko nor did he enter the chum where his son was recuperating after such a great hunt. Hadko expected to bear his father's wrath, but his own young and bright anger had still not died out. It was with a light heart and fearlessness that he came forth from the chum to meet his father.

Mebet stood in the middle of the encampment with his arms across his chest. When his son had come up to him and stopped an outstretched arm's distance away, expecting a blow or a harsh word to come, the Gods' Favorite took something from his chest and offered it to Hadko. It was a knife of exquisite craftsmanship, large with a curved blade of blue metal, like a crescent moon, and it was kept in a sheath made from leather and white bone.

Hadko's hands trembled, and the anger within him died. He wanted to fall to his knees, but Mebet grabbed him by the sleeve of his deerskin:

"Take it, it is yours now. You are a grown hunter now. You can take my new spear. And take my bow as well, it will serve you well."

This was all too much for Hadko and he collapsed at his father's feet nevertheless.

Mebet smiled and went to his chum. As he pushed the flap over the entrance aside, he turned to his son and said:

"Did Voipel obey you? After all, he obeys only me…"

"He served as my eyes, my nose, my hands, and my will," Hadko replied. Tears were flowing down his cheeks, but he did not even notice them or raise a hand to wipe them away.

"Voipel is yours now," Mebet said and disappeared into the chum.

The north wind, which rages fiercely and fearsomely and can blow through anything, is what the word *voipel* designated, and it was the name given to Mebet's best dog, which was recognized as the king among the dogs of the taiga and tundra. Other dogs knew that any fight with this broad-chested, shaggy monster with icy blue eyes could only end in death. Once they caught wind of this dread foe, they would flee from their owners. The threat of being hanged with a belt frightened them less than Voipel's fangs.

Mebet's dog was all around good in anything to do with hunting, large migrations, and battle.

THE BETROTHAL

The next morning, Hadko and Mebet set off with their two sleighs into the taiga, so that they could bring a hidden part of Hadko's catch back to their camp. This was namely the remains of an elk and two deer which Hadko had killed when he was only a short distance from the camp. The Blizzard Man had proved capable of hanging the meat from the branches of huge pine trees so that it could not be plundered by wolves. It warmed Mebet's heart to see that his son had inherited his strength. Soon this joy was mixed with pride: the deer hides were branded with red arrows, the mark of the Ivsha clan. They marked their war reindeer with a red arrow. As Mebet loaded his sled with this catch, he thought that his son's dark eyes might not be alien to his at all, only different. After all, no one knows exactly how those favored by the gods are supposed to look. And no one knew how many in this world might have been granted freedom from human custom, and yet could retain their strength and good fortune. It pleased Mebet to reflect on this, he enjoyed these musings until sundown and fell asleep calm and content.

The next day, Mebet left the chum early in the morning and found his son engaged in an odd activity that he was not able to make sense of right away, so astonished was he. Hadko was tying red ribbons to his sled, which was heaped with his catch from the great hunt. The same red ribbons fluttered in the brisk wind on the horns of two white-faced reindeer, which had been taken from the herd without even asking.

The Gods' Favorite stood there frozen and stared. He remembered what the ribbons meant. There was no doubt about it: his son was setting off to be betrothed to that girl from the Pyak clan. He was heading off, as was the custom among men, loaded with gifts and tokens of his affection.

Hadko did not wait for his father to say anything, he spoke first:

"Father, you did not give me the bride-price. I caught the bride-price on my own. You said that you would not stand in the way of what I felt to be necessary. Now I am doing what I feel is necessary, everything as it should be."

He was an impudent young man, Hadko, and he had not been afraid of falling to the ground with his face bloodied before he could say all his impudent words. Mebet remained silent. He saw the bright mark of the Ivsha clan on the hides skinned from the caught deer, and he realized that his son was not as he had imagined him just the day before: it was not through Hadko's own bravery that he had plundered others' possessions, but rather he had done so unwittingly and fortuitously.

His mother came forth from the chum with a smoking piece of meat on a large wooden plate, but upon noticing her husband's heavy silence, she was reluctant to go up to her son, and so she simply set the plate down on the snow. Hadko rushed up to take the meat and then, burning his fingers, he put it in his deerskin bag. "Thank you, mother!" he said merrily, almost shouting the words.

On this morning Hadko was not only impudent, he was also proud and probably quite pleased with himself. He leaped, light as a feather, onto the overloaded sled and so vehemently did he lash the reindeer that the animals went wild – they spun the sled around like turbulent water spins a tiny boat. The happy young man was wrapped up in a snowy white cloud, and from this cloud his loud, merry, and silly words were heard:

"Just wait until this evening! Until the evening…"

The sled and the animals hauling it vanished in the distance. The Gods' Favorite turned to his wife and studied her face for a long time.

"Where did he get the ribbons from?" he asked softly, nearly in a whisper. "Where did he get the ribbons and the meat for the road?"

Yadne averted her gaze.

Neither by that evening, nor the next day, nor the third had Hadko returned. On the morning of the fourth day one of the reindeer – the other missing – dragged the sled back into camp. The sled had been reduced of half of its contents. A few red shreds fluttered in the air. Driving the sled was a young man with a pockmarked face whom they did not know.

Under a deer hide on which one could make out a red arrow lay Hadko. When Mebet threw this covering aside, his son did not make even the slightest movement. His mother stood nearby, aghast. "He'll come to," Mebet calmly thought and gave Hadko a slap on the cheek. His son moaned, tossed about, and seemed to be trying to say something, but he was unable to. Such a stench issued forth from him that even Yadne, whom normally nothing could faze, turned away.

Finally Mebet said, "You have both visited the One-Eyed Witch."

The pockmarked young man who had brought Mebet's son back spoke quickly and apprehensively. It was a confusing tale. From his rambling account Mebet gathered that they indeed had gone to visit the One-Eyed Witch, but only Hadko had eaten mushrooms there, and a great many of them. Hadko had also drank the urine of an elk which had grazed all summer among mushrooms. The pockmarked young man had not eaten any mushrooms nor drank the elk urine, and he had tried to dissuade Hadko from this bad business, but Hadko had not listened. Since Hadko was not capable of driving his reindeer himself, the other young man was forced to bring him home, like one hauls an ailing or dead man.

"What is your name?" Mebet asked the pockmarked young man.

"Makhako," he said, somewhat embarrassed, because in Nenets this name meant "stutter," and he indeed had stammered a bit. Makhako, it turned out, belonged to the same Vela clan as Mebet, which meant that this was a visit from one of his own kinsmen, though so distant a relative that Mebet had never met him before.

Mebet took his son by the arm like an infant and turned him over, so that the stench would not be so repugnant to the nose and carry to the distant chum. He ordered Hadko's mother to light the stove there and place a pot of steaming meat broth next to Hadko, so that their son could drink it when he finally came to.

During the brief time when Mebet was carrying his son in and giving the young man's mother orders, Makhako shuffled awkwardly by the sled. It was clear that he wanted to get away from here as quickly as possible. However, the Gods' Favorite lay a hand on Makhako's shoulder as if the young man were an old friend and said:

"You will be my guest. Let's go inside, there is food aplenty. I have been waiting for you, kinsman."

Makhako, though unable to believe his luck, followed Mebet docilely and sat down at the place appointed him. It was the place for honored guests.

There, treated to a rich feast, he told the story of Hadko's betrothal. Mebet laughed then as he had never laughed before in his life.

THE REVENGE OF THE PYAK CLAN

The Pyak clan's encampment stood only a short journey from Mebet's, and therefore impudent Hadko had promised to return on the evening of the same day. He was very keen to see to this matter and he drove his reindeer on mercilessly. Along the way he came across Makhako, whom he was seeing (like his father would) for the first time in his life. People in the taiga, even if they were strangers to one another, would never meet without the exchange of greetings, or a fight, or a killing. This time greetings were exchanged. Makhako was on his way to visit relatives, but he was in no particular rush, as he had not been invited and he was not even sure that he would be welcomed there. Mebet's son, on the other hand, was in a great hurry, but once he met this passerby, he remembered that custom would not allow him to go to a betrothal alone – he had to arrive together with his father or friends. But his father had remained at home, and he had no friends around. Without thinking about it for long, Hadko suggested to Makhako that he be his friend. Makhako, who didn't think it over long either, agreed and hopped into the loaded sled, and the two sped off.

When they caught sight of the Pyak encampment, Hadko stopped his reindeer. The Blizzard Man was suddenly overcome by shyness and a sense of embarrassment. He was still a very young man, and marrying for the first time. He did not know how he should go about such a serious business. That morning, as he had set out from home, he was certain that his catch from the great hunt would be a suitable bride-price and impress his bride's parents. But now, as his reindeer were already stomping the ground near the Pyak camp, Hadko realized that he did know the right words at all, the first words that must be spoken to the parents when one arrives with the aim of leading their daughter away.

His pride now quashed, Mebet's son shared his woes with his new friend. Fortunately, Makhako turned out to know a great deal about traditional customs. Moreover, while they were making their way together, he managed to ask Hadko about the contents of the sleigh and assure him what would serve as the best bride-price and what was unnecessary. Makhako was a good-hearted young man and he loved to speak to people in a way that would please them. He knew that the most pleasing words were the ones that the other person wanted to hear.

Makhako said – and he was completely right – that betrothals must be carried out in the following way. One must come up to the bride's parents' dwelling and shout, "Hey, old man, is your daughter at home?" If the suitor has long been expected, and if the young woman herself so wants to marry him that she is prepared to jump out of her boots and run after her future husband's sled, then the parents will come out and reply:

"Our daughter is home, you have come right on time. Come in."

But usually, Makhako said, the first shout draws no response from within. Then it is important to hold one's ground and prove that one is serious. "Don't be shy," he instructed the Blizzard Man. "Shout a second time, and if necessary a third time. They will definitely come out after the third time."

"But what if they don't come out?" Hadko asked, anxious.

"If they don't come out after the third time, then things look bad for you, brother, and you'll have to figure it out. They're shunning you." Makhako laughed and then went on, "But don't be sad, brother. Ultimately, you can steal the bride away if you both agree to it, and then use gifts to buy her parents off. And if that doesn't work either, no problem. There are a lot of pretty girls in the taiga these days, and if we don't find you one in the taiga, then we'll find one in the tundra."

After hearing these words, Hadko was quite downcast, but fortunately his youthful anger surged up in him again. He lashed his reindeer and the sled flew forward, then stopped outside the large chum where the bride's father lived.

Hadko gave a shout. A shout so loud that one might think he was drowning in a swamp and crying out for help. "Hey, old man, is your daughter home?"

There was no sign of life from the chum. Only the Pyak clan's dogs gathered around the sled and barked furiously. One of them, an old white-muzzled bitch, was already prepared to attack these outsiders, but Hadko hit it with the wood of his spear. (The thought flashed through Mebet's son's head that it was a good thing he hadn't taken Voipel along, as Voipel would have torn all these other dogs to shreds and ruined all his attempts at winning this bride.)

Makhako nudged his friend as if to tell him not to be shy, to keep shouting. Hadko shouted, but not the same mighty shout he had managed the first time. After this shout, there was a fluttering at the canvas over the door, and soon old, bald Pyak appeared.

"Who are you and what do you want?" he asked sternly, almost angrily.

Hadko made an effort to shake off the shyness that was coming over him.

"I have come to ask your daughter, I have brought the bride-price. I am Hadko, son of Mebet from the clan of Vela. I want to do everything properly, with her parent's blessing…"

After old Pyak heard these words, the anger seemed to vanish from his face. He stepped out the door and spent a long while looking at the sled decorated with red ribbons. For some time no one said a word, neither Hadko, nor old Pyak, nor Makhako. Even the dogs had ceased to bark once they saw their master. Makhako was the first to break the silence.

"You'll find this an awfully great bride-price, sir. A bride-price worthy of a real chief! The furs alone add up to a whole herd. And the skins – just look! – are white as snow."

"It was a good reindeer," Pyak said. "It would have been fit for sacrifice at a big celebration. So, you are that Mebet's boy, from the clan of Vela?"

"Yes. My name is Hadko."

"Wait just a moment," the old man said. "I'll be back."

He disappeared into the chum and there was no sign of him for a long time.

"Now he's praising you to his daughter," Makhako said. He was excited and antsy as if it were not Hadko who was to marry but him. "Now the girl herself is going to rush forth, you'll see."

But instead of the bride, it was old Pyak who came out again. On his bald head he wore an iron cap, and he had become noticeably stouter – clearly he had donned armor under his deerskin.

"So you, son of Mebet, want to marry my daughter," Pyak said, his tone nearly solemn, as he drew a bow from behind his back. A feathered arrow was placed at the bowstring, and now the shooter lifted the arrow to the height of Hadko's eyes. Hadko could clearly see the triangular tip wrought from black iron. As the old man drew the bowstring back, he continued:

"You want me to give my daughter to you, Mebet's whelp? Son of a man who does not honor the gods, who scoffs at the laws of man, who hunts animals wherever he pleases, and who thinks that everyone ought to be afraid of him? When you arrive back home, tell your father that old Pyak is not afraid of him."

However, when the old man had said this, he lowered his weapon, though his fingers still gripped the white feathers on the arrow tightly.

Now Hadko spoke up. "I have brought the bride-price. I gathered all this myself on a great hunt."

But immediately the black triangular tip of the arrow was brought back up to his face. The old man was shaking with rage.

"Do you want every clan to know that Pyak accepted a bride-price of stolen goods?! You are flaunting skins with a red arrow on them, and you think old Pyak doesn't recognize that this is the Ivsha clan's mark? You stole them. You are just as much a scoundrel as your father."

The attempt at a betrothal had been for naught. Hadko's hands reached for the spear that was lying nearby, and when the old man saw this he stepped back.

Everyone knew one more famous trait of Mebet. He did not care about insults. When people said straight to his face the sort of words that other men can never forget and seek to get revenge for, Mebet would only laugh. But if ever a man tried to lay a finger on Mebet or his property, that man would not get away alive. Two winters before, five outsiders, exiles from their own people, came wandering across the taiga and attacking the Nenets' dwellings. They vanished without a trace after they headed towards the encampment of the Gods' Favorite. After spring came, hunters found in various places heads with tattooed faces: Mebet had buried them in the snow at the borders of his own territory.

Old Pyak was aware of this. He saw that there was more here than just Mebet's possessions, that he was dealing with the very son and heir to the Gods' Favorite, and therefore he threatened Hadko no more than was reasonable. He would sooner gnaw his own arm off than slay the son of a man who had no equals anywhere, whether in the taiga or in the tundra. Pyak hoped nevertheless that this undesirable suitor would show himself to be a coward.

Hadko gripped the spear. Mebet's son felt how the dull rage, surging up from somewhere deep inside him, came to a stop in his chest. The old man with his experienced eye saw this and, in order to avoid losing face, he said sternly and angrily like when the two had first met:

"Get out of here. Otherwise one of us is not leaving here alive."

Makhako, who had been lying this whole time on the sled, took his goad and poked the reindeer on its right flank. The draft animals set off and the snow runners whirred over the slightly melted snow. The reindeer made their way calmly, without being driven on – Hadko no longer had any reason to hurry. The sled departed ever further from the encampment, and Hadko watched indifferently as it receded and old Pyak shrunk to a tiny, blurry figure. Suddenly, someone rushed from the chum and tried to catch up with Hadko's adorned sled. Astonished, Hadko stopped his reindeer.

It was a young lady that was running after them, old Pyak's daughter. "Stop, Mebet's son," she shouted. "Wait for me!"

Hadko could already make out her face: a sweet face with bright black eyes, like wet stones along the river. It was the same face which he had seen once at a big celebration and would remember forever. The young lady's features remained in his mind day in and day out, shining like the summer sun.

She came up to them and stopped. Hadko saw how Pyak's daughter was struggling to hide her smile. She took in a deep breath of air, spat loudly at the sled, and then immediately rushed back whence she came, laughing all the way. When she had arrived back at her father, she asked, suppressing her laughter:

"Father, did I do everything right? I did what you told me to…"

Old man Pyak said nothing in reply and went back inside.

The whole way, as the reindeer bore the decorated sled towards who knows where, Makhako brooded:

"Oh, it's a shame about these skins. A real shame. I saw that they were branded, but I assumed it was your own mark. You and I were silly like wolverines: you should have said that you bought those reindeer. Or that they were given to you as a gift."

THE ONE-EYED WITCH

"So she just spat?" Mebet howled.

"Yes," Makhako said. "She just spat."

Mebet fell to the skin on the floor under him, choked with laughter.

"The only thing is," Makhako went on, slightly embarrassed, "the spit should have hit Hadko. After all, he was the one who wanted to marry her. But for some reason she spat on me."

Mebet said nothing in reply, he was still laughing and incapable of speech. But when he could speak again, he began to question Makhako about how they had ended up at the One-Eyed Witch and whether they had a good time there.

If the one-eyed woman was not known to every single person in the taiga, then at least a majority of its inhabitants knew of her. She was descended from a line of shamans, and at some point she became a shaman herself. But once she violated some grave taboo, and then the power left her and never returned. The spirits refused to speak with the Witch, the gods barred their door whenever she called on them, and her soul was not welcome among any of the other worlds. Thus she was no longer able to perform the shamanistic rites, nor to prophesy or heal the sick. At first people remained unaware of this tragedy that had come upon her, and by custom they continued to visit her, or to invite her to their camps and treat her lavishly. But as the years went by, they visited her or invited her over less and less, as they could see that it brought them no benefit.

The One-Eyed Witch was left alone in her chum. She took the white ribbons down from its exterior, scraped off the shamanistic signs, stomped on her magical drum and forgot its name, flung the drumstick away, and fell in a deep melancholy. She simply wanted to die and was sure that this would happen soon, but death never came – clearly this was just another way that the other worlds were showing her their scorn.

Once upon a time she had been left with only one eye, but this did not happen in the same way as with other people – from an enemy's blow, a sharp branch, arrow, or sparks. The eyelid over the Witch's left eye had fused together, and only a winding line of little hairs, like a secret sign, served as a reminder that she had once possessed eyelashes. People thought her strange disfigurement to be some kind of sign, but with time it ceased to concern them and was forgotten.

She still remembered the spells that she had inherited, but now these words, which had once forced ethereal beings to respond to her and do her bidding, were no longer needed. The One-Eyed Witch understood this, and were it not for a whim of chance – and chance is a message sent by a higher power, the power that traces the fate of every mortal – she would have withered away from her melancholy, from the sole thought that had gripped her now for years and had driven her crazy.

Once the One-Eyed Witch had gone deep into the taiga, to where thawed bogs give off their stench. While there, she slipped on a hummock and injured her leg in a way that left her unable to walk. She lay immobile for a day and a night, and when the sun rose again, she crawled home. Every movement drew pain, but the Witch crawled on nevertheless – she knew how to bear pain. The death which she, sitting in her chum, had awaited like an invited guest, now came quite close. But the Witch had suddenly lost her desire to die. Shamans travel across the various worlds and so they do not fear death; the abodes of the dead are just as familiar to them as the dwellings of the living. But it was obvious that, now stripped of her gifts, the One-Eyed Witch had become entirely human and so she wanted to live, and she crawled forward with her last strength. She moistened her lips with swamp water, and she ate of the still-unripe and bitter berries which grew here and there. The berries caused an unbearable pain in her stomach. The One-Eyed Witch lay there among the swamplands for another night.

When she came to again she saw, through the one eye she had left, a mushroom growing right in front of her. It was an early puffy mushroom and it had a cap that was dark-brown like a reindeer's liver. Her head and her stomach felt empty and ravenous, and without thinking the Witch plucked the mushroom from the earth and ate it. Sleep came over her, a brief and rosy sleep like her long-ago childhood. When the sleep passed, the Witch suddenly felt that the pain in her leg had abated, and her body, which resembled the moss heavy with the moisture of the marsh, was no longer shaking with chills. Nearby another mushroom was growing, of the same kind as the first but smaller. The Witch ate it, and the pain vanished entirely – even the very memory of it was gone. But there was something else within her now, something even better than the pleasure at the departure of the pain:

her melancholy at the loss of her shamanistic gifts had left her now. The One-Eyed Witch was happy, though at first she did not realize what exactly had happened to her.

She tried to stand up, and now she proved able to walk. Her injured leg was swollen and some of the threads holding her boots together had torn, but there was no longer pain, and no longer any melancholy. The world had suddenly become worth living in.

She eventually reached her chum when an enormous moon was hanging in the sky. Nights at that time of year had become ever shorter and brighter. A half-eaten reindeer bone and a bit of meat broth remained in her pot. In the corner under an old deerskin she kept some dry firewood. The Witch started a fire in the stove and spent a good while relishing the smell of the hot smoke. She ate everything that was left in the pot, without even a thought about what she would have to eat the next day (her larder had long since been emptied). Then she crawled under the furs and slept for a long time.

She was aware that those two miraculous mushrooms had brought her deliverance. Truth be told, it would have been hard for her not to realize that.

The people of the taiga had long known of intoxicating mushrooms, but only a very few knew which ones they were, and how much one could eat without causing sickness or even death. At times there was no one left who was expert in these matters. But people remembered how a certain family from the upper Sated River was found in their dwelling with their throats torn open. Initially it was thought that wolves had done this, but the wolves were not to blame: the people themselves had bit at one another. Later people found out about a stranger in a conically shaped hat, who had gorged on mushrooms, sat astride on a big log, and dozed off. His reverie was so profound that he did not notice how he had eaten to literal bursting, and thus he died. This was talked about for a long time, because a strange and curious death is always remembered better than others.

The One-Eyed Witch waited impatiently for the swelling on her injured leg to go down, and when it finally did, she headed for the same swamp, so that she might look for those mushrooms whose caps were the color of fresh reindeer liver. Just as dogs run to meet their returning master, so did these wondrous mushrooms seem to rise forth from the swampy ground when the One-Eyed Witch drew near. The first time she gathered a great number of them, a whole bagful. Then she hung the bag from an old bowstring over the fire in order to dry the mushrooms.

These mushrooms which drive melancholy away became her chief occupation for the rest of her life. She taught herself how to cook them in a special way, she knew how much of the mushrooms a person should eat in order to lead his or her soul into the desired state, whether it be gentle oblivion, a childlike joy, complete insensibility, a good cry, self-pity, indifference, elation, or even becoming temporarily blind or experiencing paradisiacal visions. She also became familiar with the dangerous aspects of mushrooms, when elation can give way to fury, self-pity to suicide, and gentle oblivion could turn into sleep eternal.

From that time on, no longer did the One-Eyed Witch even remember the melancholy she had felt at the loss of her talents, and she forgot all about her shame before her shaman forebears. Her life took a whole different course when she treated another person, a man who had accidentally come across her camp, to the mushrooms. This Nenets was heading back from the hunt and carrying his catch: several sables caught with a snare. When he departed, he left her all of these and did not seem to mind at all. When the One-Eyed Witch saw that her guest had left, she caught up with him and told him that he had forgotten something. A firm rule of not accepting too much from people was the last thing that remained of her lost shamanic powers. But the hunter only looked at her with a vacant, uncomprehending stare, and then he took off his deerskin and stood bare-chested.

"Take this, too," he said and then wandered off into the taiga.

The hunter was only the first of a large number of people to visit the One-Eyed Witch's chum. Whoever tried the miraculous mushrooms almost inevitably came back a second time. The Witch asked nothing from the people who visited her – instead they readily left with her whatever they had. Soon her storehouse was full to the brim with tokens of gratitude, and she had to build a second storehouse farther away.

However, besides these generous people, there were many others who believed that the Witch's mushrooms were a source of trouble in the taiga. Several times the Witch's camp was attacked, but each time she managed to get away and hide. Once an arrow even hit her, albeit only at the end of its flight. It did not kill her, but it struck her powerfully in the neck and the Witch fell down unconscious, though the attackers did not move in for the kill. Whether some members of this war party themselves eventually came to visit her and therefore tempered their aggression, or whether some supernatural power had remembered the Witch and came to her aid, she was never disturbed again.

Some time after the attack, people began to visit the One-Eyed Witch again. Her life was peaceful and content, until the day when two white-headed reindeer came up to her camp hauling a wedding sled, with an offering for a bride on it left untouched, and a despondent Hadko.

Hadko spent three days and three nights with her and he asked her to help him forget everything. For this, he gave her one of the reindeer and over half of what he had intended to give to the parents of his future bride. On the way back, the Witch gave him a flask wrought from birch bark and leather with a foul brew inside it: elk urine. The elk's talents for finding the miraculous mushrooms exceeded even the Witch's, and therefore she chose the elk as a symbol of her new life. She decorated deerskins with elk motifs and before these depictions she secretly uttered a prayer that had come to her once in a dream.

It remained forever a mystery how the One-Eyed Witch had got an elk, a mighty forest creature which not every bear is willing to attack, to give her its urine. That is why people ascribed fantastical properties to the drink and quietly boasted to each other that they could down it without any disgust.

MEBET'S TOKENS OF APPRECIATION

The Gods' Favorite had welcomed this pockmarked relation into his home. Now Makhako was telling his story more readily and eating with great satisfaction.

"Your mouth must be having a hard time," Mebet said. "It has two jobs to do: eat and talk."

"I'm used to it," a cheerful Makhako answered.

"So, tell me: how did Hadko know where the One-Eyed Witch lives?"

Makhako's jaws froze in mid-chew. From the moment he had arrived at the camp he had been worried that Mebet would start asking about how his son had ended up in such an unholy place. His fear had abated at his host's showing him such warmth and generosity, but now it rose up again. Makhako was well aware that he was a bad liar, and thus he worried that he would be unable to hide the truth – it was him, and no one else, who had recommended to Hadko that they visit the chum decorated with elk motifs.

Makhako barely managed to avoid choking on his morsel of food and save himself. He began rambling about how, well, many people knew of the One-Eyed Witch and so why wouldn't Hadko know about her, too? Now he himself, as he had been saying from the very beginning, had spent the entire journey there trying to dissuade his friend from this foolish business, and he had not eaten any mushrooms or drank from the flask, which was the honest truth and he was prepared to swear to it on a bear's head.

"So be it, then," Mebet said amiably. "Hadko has long since been roaming the taiga on his own. He's a grown man now. I am grateful to you and I would like to repay you somehow, since you brought my son back to me alive."

At hearing these words Makhako's spirits soared. The joy rose to his head and burst out upon his face as a blissful smile. Mebet continued:

"But I want to ask one thing of you…"

"Ask of me whatever you want," Makhako said boldly, for after all, he was poor.

"Stay here as my guest for a few days more, while Hadko recovers. I need to leave for just a short while. Eat and drink, do whatever your heart desires, but wait for me because, before you head home, I would like to give you a worthy token of my appreciation."

The Gods' Favorite paused for a moment and then added solemnly:

"After all, isn't that the custom among good people?"

Makhako could not believe his sudden good fortune.

Before dawn Mebet went off into the taiga. Yadne, half-asleep, heard the whir of sled runners over moist snow. By the time she ran out of the chum, the sled was already nowhere to be seen. Deep reindeer tracks attested to the fact that Mebet had managed to leave the camp. A little while later the dogs came back from the taiga, Voipel running at the head of the pack. Their owner had not taken them with him, but he had taken a spear, a shield, and two bows with a large quiver full of new arrows.

Mebet had never been accustomed to telling his wife where he was going and why, and this time too he left her unaware. Early in their relationship Yadne had worried for her husband and waited anxiously for his return, but she soon stopped: she knew that there was no power capable of harming this man whom the gods loved. But now her old alarm, though she had nearly forgotten it entirely, came rising back up again.

By midday Hadko began to come to. All night he had been vomiting some dark-red matter, which frightened his mother, as she thought that it was blood. After purging the contents of his stomach, her son fell back into his daze and muttered things. His mother could catch bits of words and people's names, but she could not figure out what they meant.

Yadne had spent the entire previous day preparing food for her husband and his guest. She brought to their chum birchbark containers full of fish preserves and reindeer meat in a thick broth. She had heard Mebet's thunderous laughter, and the chuckling of his guest which sounded like a loud hiccup, but she did not know what exactly Makhako was recounting. Even without words, however, she could easily understand her son's woes: old Pyak had driven this suitor away and scoffed at his bride-price.

Hadko was eighteen years old then. For the peoples of the taiga, this is the age when one should already be bringing up children, not just seeking marriage. Yadne had silently reproached her husband for not seeking a bride for his son, and a few times she even said so aloud, but Mebet either answered nothing or merely laughed, and ultimately he told his wife to mind her own business. This offended her, but soon the offense fell away like a dry branch.

Yadne looked into the large chum where Makhako, wrapped in furs, lay snoring next to a fire that had gone out. She started a new fire and then went to see her son.

Hadko was awake now and resembled a dead man returned to life. He refused the steaming broth which his mother had brought him in a wooden bowl. He lay there silently, his eyes open, and his silence was so heavy that Yadne decided to say nothing.

Towards sunset her son himself spoke up: was father home? His mother was patching a summer deerskin mantle and answered him without interrupting her sewing:

"He left this morning. He didn't say where to."

Hadko crawled out from under the furs, slowly rose to his feet, and stumbled out of the chum. He was gone for a long time. In the middle of their camp his sled decorated with ribbons still stood, along with what remained of his offered bride-price – Mebet had not touched it. Hadko went into the large chum. Pockmarked Makhako, who seemed to have slept well, was sitting up with his legs crossed and eagerly gnawing at the meat left on a bone.

"Hello there, brother," Makhako said loudly. "You slept a long time. I've been waiting for you to wake up."

Hadko sat down opposite him.

"Those must have been some powerful mushrooms over at that Witch's place," Makhako laughed. Then, leaning towards this son of the man whom the Gods favored, the pockmarked youth whispered, "Me and your dad are friends, good friends. He fed me and listened to my story, and said some really nice things. I have never been treated so well as a guest. I love visiting other people and talking with them about whatever. But my own folks are like greedy little chipmunks: sometimes they'll feed me, but sometimes they won't even throw me a bone. You're just loafing around, they say, you aren't tending to your own home. But I'm no loser, I'm outgoing and I help people out. I helped you. Your dad, Mebet, really thanked me for bringing you back alive from that Witch. You might have just died back there, froze to death, if you hadn't had me with you. There was this one time – I was visiting relatives then – when I hear dogs barking, and reindeer come hauling a sled up to the camp. Some strange guy is sitting on the sled with his head bent. 'Hi there,' I say. 'Who are you?' and he doesn't answer. It turned out to be a dead man! While he was making his way somewhere, he fell asleep and froze to death, the fool. Believe it or not, we had to hold that guy over the fire until he straightened out. You can't bury someone all scrunched up like that. Who he was, I have no idea. Grandpa said that he might have been one of those Yaptiks from the tundra, but I had never seen him before and he was a mystery to me. So, the same might have happened to you if it wasn't for me."

Makhako lay on his side, seeming like he was at complete ease, and then he asked in his normal loud voice:

"Do you know where your father went off to?"

"He went off somewhere."

"He went to get me a gift. He said that he really appreciated how I brought you back alive."

Hadko suddenly became nauseous and felt a thick lump in his throat. He rushed outside and fell to his hands and knees next to the sled on which he had gone off to get his bride. Deaf and blind, he shuddered with convulsions and did not see how Yadne, frightened, came rushing up to him. When his vomiting finally abated, his mother helped him to stand up and, nearly carrying him, to go back inside. There Mebet's son collapsed onto the bed. Yadne covered him with furs and then rushed to get firewood so that she could make the fire burn hotter. When she returned, she heard a strange and frightful sound: Hadko was sobbing. Among the peoples of the taiga, even children rarely cry, and she could not remember a grown man ever crying. This frightened Yadne, but her fear quickly passed. In her heart, she saw under the furs not a great hunter worthy of his father, but rather a mere baby. Just as she had once bent over his cradle filled with goose down, now she hunched over her son in the bed and stroked his shivering head, the black hair drenched with sweat.

Yadne leaned down and gently whispered into his ear like the sound of a warm summer day. Hadko drifted off to sleep without even understanding what she was whispering.

His mother had uttered a spell, the only one which still remained in her memory from back before she became the wife of the Gods' Favorite and still lived among her own family. These were the words she spoke:

> I am the white partridge, I am the white partridge,
> I'm flying towards the sunrise, where the sun lives,
> I'm flying towards the sunrise, where the sun comes up,
> I'm flying towards the sunrise, where the rivers flow from,
> I'm flying towards the sunrise, where the gods live,
> I'm flying towards the sunrise, where I'll make my nest,
> I'm flying towards the sunrise, where I'll hatch my chick,
> My one chick, white like me.
> Hide me, snow, from the foe's fangs,

Cover me, snow, from the white-plumed arrow,
From the eagle-plumed arrow,
From the owl-plumed arrow, the hawk-plumed arrow.
Tree branches, keep me safe,
Tree branches, keep me safe
From the foe which walks on the ground.
Blue sky, protect me,
Blue sky, protect me
From the death which moves through the branches.
River spirit, defend me,
River spirit, defend me,
Keep me bound for the bright sunrise.
Wind spirit, lift me up,
Wind spirit, lift me up,
Support my wings when strength falters,
Bear me not towards darkness,
Bear me not towards ice,
Bear me not towards the harsh frost…
My nest I'll make of fragrant grass,
My nest I'll make of soft fir-needles,
My nest I'll lay with snow-white down,
To keep my chick warm.
My chick will look towards the sunrise,
My chick will see where the sun lives,
My chick will see where the rivers flow to.
My chick will grow higher than a mountain.
Its wings will grow vaster than the river.
The Kars bird will not threaten it,
The black bird which sparks terror.
But until then protect me,
Until then keep me safe –
snow spirit,
wind spirit,
spirits which live among the branches…
I am the white partridge,
I am the white partridge,
I'm flying towards the sunrise to hatch my chick,
My sole chick, my white chick…

The night had passed and morning was already turning into bright day when Voipel started barking – Mebet's sled had appeared far off. Everyone – Hadko, Yadne and their guest Makhako – came out to the middle of the camp to greet Mebet. The two draft reindeer gradually drew nearer. It was clear that Mebet was sitting low, so the sled must be empty, without any large hunting catch on it. Once the Gods' Favorite had arrived back in his camp, he was obviously in merry spirits and, as always, pleased with himself. The two people of his household and their guest bowed courteously in greeting.

Mebet responded only to Makhako's greeting, however, and immediately said to him:

"I am happy that you show me such respect, good friend Makhako, and that you have awaited my return. Forgive me that I took so long – I had a lot of hard work to do. Did they feed you well while I was away?"

"I have never eaten so well or slept so soundly," Makhako replied.

"I have brought you a gift like I promised." Mebet took a deerskin sack from the sled, its contents heavy and bulging. He did not give it to Makhako, however, but only laid it down on the snow.

"Take this and see what's inside. Come on, don't be shy."

The guest came up, very pleased and slightly bowing as he hurried forward. He knelt at Mebet's feet, grabbed the sack and, looking around at everyone with elation, he shoved his hand inside. He froze at what he found there. A smile flashed across Mebet's face. Makhako drew a hand from the bag, his fingers bloody.

"Show everyone my present," Mebet said with his invariable amiability.

A baffled Makhako poured the sack's contents out and leaped away with a cry. The One-Eyed Witch's head came tumbling forth and loudly struck the trodden snow. Makhako could clearly see the curved line of little hairs where her eyelid had fused together, and the Witch's hair which was now the color of her blood.

"Do you know what the one-eyed woman said to me before she died?" Mebet asked. "She said that she never gave you any of her amazing mushrooms. Not because you had nothing to repay her with, but because stupid fools are already happy the way they are. That is why you arrived here in sober mind, and you brought my son back alive. Thank you, good friend Makhako. You can take your gift with you when you go."

Makhako did not hear these last words, for he had bolted off into the taiga, without even taking his skis which remained in Hadko's sled. As he ran, he wailed in dismay.

Neither Mebet, nor Yadne, nor Hadko ever saw Makhako again, the frivolous man who did not tend to his own home and had come to them as a distant relative.

THE BLIZZARD WOMAN

The One-Eyed Witch's head lay before Mebet's feet and he kicked it away. The head rolled and came to rest in a soft bank of snow where it could hardly be seen. Mother and son stood silent and petrified. Only the Gods' Favorite retained the power of speech, and now he turned to Hadko.

"When you were tying those ribbons to the sled, I remembered one story which would have been quite fitting, but I didn't tell it to you. I'll tell it to you now. Old Pyak and I are nearly the same age. Once, long ago, he and I wrestled at the bear feast. As a joke, I grabbed him by the hair, lightly tugged and left him bald over half his head. His hair never grew back after that. Old Pyak got awfully angry at me, and he will bear that anger with him all the way to the other world." He laughed. "And many years later you, son, go courting his daughter. A person could hardly imagine something more audacious than that. But I'm happy for old Pyak. He told you off good and at least he got some satisfaction out of that."

Hadko stood motionless and without a sound. At that moment, the one they called the Blizzard Man came to hate his father.

Mebet went on:

"There's a present waiting for you, too. It is better than the one that I brought for Makhako."

Only now did Hadko and Yadne see that Mebet had not come on an empty sled after all: something was hidden there under furs. As the Gods' Favorite threw the furs back, he said with mock affection:

"Come on out, dear, you're already at your new home."

Under the furs he had hidden a girl from the Vaynot clan. Mebet had brought her as a wife for his silly, clumsy son. He had abducted her easily, just like he caught everything that his heart ever desired.

The girl was beautiful, certainly even more beautiful than Pyak's daughter. Mebet had chosen her according to his own tastes. Coincidentally, she bore the same name as his son: Hadne, "Blizzard Woman".

They set the bride up in the small chum. For several days she was completely numb, unwilling to touch her food, and she did not utter a word. Yadne constantly visited the chum and cared for her like she had recently cared for her son.

As far as Mebet was concerned, he expressed no particular feelings one way or the other, neither pride nor happiness, let alone worry. He had simply carried out a task that he thought necessary and worthy of himself. The Gods' Favorite regretted only that his son had not carried it out, but it was unlikely that Hadko would ever dare such a thing. Mebet now forgot once and for all his recent happy musings that Hadko would grow up to be just like him, though in his own different way. His son took all matters of human beings very seriously, and therefore he could never become a favorite of the gods. He may well be a fine hunter with strong arms, but there are many such skilled hunters and strong men in the taiga.

Yadne was so concerned with tending to the girl that she did not even notice her husband. Mebet thought that his wife was harboring a grievance against him, but that was not the case at all. His wife's concern for the girl was mixed with fear. Once Yadne was carrying an armful of firewood back to their home and, when she ran into her husband, she looked him in the eye and said with clear reproach:

"Look at what you have done, Mebet, just look. The Vaynot clan will get revenge for abducting this girl. It won't be just two or three of them who will come, it will be a whole war band. You know how resentful the Vaynot men are."

"Let them come, then," her husband replied indifferently.

Yadne only shook her head and repeated, "Just look at what you have done, Mebet…"

She went inside and there, as she broke the twigs and fed them to the fire, she sank into the anxious thoughts which had started coming to her long before Hadne had been abducted.

One can endlessly repeat that the Gods' Favorite was a singular human being, or perhaps not a human being at all, but simply repeating that gives rise to doubt. Mebet was already gray-haired, and therefore Yadne wondered more and more how much time he still had allotted to him. The summer sun was now heading for its long setting, and shouldn't the strange favor which the gods showed to this one single man also end someday? Or perhaps he was immortal? But then why would old age, so merciless to everyone else, manifest in him as well? And how much longer could the people of the taiga suppress the sense of envy and humiliation they felt before this man elevated so high above them? When would they put an end to his free-roaming ways? He could still catch an arrow in mid-flight, but what about two arrows? Five? A dozen? A hundred? Could he catch a hundred arrows launched right at him?

Yadne also wondered about whether Mebet could be called an evil man. No, he could not. He was cold to other people and showed little affection for them; he had been the same in his youth. But her husband never humiliated her out of the mere pleasure of it, and he never beat her. Among the other men of the taiga, wife-beating was considered among the most readily accessible entertainments.

Sometimes he was harsh, cruel. But ultimately, what seemed to be cruelty was actually beneficial and for the best. Mebet had killed the One-Eyed Witch and turned the dead woman's head into a mere toy, but was this cruelty? In one short day he had managed to see to something which no one else had bothered to see to in all these years.

Yadne remembered what Mebet had said when he was still young, she remembered how he responded to the reproaches of honored people that he did not live according to the accepted laws:

"I understand what you want of me," Mebet said. "You want me to temper my strength and become weak like everyone else. But can strength really be reduced to weakness? For because it is strength, it is impossible to subdue."

The life which Mebet had led before he said these words, and the life he lived afterward, made it clear: there are many mysteries in this world, and the Gods' Favorite is an enigma beyond the minds of others. The honored people came to accept this, and subsequently so did everyone else.

THE WAR REINDEER

Yadne was right: revenge came for the girl's abduction. On the day when the master of the house and his son were making a new sled, a reindeer came wandering into the camp and on its white side was a black arrow – this was the Vaynot clan's sign of war. As the Gods' Favorite looked at the reindeer, he told his son:

"They wage war like they throw weddings: everything is done according to the rules."

Mebet went inside so that he could change into a new deerskin. Though he scoffed at human conventions, he was yet well aware of them. Shortly after the reindeer had come, emissaries from the hostile clan should arrive so that they could discuss the terms of war and designate a site for the battle to come. To refuse to accept these emissaries would mean defeat before the first arrow was ever launched to begin the fighting.

Mebet wished to greet these imminent foes in a worthy fashion, and so he changed his clothes. Hadko had guessed at what this all meant, but he continued the interrupted work alone. He still remembered that brief, unspoken flash of hatred he had felt for his father.

Voipel growled and subsequently the other dogs began to bark: the emissaries had appeared far off. A pair of reindeer were swiftly hauling a sled under a red flag. On the sled sat two old men, now fit only for discussing the terms of war.

Mebet bowed. "Greetings, honored ones," he said.

The old men took his greeting for mockery (and they were right in this) and they did not reply.

"Everyone's patience is at an end with you, Mebet," began one of the old men, lean and with a face that seemed triangular due to his enormous cheekbones. From that face long mustaches, twisted like thin thread, and a braided beard hung down. "Let our Vaynot clan be the first to stop you and, if need be, to cut your life short."

"Why did you take the girl?" the second old man cried, shaking his fists. "Or do you lack the reindeer to pay the bride-price?"

"Or are your storehouses empty?" the first added.

The old men shouted at Mebet in turn, unleashing all their fury on him and making it clear how angry and offended the Vaynot clan was.

"All those animals you have killed in others' hunting grounds!"

"All those girls you have abducted!"

"And you never came to make peace afterward!"

"It brings you pleasure to humiliate others…"

"You enjoy bringing other clans low…"

"But soon an end will come to all this…"

"Soon, very soon now, we will stop you…"

This went on for a long time. Finally, Mebet replied to the old men in a tone that was nearly warm and friendly:

"I cannot understand why you are so angry, honored visitors. Yes, I abducted the girl, but did I not kill anyone while doing this?"

After Mebet said this, the old men began whispering to one another, but so loudly that all could hear what they were discussing:

"He is mocking us…"

"He is simply asking to die…"

"Does he really expect us to thank him for not killing anyone?"

"The man's crazy."

Mebet interrupted this feigned deliberation between the two emissaries. "As far as abducting girls goes," the Gods' Favorite said in a voice that was now less and less friendly, "I completely admit that. But I can hardly be considered a brigand. I only stole women away to help those who could not purchase a bride of their own. I have abducted only a single woman for my own self – that was my wife Yadne, who now stands before you. I didn't abduct your girl for myself either, but for my son. He cares too much about doing things right, and that is why he ended up in a difficult position and nearly died from his grief."

Mebet knew that old Pyak, who now lay in his dwelling and had regained his composure, considered himself the victor and had been spreading the story of Hadko's doomed courting of his daughter widely among the clans.

"There is no reason for you to rebuke me so harshly. In one thing you are wrong, honored visitors. It does not bring me pleasure to humiliate others and bring other clans low. If only because no one has let me know that he feels truly debased and humiliated."

Mebet spoke in the way he was accustomed to, that is, he spoke the truth. Traditional custom allowed abducting a bride, but the same traditional custom demanded that war then be averted by striking a peace with the abducted girl's parents – the man should visit their camp with gifts and ask for forgiveness and for the parents' blessing. Ordinarily, if no long enmity long existed between the two clans or families, and if the offered bride-price was found suitable, then the abductor could have his bride. To give one's grown daughter away at a price lower than expected was considered a better deal than keeping her at home, feeding and clothing her, and simply waiting until she became an old maid that no man desired.

If the abductor had not come to visit within one year of his deed, then the bride's family could consider themselves well and truly offended and they had a recognized right to get their revenge. It sometimes happened that they did take revenge, particularly if the girl was a beautiful one from a wealthy family, and her father had planned to increase that wealth by arranging a successful marriage for his daughter. Among the poor, things were much simpler, but they too recognized the right to cleanse stained honor.

The Vaynots lacked the patience to wait a whole year; they saw no sense in that. One could sooner expect the dead to awaken than Mebet or his son to come bearing a peace offering and asking for forgiveness. Therefore, the Vaynots decided to send the war reindeer earlier than the set period.

Mebet, who had taken part in a bridenapping on multiple occasions, had never before been the target of revenge. Previously, as soon as the offended party heard the name of the abductor, they tempered their fury and ultimately forgot about everything. No one wanted to test the luck which was shown forth on the Gods' Favorite. People did not quickly forget their shame, of course, but to themselves and to their circle they made the excuse that whatever happened had happened, and ultimately it was for the best – especially if the family was poor and weak in men, so that even if the young lady were a veritable goddess the family could hardly hope for much wealth from a successful marriage. After all, only those of great wealth or great strength could allow themselves to choose a woman on the basis of her beauty, let alone love, and there were few such men around recently. Mebet was the only one for whom the gods' favor replaced any need for riches and to whom everything was granted.

The abducted Hadne, the Blizzard Woman, was beautiful indeed, and the Vaynot clan was rich and strong in manpower. Mebet knew this and so he was not surprised that Hadne's abduction did not end as usual with a cowardly peace being struck, like all his previous cases of abduction.

After a silence, the old man with the braided beard spoke up again. He was no longer openly showing his anger. "We know, Mebet, that you can still catch arrows in mid-flight, though you be with gray hair now. You would probably be pleased to live to such an age that your head turns completely white like ours. But think carefully! The summer sun is setting now, and the green forest will turn black for the whole long winter…"

This startled Yadne – the old man spoke aloud what she had been thinking the day before, as if one of the spirits had conferred these thoughts on him without missing a word.

"Your strength has not left you, Mebet," the old man went on. "And fortune has always been with you like a loyal dog. It has never left you in good times or in bad. You do not even know the limits of your strength and your good fortune, but as I'm sure you'll agree, you shouldn't think these things are your doing alone. The spirits have not yet sent you such a trial that would reveal the limits of your strength. Clearly that is their will, and it is not for us to dispute it. But I, a mortal man, will reason like a mortal man. You can catch one arrow, or two arrows, even three. But can you wave a dozen arrows away? Can you shrug off a hundred arrows? Think on this, Mebet…"

"Think on it," the other man spoke up. "We have sent you the war reindeer, and that means that we do not intend to merely toy with you and leave this matter unresolved. The men of the Vaynot clan are many and, if necessary, we will not be ashamed to come at you with every man we have. We have been offended, and this is no feast where just two men wrestle one on one. You have a family, a wife and a son who still lacks experience. Do not put their lives into jeopardy either."

Mebet could guess what the old men were getting at, though he ascribed no great importance to their words. According to the rules, the men sent to negotiate were obliged to mention the possibility of striking a peace, and if no peace could be agreed, then they would have the right to make war. The Gods' Favorite knew that now they would suggest that he return Hadne, or that he set off to her parents bearing gifts and asking for forgiveness. Yet the old men would hardly be satisfied if Hadko did this, for the repentant youth would not satisfy the Vaynots' wounded honor and thus the revenge would be unfulfilled and ultimately shameful. A repentant Mebet, however, would be something else entirely.

Ultimately the Gods' Favorite tired of these deliberations. He bowed to the old men, turned, and went to the farther chum, then he soon returned with Hadne. She had not heard what Mebet and her kinsmen were talking about, but from the sounds – the scraping of the sled, the barking of the dogs, and snatches of conversation, she could guess what was going on. Thanks to Yadne's tender care, she had come out of her initial shock and she had begun to eat and to speak a little. Hadko, her future husband that she had never expected, turned out to not be so terrible. But Mebet she was afraid of.

It was a mute and immobilizing fear. It came upon her after the Gods' Favorite had first got ahold of her.

Mebet had abducted the Blizzard Woman with almost magical ease.

Early in the morning, not far from her encampment where the forest stands some distance away from the riverbank, Hadne saw a remarkable thing. Three pink partridges were leaping out of snowdrifts and, after flying at a low height, falling back down into the white snow. Hadne, enchanted, watched these odd birds, and the sight seemed to augur well. In order to get a closer look at the birds, the Blizzard Woman ran up to where this peculiar dance was taking place.

A partridge fell almost at her feet. Immediately the snow behind her, which had been polished by the wind, surged up and an irresistible force pressed down on her shoulders. A fur mitten covered her mouth. Hadne was oblivious to how exactly she had ended up in the sled under the furs: she could not see or hear anything. The force did not hurt her but put her into a swoon.

The whole way, the young lady lay there in the darkness and did not dare to move a muscle, so there was no need to bind her. Hadne could feel how the reindeer were running along, and she heard the cries of people coming from somewhere. But all this went past her, it all seemed to be happening to some other person that had awkwardly ended up in her own body.

After Mebet had abducted this bride for his son, he was pleased with himself – he had never done something quite like this before. He again admired the favor which the gods showed him, and the ethereal powers (they were undoubtedly involved in this enterprise) had carried out his plans even better and more elegantly than Mebet had ever hoped.

As Mebet headed towards the Vaynot clan's territory he made a wish that he might see a pink partridge, a sign of luck, and when he stopped for a brief moment to let his reindeer rest, he saw not just one but three such birds. He set up three snares without any especial effort and covered them with a dusting of snow, and soon thereafter he held in his hands three warm, slightly shivering birds. These birds proved to be remarkably docile and they did not try to escape. Not far from the camp Mebet stopped his sled again, he put a long rope around the leg of each bird and set them in the snow. The Gods' Favorite then buried himself in a snowdrift like a bird and he lay there, breathing through a dried stalk of the *porys* plant, until the wind had made the snow over him smooth and shiny. He held the ends of the ropes in his hands and the birds meekly awaited his signal.

The sky had just begun to brighten. People awoke and stepped outside, and when Mebet made out the voice of a young maiden, he began to jerk the ends of the ropes in turn. The pink birds fluttered up and fell back down. The two white-headed reindeer were waiting for their owner nearby in the forest. They came forth at the call known only to one man, Mebet.

People saw the sled that seemed to surge forth from under the earth, and then they noticed that Hadne, daughter of the most venerable and elderly of men, had disappeared. They set off in pursuit. The Vaynots did not manage to shed a single drop of Mebet's blood, but he never missed. His bow shot off arrows with a dull tip, they struck their targets in the head and Mebet's pursuers dropped to the ground, stunned. Afterwards, they were left with a terrible headache, as if they had eaten of the One-Eyed Witch's mushrooms.

Now the Gods' Favorite and the bride he abducted stood side by side for all to see: Hadko, and Yadne, and the emissaries from the Vaynot clan. Mebet had no need to grip Hadne tightly, in fact he did not touch her at all. Even seeing her kinsmen on the sled beneath the red flag of war did not faze her in the slightest. Thus they stood there for some time without speaking; when the silence became too oppressive, heavy like the spring snow, one of the old men could bear it no longer:

"Hadne, my girl, you will be home soon and back with your father. We will bring you back, Hadne…"

The old man's words went unanswered. Hadne did not budge.

"You see, she does not want to go back. Leave now!"

Everyone except Mebet were startled at hearing this voice, because it was the voice of Hadko, who so far had not said anything.

"She does not want to go back," Hadko repeated firmly.

The emissaries were taken aback. The old man with the braided beard was the first to regain his composure. "Since when, Mebet, does a whelp decide matters of war when his father is present?"

"He is no whelp," Mebet replied, "but a man."

War was inevitable, there was no longer any doubt about that.

"You are bringing ruin on yourself and your family," the old men said. "If necessary, we will come as a large host."

"Come, then," Mebet said coolly.

The emissaries, as was appropriate in such a situation, got down to discussing the terms of the war. They asked the foe where the most suitable site for battle would be: on the river ice or on the snowy field, the same where Hadne had been abducted.

Without showing the slightest unease, Mebet replied that the ice was no longer as strong, and so it would be better to fight on the field. "Especially considering that it is a place that I know well," he added.

The old men proposed that the two sides face off after three moons had come and gone, and that they would fight between sunrise and sunset but not take up arms at night. The dead were to be left on the field of battle, the wounded were not to be taken captive and were to be released back to their own people. These terms immediately met with their enemy's agreement. The matter was finished, the emissaries could now head back. However, their bafflement only grew stronger. Mebet may well be a remarkable man, the peoples of the taiga and tundra thought, but it had never before happened that just two men accepted a challenge from an entire clan. To make themselves feel better about this business, the emissaries told themselves that the Gods' Favorite would call on helpers. But they had forgotten that Mebet had no friends.

The most astonishing thing of all was that Hadko had called for this war. The old men saw this as the foolishness of youth, blended with insolence. But the fact that Mebet had approved his son's action left them downcast and with a sense of foreboding.

When the sled with the red flag had vanished from sight, Yadne fell to her knees, flung her arms around her husband's legs, and wailed. She begged him to catch up with the emissaries and to tell them that her son alone was to blame, his pride and foolishness, and that they should come back and reach a peace agreement. Otherwise, it would come to death and slaughter…

Mebet bent down and freed his legs from Yadne's grip. He picked his horrified wife up and clasped her to himself – she could not remember a time when Mebet had ever held her close like this. They stood there in that embrace until Yadne's crying ended.

"Go inside and cook a lot of meat," the Gods' Favorite quietly ordered her. "We all need to eat very well."

His wife, with her head hanging low, went to do what she had been told.

Mebet also ordered that Hadne was not to be disturbed. No one was to speak to her or burden her with chores, but only to keep her safe. This abducted girl from the Vaynot clan had still not truly entered into his family.

She was a piece of disputed territory from which nothing could be taken until the matter was resolved by arms and victory in battle.

In vain the two old emissaries pondered why the Gods' Favorite had accepted this awkward war. They assumed that he had some insidious design in mind. In fact, Mebet did not have anything in mind at the moment. He did not know exactly how he would fight.

It was not the war which occupied his thoughts but Hadko.

His son's boldness puzzled him. One could hardly imagine that Hadko had fallen in love with Hadne, for the two had hardly seen one another. Suddenly Mebet realized that it was not the beauty of this unexpected bride which had acted on Hadko, nor any trace of his former lovesickness. What had awoken in him was that primeval bestial lust for war which preceded all other wars whether for land, wealth and power, revenge, glory, or a simple desire to kill. It was the drive to wage war for a woman. Male animals tear each other apart in competing for mates, the gods vie for goddesses' favor. Women are the first thing plundered by any clan which fate has cast out into the wild. If the raid proved successful and the clan's continuation is guaranteed, only then traditional custom enters into force. But that primeval lust for war remains hidden deep in men's blood and manifests itself when everything must be begun from the beginning…

His son's action revealed to Mebet that within Hadko there lived two men, one of which was the leader of a clan which fate had cast out into an unfamiliar place. He acted according to some inner commandment and did not hide behind custom.

That is what Mebet thought, but he was wrong…

FORKED ARROW

After three moons had passed, the warriors of the Vaynot clan went forth to the snowy field that stretched from the edge of the forest to the riverbank. It was still before dawn when they stopped and waited for the enemy. Their camp stood nearby. Initially the elders had not planned to move from their site, but the previous night they changed their minds and ordered that the chums and possessions be gathered up, and that all those who could not fight be sent to higher ground some distance away.

The Vaynot clan's decision to move away from the area may seem peculiar, just like the war itself where two men had accepted a challenge from an entire clan. But when the elderly emissaries returned, they brought their fear along with them, though they tried to hide it. After long deliberation, the Vaynot men no longer doubted that Mebet, who was not so strong and not foolhardy, would bring more than his son along to fight with him. They were convinced that the Gods' Favorite would call on others, and those others would set off with him either for pay or out of fear.

No one among the Vaynot clan could have any idea of the enemy's numbers. According to the customs of war, they had sent out a scout, but he had still not returned and this only fueled the elders' fear. To capture a scout and smear his blood over the runners of one's sled was considered an anticipation of victory. Some of the Vaynot clan's warriors quietly mused about whether they would soon see a red track on the snow.

The sky slowly and gradually turned brighter. The sun, as if unwillingly, would finally crawl forth from behind the distant hills with their black snatches of forest. The Vaynot's war leader looked at the sky and then ordered that a tiny toy chum be erected with a little red flag atop – traditional custom required that the site of the looming battle be marked. The flag was set nearly at the same place where the white partridges had leaped up out of the snow at Mebet's command. The war leader had ordered that this be done so that their clever choice would discourage Mebet and, more importantly, so that any shameful hopes in his own warriors' hearts would be snuffed.

The war leader had seen these hopes on their faces and in their talk, for he knew war like an old man knows his old woman.

The sun was already half up, but their opponent had still not shown up. The waiting became unbearable, though it was now mixed with a faint hope that during the three days designated for preparations for honest fighting, Mebet had changed his mind, given his impudent son a thrashing, and perhaps even intended to back off. Regardless of whether Mebet brought other fighters along, if he or his son died in battle, or if just one of them was cut down on the bloody snow, the consequences for his family would be horrific. There would be no one to support Mebet's wife, the abducted Hadne would be returned to her parents, and Mebet's son (again, assuming he survived and was not left a cripple) would no longer be able to find himself a wife, except by abducting one as his father had been accustomed to do. Their herd and all their possessions would go to the victor as spoils. Mebet's family would be reduced to vagabonds with no home of their own, and they would have no choice but to enter into servitude among wealthy people. Yadne in her old age would have to do the dirtiest, most laborious chores. Hadko would be hired to tend herds in return for the occasional chunk of meat, given to him along with contempt and abuse. Mebet's pride would never survive such an outcome. Any strength, even his, has its limits, and luck can betray even those on whom it had settled. The Vaynot clan's forces were great, and no one would accuse them of lacking good hunters and brave warriors.

These thoughts wandered through the minds of many Vaynot men and some were nearly convinced of them entirely, when suddenly a cry was heard from above. It was a lookout placed in the highest tree:

"They're coming! I can see reindeer, two reindeer, and a sled…"

The Vaynots' war leader craned his neck up. "Where is Mebet?" he shouted. "How many men does he have with him?"

"I cannot see any people," the lookout answered. "Just the sled and nothing else."

"Take a better look, you blind owl," the war leader shouted grumpily. "There should be people."

"There aren't any people, Nyaruy. I can't see any…"

Nyaruy, "Forked Arrow" – such was the Vaynot war leader's name – ordered the lookout to stay there in the tree and immediately announce if he saw anything suspicious. The two draft reindeer were moving slowly and still far off. But even as time went by, the lookout sitting on the branches still had not seen any people.

The warriors gathered around Nyaruy and wondered what this empty sled might mean. Surely, one said, the sled was not bare, and Mebet and his son were hiding there under skins, and maybe others as well. Another man suggested that the foe had perhaps sent gifts to buy his way out of fighting.

"Foolishness," the war leader said. "Do those reindeer really know the way to our camp?"

The men retorted that Mebet was not like other men, and so his reindeer were not like other reindeer. But the war leader did not manage to reply to this, for a shout came from high in the tree: there really were no people in the sled. Not a single person.

The pair of white-headed reindeer approached the Vaynot host. They were hauling a sled with remnants of red ribbons – the same sled of courtship. There was nothing else on the sled but an old deerskin. The war leader examined the animals from all sides: on the dark-gray flank of the right-hand reindeer he saw a white arrow with a circle around it. The paint was still fresh and the mark, which the Vaynots had never seen before, might be taken for Mebet's own war mark.

The host of warriors had so far remained in the forest, but now they went out into the middle of the white field. They stopped there and remained silent, uncertain what to make of this ruse. Everyone waited for Nyaruy to say something, but he did not utter a word. Finally, when the silence had dragged on for a long time, one of the warriors spoke up, laughing at his own words:

"Maybe Mebet tried to buy us off with a pair of reindeer, a ragged old deerskin, and this sled – isn't it a new sled, after all?"

"Quiet, you stupid wolverine," Nyaruy roared.

Again there was silence.

"I have had enough of these riddles, I am tired of his mockery," the war leader said. "We did everything as it should be done, but now I spit on traditional custom. We shall wait a little while longer, but if Mebet does not show, we shall go to him and put out his fire. People can think whatever they like about it, but that is what I will do. Mebet deserves what's coming to him."

Nyaruy's determination dispelled any doubt and uncertainty. The host of warriors leaped up, gave a joyful shout, and banged their iron. When the bottom tip of the sun was already visible over the horizon, the Vaynots set off for Mebet's camp. Behind the host several reindeer-drawn sleds followed, empty so that the Vaynots could haul off their lawful booty and, if necessary, any wounded.

Mebet lived quite close, only half of a day's walk. Nyaruy expected to be there by noon. They walked quickly, even merrily, and this pleased Forked Arrow. Only one thing troubled him: their course lay through forests and along small rivers that had still not begun to thaw, but nowhere could Nyaruy see any tracks of human beings – only snow which the wind had polished to the smoothness of bright metal.

Nyaruy's experience told him that an enemy in Mebet's position had no choice but to try to lure the Vaynots into the taiga and besiege them there. However, it would not make sense for just two men to lie in ambush. And hiding many men without leaving any tracks would be very difficult, nearly impossible – after all, any man of the taiga is capable not only of spotting tracks, but also hearing the breathing of snakes, pointing to the most distant star, and distinguishing between the scents which the wind brings.

Nevertheless, the reindeer which had arrived at their camp had borne the mark of war, and that meant that Mebet had accepted his enemies' challenge. How the Gods' Favorite intended to respond to it, Nyaruy did not know: neither the snow, nor the wind with the scents and sounds it bore, gave him the slightest clue.

They had nearly arrived at Mebet's camp. They could already see smoke rising from a hearth somewhere near a riverbank. With a gesture the war leader bade his men to stop. There were no apparent signs of danger, but Nyaruy suddenly recalled how their scout had vanished. Without wasting time on making a decision, but simply giving into his innate warrior instincts, he decided to attack at once and with all the forces he had.

The Vaynots, who had prepared their weapons for battle, arranged themselves in a single long line with some space between each man, and they began moving towards the camp. When the top of the larger dwelling appeared in the distance, Nyaruy stopped and launched into the air the first arrow, one with a black feather that would serve as a signal. The men could see the arrow, shot off by Nyaruy's deft hand, cut through the black smoke from the hearth. The Vaynots waited for the enemy to reveal himself or at least shoot off an arrow in return, but neither happened.

"It seems to me," Nyaruy shouted, "that there is no one in the camp. Mebet and his brood have fled." He gestured for his men to continue onward. With quick steps, the entire line of armed men approached Mebet's homestead. The camp really did seem deserted. Only three reindeer stood some distance apart from each other, chewing on dry moss that had been laid out for them.

In the big chum from which smoke issued, the Vaynots found Yadne. Their foe's wife was sitting at the hearth and occupied with her sewing. She did not show the slightest unease at the appearance of the armed men. The two other dwellings were empty – even the fires there were cold.

"Where are your husband and son?" Nyaruy asked. "Where is our girl Hadne?"

"How should I know?" Yadne answered nonchalantly. "I suppose they went off to fight you."

"They didn't show up."

"Well, how would I know?" Yadne answered with the same indifference. "Men don't tell women where they intend to fight, that is men's business."

"Get up and come with us." Nyaruy went up to his foe's wife and grabbed the hood of her deerskin coat. The Vaynot war leader was getting angry.

"Apparently Mebet loves you so much that he abandoned you to the whims of the enemy on the first day. Perhaps you have grown too old for him?"

He tore at the hood, upon which Yadne fell to the ground, but she rose unaided and then walked outside.

By this time all of the Vaynot men had arrived at the camp. The warriors staggered about randomly, still unable to fathom what was going on. Some had already got down to plundering the camp. Mebet's chums were well-made from new skins, and even at the bottom he had not laid birchbark as the men of poorer households do. The chums held various appealing items: pots, clothing, skins, furs, and perhaps they would even find weapons. And Mebet's wife was not so old and she too would be completely appropriate spoils.

Nyaruy's thoughts were far from these mercenary concerns, however.

"Listen, woman," he said quietly. "I don't know where Mebet and his son are hiding and where they have hidden the girl of ours they stole. But I can't believe that you don't know. The god of war is an angry god. Do not mock him, Yadne. He doesn't like when people mock him, especially women."

Mebet's wife suddenly smiled at the enemy's words.

"No use," Nyaruy shook his head. "You will tell us where Mebet, his son, and our Hadne are. It's just that before that, we will do something to you which even men could not withstand. We'll begin to break your bones, to make a mask for feast days from your face, and many other things. We have some great experts among us…"

A warrior ran up:

"Shouldn't we be gathering booty now, Nyaruy?"

In reply the war leader yelled at him with such vehemence that the warrior leaped back:

"You are as greedy as chipmunks and foolish as wolverines. The war has not even started yet, and you are already talking about booty."

He was right, the war had not even started yet. With the same loud and angry shout Nyaruy ordered his warriors to examine every part of the camp and study every track, every fallen branch, and report to him about everything. The warriors dispersed to carry out their leader's orders.

"Just think it over," he told Yadne. "I will give you some time to reflect on things."

Again the war leader was reminded of how their scout had vanished. And that eerie and foreboding stillness… No, the war had not even started.

The men he had sent to thoroughly examine the camp now returned.

"Look at what I have found, Nyaruy. Over there, in the forest."

In his hands the warrior held a slender pine trunk. It was long, nearly twice the height of a man, and at its lower end it was as thick as a grown man's arm. It was sharpened to a point at the tip.

The war leader studied this find and he felt a sudden flash of alarm. This was not simply a pine trunk – the wood was still so smooth and bright that it had clearly been chopped down and sharpened to a point quite recently, perhaps the day before. This tree undoubtedly represented some kind of weapon, a product of Mebet's ingenuity that had been accidentally dropped.

"What is this for?" Nyaruy thought out loud. "What is this for?" he then asked Yadne, nearly shouting the words. "When did your husband cut these trees down? Tell me. Tell me!" He drew his curved and shiny knife from its sheath. The knife was very similar to that which Mebet had given to Hadko after the latter's great hunt. The war leader held the blade up to the woman's throat. "Is this a stake for bear-hunting?"

"Maybe," Yadne whispered through her clenched jaws.

A slender stream of blood snaked down her throat and stained the collar of her coat.

"Let me go, put your knife away, and I'll tell you everything."

Nyaruy drew the knife away. Yadne wiped her neck with a handful of snow and then threw the now-pink lump aside. But instead of giving the war leader any answer, a powerful and piercing whistle issued from her lips. The one they called the Forked Arrow winced from the unexpectedness of it all.

Neither Nyaruy nor the other Vaynot men had time to see how the three reindeer, which had been meekly chewing on moss, sharply bolted at their mistress's whistle. The reindeer pulled sharply on long ropes which had been cleverly concealed under the snow. Immediately a dense row of sharpened pine trunks came shooting up terrifyingly from under the snow and all Mebet's camp came to resemble the jaws of a giant pike. The warriors cried out as one. The Vaynots' reindeer, spooked, bolted off without even knowing where they were going, and they were the first to be impaled on this deadly fence.

Thus the war began.

Men rushed about like blizzard snow as arrows came flying towards them. The arrows came from every direction, some from above as if straight down from the sky hard and unceasingly, like thick drops from a terrible black storm cloud. The hand of a great archer generously distributed death among the Vaynots and men fell, struck in their faces and necks. Some managed to break through the dense encirclement of stakes, though shreds of their clothing remained on the sharpened tips. Amid this fighting and panicking retreat, Nyaruy did not see where Yadne vanished to. The war leader regained his self-composure after a momentary lapse. With shouts and blows he stopped his frantic warriors from panicking and, finally, he managed to get those who remained into formation in a circle and ordered them to launch their arrows. The Vaynot men shot without seeing the enemy and they died. When the host of warriors, which had been quite large for such a peculiar war, had been reduced to a mere five men, the steady flow of arrows from the sky suddenly stopped.

The camp was littered with bodies. An opening gaped in the encirclement of stakes, where the reindeer had broken through with their heavy bodies and then died. None of the remaining Vaynot men took advantage of this opening to flee. The gap had proved useful to Yadne – while the arrows were still coming down, she had run out from the distant chum in which she hid and, leaping over the reindeer carcasses, escaped into the taiga.

An arrow had followed her from behind, however. It hit her in the back and cast her face-down into the snow. In the place where Yadne fell, only the slender wood of the arrow with its brown feather could be seen.

Nyaruy had not noticed which of his men had launched this arrow. But he did notice when the twang of a bowstring rang and the red-mustached warrior to his right fell forward with an arrow through his neck. Nyaruy now recalled that it had been the same man who asked if it were time to begin gathering booty.

"That was the last of them." The voice came from the direction from which the arrows had flown.

"And my own quiver is empty," came the reply.

Heavy clumps of snow slid off the branches of the large larch trees and plopped down onto the ground below. A man then jumped down from the branches and walked unhurriedly towards the camp. Nyaruy saw that it was Hadko.

The same sound was heard, and then Mebet descended. The two men were in cheerful spirits and, though they stood at a distance from one another, they spoke freely and loudly to one another.

"I told you that using the bone-tipped arrows, too, would be fine, but you didn't listen to me. During a war, just like at a wedding, you have to be lavish."

"Next time I will be even more generous than you, father…"

They walked up to what remained of the Vaynot host and then threw their bows over their shoulders, making no attempt to defend themselves or hide. The warrior standing next to Nyaruy raised his own bow and placed the white-feathered arrow close to his right cheek, but then with a sharp gesture Nyaruy knocked the arrow away and the bowstring went limp. The war leader himself did not know what had led him to stop his man from shooting.

When Mebet and Hadko had come up to the outer edge of the encirclement of spikes, which posed no danger, the Vaynots still crouched with a bent knee, in position for shooting off their arrows. But now they had lowered their bows and the arrowheads stared limply at the ground.

Mebet was the first to speak. "Greetings, Forked Arrow. That is what they call you, isn't it?"

Nyaruy did not respond.

"Now there are five of you and two of us. A fair proportion for an honest war. After all, don't you Vaynot men insist on an honest war? Your elders were right, I have heeded those esteemed men and, in order to avoid tempting fate, I decided to start things off by slightly reducing your forces. I realize that this was not our agreement, and the site of the battle is not what was declared earlier, but I think that isn't so important anymore. Now we – my son and I – will fight you with spears."

Nyaruy was a magnanimous man. "I think it an honor to fight with you, Mebet, one on one. But don't you speak to us of an honest war."

"Was I the only one to breach our agreement?" Mebet asked.

"I don't mean the agreement. You set your wife out as bait, like a piece of meat to lure a fox. Look." Nyaruy gestured across the encirclement of stakes, to where snow drifted over the open white expanse. "Your wife is lying there with an arrow in her back. It was a miracle that your own arrows did not get her killed at once, but now she is probably dead already."

Mebet turned pale. He had seen Yadne run out of the camp, but he had not been aware of any arrow. Moreover, Nyaruy's remark about a piece of meat was right, though Yadne had herself asked her husband to let her play a role in the war.

"Mama! Maaama!" Hadko cried, but no sound came from the place where the Vaynot war leader had pointed to.

"Go to her," Mebet hoarsely ordered his son.

Hadko was visibly wracked with anguish. "You will stand alone against five men," he said.

"Don't you worry about me," Mebet replied.

"There are five of them…"

Mebet roared so fearsomely that it nearly knocked Hadko down into the snow. "Go to her!"

But before Hadko could take a single step, a tree quivered and dropped a sprinkle of snow onto the ground. A small figure fell from the tree's branches into a snowdrift and, throwing a correspondingly small bow over its back, ran across the white field. The snow nearly came up to the person's waist and they could see the figure continually fall and disappear into the white, only to rise again and keep running.

It was Hadne.

Later in the day after the Vaynot emissaries had left, the Gods' Favorite really had no idea at all about how he would wage the war. He needed solitude. Mebet went to the riverbank not far from his camp, and there he sat on a stone and sank into thought. No one would dare approach him at a time like this.

Then suddenly, something strange happened, and it left Mebet startled. A large black bird fell to the ground nearly at his feet. It was a crow with an arrow through it, and it was one of Mebet's own arrows, with a notch on the wood and an eagle feather. The Gods' Favorite turned and saw Hadne standing a dozen paces from him and holding a bow in her hands.

"This is too heavy for me and the bowstring is too tight, I'm not strong enough to use it," Hadne said, her eyes kept pointed to the ground as a sign of respect. "Do you have some smaller bow that would be good for me?"

It was one of those rare occasions when the Gods' Favorite was so thunderstruck that he could not even imagine that someone else – let alone a woman – had dared touch one of his weapons.

"You are my people now," Hadne answered before Mebet could even ask the inevitable question.

On that same day Mebet found a bow for the young woman.

When she was a child, her elder brothers had fun teaching her to use a bow. This schooling came in handy: Hadne, hidden among the branches of a larch, had shot arrows at the Vaynot men, at her own kin. Hadne had no idea how many men she killed then, but there was no doubt that she left many families bereft of a husband and father.

All of the men – Mebet, Hadko, and the Vaynots – had suddenly forgotten about everything and only stared as Hadne ran off. Now she stopped, took the bow from behind her back, flung it away, took several more steps, disappeared into the snow, then rose to her full height and shouted something at them, waving her arms. No one could make out exactly what she was shouting, but there was no need to: Hadne had found Yadne. She helped the other woman stand up and now two figures, one appearing and the other disappearing, came across the white expanse. Mebet's wife could walk, and that meant that she was still alive.

Hadko dashed over to his bride and his mother. Mebet stayed put, one man against five of the enemy. But as his son was running across the field, the war was already over.

Nyaruy was the first to realize it. Shame came over him now as if he had been sucked into a bottomless abyss, into a stinking swamp. It was the shame of his foolish defeat in the war over the abducted girl. The man they called Forked Arrow felt empty inside now, there remained not even the smallest trace of anger at the little woman who had betrayed her clan and killed her own kin.

Nyaruy rose to his full height and thrust the butt of his spear into the brittle snow that was stained crimson with blood. He put his throat over the spear's sharp blade and then he fell forward. He had been a good war leader. For many years the Vaynot clan had entrusted matters of war to him and they had never experienced a loss before.

The empty sleds which Nyaruy had brought along for hauling off booty now proved useful for carting off the dead. Mebet and Hadko themselves helped to load them. A few frantic reindeer, which had remained miraculously unscathed under the hail of arrows, pulled this caravan of the dead down the established path. On each of the two sleds, two of the surviving Vaynots rode. The goads to drive the reindeer on were left somewhere at the bottom of the sleds; the men had forgotten them as they piled the bodies on. This did not bother the sleds' drivers, as their reindeer knew where to go, and all that mattered was that they get away from this terrible camp.

MEBET'S GLORY

Word of the victory over the Vaynot host swept like a snowstorm across the taiga and the tundra. So astonishing was the news that for a long time people were unsure of what to make of it.

One thing was clear, however. The myth of Mebet, the one whom the gods favored and a man not of this world, became ever stronger and turned into firm belief. But this firm belief gave people no comfort. Again the old men and women of the clans puffed on a pipe filled with dry moss and wondered who among the gods had seduced Mebet's mother. They recalled how Mebet had hunted and slain a bear several years in a row, refusing any helpers in doing so, and even as a youth he sat in the circle of elders at the bear feast, which earned him the envy of other hunters. When Mebet grew weary of being shown this honor, to their envy was added contempt.

This strange man of the clan of Vela did not honor the gods or the spirits, he did not perform sacrifices, he did not visit the shamans, and there was no taboo that he did not violate. He had entered the unclean chum of a woman giving birth, he allowed his wife to slice the pike fish up, he did not pray before hunting, and he would leave a wounded animal to rot if he found better and bigger prey. His chum had no sacred height nor forbidden lower portion. He himself was the entirety of his home, and people and possessions were arrayed in his home as he, Mebet, willed them to be.

People came to accept that it was not their place to criticize the Gods' Favorite. But it troubled them that Mebet was never punished by the gods and the spirits. When the taiga was struck by a plague that decimated whole herds of reindeer, or an illness that killed people, or years of famine that brought animals out of the forest, these woes would briefly visit Mebet's camp, too, but they would quickly depart as if reluctant to take too much from him.

Even in the years of great hardship, Mebet never once threw his mittens down at his wife's feet as a sign of an unsuccessful hunt. Even if he caught no big animals, the taiga would give him at least some small birds, and thus his family could survive. Mebet accepted equally the woes and the blessings which the supernatural powers sent, and he did not suffer from the age-old diseases of humankind: envy, a thirst for glory, greed, and revenge.

People suffered. After that remarkable war, their world was again torn apart. The very existence of this inexplicable man from the tribe of Vela led them to blasphemous thoughts that perhaps the spirits' power was exaggerated and their very names were mixed up, and so any sacrifices or incantations were just wasted, the old traditions were false, and the old laws pointless.

The terrible and shameful fate which the Vaynot clan suffered elevated Mebet even higher in people's eyes. He was aware of this, but he felt no particular pride or pleasure at it, except that the thought caused a smile – the same light and divine smile which had been with him since his youth – to flash across his face. To seize authority over people, to become one of those great leaders whose memory lived on in the stories of the old, would have been easier for him than picking up a dropped mitten. To pick up the mitten Mebet would have bent down without a second thought, but he did not want to bend down for anything else. What he already had was enough for him, or perhaps already too much.

When people would gossip that Mebet was descended from one of the gods, this initially entertained him. But after some time, he almost took the notion seriously. However, it simply amused him, for Mebet did not know the anxiety which the successful person feels, that sooner or later his luck will run out. Now, when Mebet could look back on already a long life lived, one thought grew ever clearer and more straightforward within him. His good fortune did not lie in his being stronger and more successful than others. His good fortune lay in his ability to forget almost entirely any suffering. Mebet's memory retained some fleeting instances of anger, brief moments when he desired revenge, or temporary annoyances, but the suffering that draws other people to compose endless and wistful songs, never stayed with him long enough to leave any clear traces.

Mebet would look at other people and see how they made each other suffer, and how they would hone in their minds reasons for new suffering. And when the whole consequences of what they had wrought fell upon them, they would weep and complain to the spirits, or castigate them with a showering of curses. Therefore, as Mebet thought with a smile, the spirits were more needing of sympathy than the dead.

The further Mebet's thoughts receded from other people, the less place there was in his heart for suffering, which now was reduced to a pale, nearly nonexistent ghost. Mebet knew this about himself, and he wished the same for the people around him. To stand apart from other people was his own form of goodness, and he knew no other. Only one thing troubled his heart, and this was that the people close to him would not accept this goodness in him sincerely, but rather only out of the ingrained habit of honoring those who are older and stronger.

Of course, it is not only human beings who conceive ways to make one another suffer: there also exist illness, hunger, and frost so severe that it can turn birds to stone. Death exists, and it was not human beings who came up with that. But the right to live is granted to the one strong enough for it. Musing on death is a waste of time and energy. While a person lives, death is absent; death comes, and then it is the person who is no longer there. What is there to think about? In truth, Mebet did not believe in death. He could see that his hair was turning gray, but he was not losing his strength – if anything he was growing stronger. And if the spirits had never refused him any small thing all his long life, would they refuse him any big thing?

Wisdom, which people so exalted, was for Mebet simply a consequence of one's legs growing weak as usually happens in old age. That old man who long ago, thirty years before, had called Mebet a fool and said, "Don't you know that sooner or later your heart will break?" was no longer capable of walking at all. When once in a while the Gods' Favorite remembered him, he smiled: "That must have meant that he was a man of great wisdom…"

He considered his victory over the Vaynot men to represent the victory of his dazzling mind. It was that mind which had brought forth the image of a pike's jaws, and that image gave rise to the deadly encirclement of long, sharpened pine stakes hidden under the snow, and then raised at once by the three reindeer bolting at Yadne's whistle… Luring the enemy into the deadly heart of this flower was also the product of his dazzling mind.

Yadne should have inevitably died – Mebet was aware of this, though he did hope for a chance to save her, though it was only a tiny chance. He had not even given her armor to wear under her coat, for Nyaruy was an intelligent and experienced man and he would have discovered the ruse immediately. It would have been fairer to place Hadko there as the bait, after all, he was the one who unleashed this war with his words. But Mebet's son was a good shooter and therefore he needed to be hidden among the branches where he could launch his arrows. His mother had never held a bow in her hands, and moreover, she had herself asked to serve as the "piece of meat". She was a peculiar woman…

But would anyone dare accuse Mebet of cruelty? What use was all this talk now of phantoms: cruelty, mercy, the law? The simple truth is that the Vaynots had been thoroughly and horrifically defeated, Hadko had received a bride, and Yadne had survived.

The arrow hit Yadne as it was at the end of its flight. It had pierced her coat made from two layers of skillfully wrought deerskin, penetrated under her shoulder blade to the depth of the arrowhead, and there it came to rest. This proved his wife's salvation. Yadne was weakened from pain and loss of blood and now hardly able to walk. His son carried her in his arms into the chum.

It was Mebet who took the arrow out. He ordered his son's bride to make the fire in the hearth hotter. Hadne deftly did what she had been told. Hadko stood nearby, anguish and perplexity visible in his face.

"Everyone leave," Mebet said. "I have to undress her."

Hadko and his bride stood outside, waiting fearfully for Yadne to cry out, but no cry came. Yadne made it through all of this without a sound.

Mebet broke the wood of the arrow close to the tip. Carefully, so that he would not disturb the iron lodged in Yadne's back, he removed her coat. When pain struck her, Yadne moaned, but the moan did not make it past her lips which were closed so tightly that they had turned blue. In the same way, without crying out, she shuddered when Mebet, with a sharp movement, pulled the arrowhead from the wound. A red trickle issued from the place where the arrow had been lodged – clearly Yadne still had some blood left in her.

Mebet studied the arrowhead. He then held it over the fire for a moment, took his knife out, and scraped something off the iron. Carefully holding his wife's head with his other hand, he brought the knife to her lips. A tiny piece of hot fat bubbled on the wide and shining blade.

"Eat it," Mebet told his wife. "This is flesh from your wound. I heard that it can help."

Without opening her eyes, Yadne brushed her lips against the blade and then fell back, unconscious. She did not come to for a long time, and now it was Hadne who unceasingly stayed by her side.

HADKO'S WEDDING

For the people of the taiga, no less astonishing than Mebet's victory over the Vaynot clan was Hadne's betrayal. She was the daughter of honored and wealthy parents. It was not particularly rare to find in the taiga a woman who had mastered the art of the bow, but Hadne had shot at her own people. She had killed her own kin who had come to free her and to avenge her. Such betrayal was something that no one had ever heard or seen before, and therefore they found it almost unbelievable.

People talked of how the abducted girl must have been afraid of Mebet, how she was suddenly inflamed by passion for his son, how she long held a grudge against her parents and clan, how her mother-in-law had put her under a spell, how she must have been bribed, or how women were naturally evil. Each of these versions had its grain of truth. If her mother-in-law had enchanted her, then it must have been with kindness, and her sudden feelings for Hadko were simply her submission to a marriage that was now inevitable.

But the main reason was much simpler: Hadne was with child. It was with this burden in her belly, however light and nearly imperceptible it still was, that she had hid in the branches of a larch and launched her arrows. It amazed Mebet that she did this like any routine task. The Blizzard Woman did not show the slightest mercy to her kin; her mother-in-law's wound worried her much more. Hadne tended to Yadne selflessly and took over all of the chores around the home.

Yadne had been the first to know that the bride was pregnant – Hadne had told Yadne herself. Then Mebet learned of it and finally Hadko.

This solved the riddle which had preoccupied the Gods' Favorite in recent days: why had Hadne snapped out of her daze and a woman who seemed to have been completely crushed, suddenly came to life, began talking, entered into the life of a new family, and even begged him to fight? The tears which flowed when she saw the elderly emissaries from the Vaynot clan were the last tears she ever shed. Hadne had stepped over a threshold dividing her new life from her former one, and she could never go back. At that time only she was aware of this, and she was ready to accept whatever fate brought her. Fate brought her treachery and fratricide, but Hadne readily accepted these and she insisted that Mebet trust her to use a bow.

Perhaps she suffered from remorse at this, but her pregnant womb proved stronger than her conscience. When Hadne fell pregnant in a strange new home, her womb told her that she was no longer of the Vaynot clan, and there was no law that could convince the Blizzard Woman that she had done ill when she committed those inexpiable acts. Hadne was in the right, like a she-wolf who was ready to bite at the throat of any creature that approached its squeaking litter of cubs, whether it be its own brother or the leader of the pack. Though her pregnancy had barely begun, Hadne lived with an animal sense of what was right, and she found in it strength, justification, and all that is exalted among human beings.

As for when Hadko had visited his bride and made her – though unlawfully and without the customary rites – his wife, Mebet and Yadne could only speculate. They did not ask their son, and they comforted themselves by saying that such a thing was bound to happen sooner or later anyway.

Yadne was enthusiastic at Hadne's announcement that she would bear a child, but Hadko became taciturn and sullen. He spent more and more time away from the home. He usually said that he was going hunting, and indeed he would come back with some catch. But sometimes he returned with just a couple of grouse that he had apparently just killed along the way. In recent days he had come home empty-handed and was avoiding Hadne and his parents. Clearly something gnawed at him.

"Why are you so glum?" his mother asked him.

"Poor hunting…"

"Aren't you happy that you have a lovely wife and she's with child?"

"I'm happy," Mebet's son replied gruffly and, to escape this conversation, he immediately went to find something to do, preferably far away from the camp.

Hadko had taken Hadne forcibly and cruelly, on the very next day after she had arrived at their camp. Mebet had ordered the abducted girl to be set up in the small chum, and then he himself went into the taiga. Yadne was off in the forest chopping wood, Hadko, who had been ostensibly engaged in repairing a sled, now resolutely walked toward the dwelling, threw back the flap over the entrance, and stepped over the threshold. Hadne was sitting on some furs behind the hearth, with her head bent and her fingers bunched into tiny, strong fists. He almost could not see her face, as it was hidden behind her hair that reached down to her shoulders. Nevertheless, Hadko got a brief glimpse of his bride's beauty and his heart pounded evilly. With a single leap he pounced on Hadne and held his hand over her mouth. The dull sound of an ax carried from the nearby forest, but Hadko was not even thinking about the chance that his mother might return.

He expected Hadne to cry out, attempt to break free, or at least bite his hand, but under his palm he felt only tightly closed lips. Hadne did not make a sound or the slightest movement, her lips under his palm softened – and Hadko began to tear Hadne's clothes off.

The sound of his mother chopping wood still carried when Mebet's son had done what he came to do.

Hadne put her clothes back on, rolled over on her stomach, and pressed her face to her fists which remained tightly closed. Hadko stepped out and continued to repair the sled. His thoughts were not focused on anything in particular, but his heart warmed and slightly tingled from having taken revenge. Hadko's unremitting pain, his sudden hatred of his father, and that awful daughter of Pyak's were the cause of what had happened in the chum. Hadko did not regret what he had done in the slightest.

On the same day when his father had mocked foolish Makhako, when he presented his son with his own living gift for him, Hadko immediately decided that this gift would serve for revenge. Perhaps the gods had shown him mercy by arranging for everything to happen this way. Hadko's mind was filled with terrible visions: the Pyak family's dwellings were engulfed in flames, their structural elements now visible, and then collapsed, the hot hearth stones hissing in the snow; the Pyak's dogs with arrows in their sides, whimpering and pawing the air as they died; the spooked reindeer running off into the forest; old Pyak crumpled up like a fat worm, a spear sticking out from his back, the sharp blade having penetrated flesh and bone... And Pyak's daughter – Hadko only later learned her name, which was Myaduna, "Born among Guests" – lying twisted on the ground and crawling away from him. He found the terror in her eyes delectable, and the anticipation of doing the right thing – executing the woman who had so heinously and foully rejected his mad love – stifled any hesitation and spurred him on. Hadko would spit in Myaduna's face (he always reminded himself of this, spitting was a must), laugh as carefreely as she had, and then raise the iron blade over her head...

Perhaps his visions would have come true. But then the war with the Vaynot clan came, and Hadne had ceased to reside in the chum designated for women during their unclean time of the month, which gave rise to her mother-in-law's first suspicions.

Once Hadko's desire for revenge had been satiated, he forgot about it. But then something else came upon him, something more terrible still. Hadko was wracked with guilt. It tormented him just as bitterly, it sapped him of all motivation, made him irritable, and it led him to shun human beings, all conversation or work. The worst thing of all was that Hadne had shown no resentment, anger, or tears. She did not shy away from this husband she had never asked for, but she did not come to him either. Hadko was tortured and he hoped that she would be the first to say something, just a single word or trifling remark, like asking him to bring water or quiet a barking dog. He would look for something to do in the home, even if it were not really necessary – he checked to see that the straps on the sled were tight, he would do women's work like chopping and carrying firewood. He hoped to the end that Hadne would call him to eat, and he did not require any sweetness in her words, just the mere words themselves… But it was his mother who called him to eat and grumbled that he always kept her waiting.

They were already sleeping together: Hadne showed no fear or disgust towards him – she simply rolled over, drifted off, and slept an untroubled sleep. Hadko could only get brief snatches of sleep and he got up long before dawn. His arms, so strong and capable of battle and great hunts, felt deadened. He was ashamed of his hands, ashamed of himself.

Never did he touch Hadne now, not even her clothes.

It was desperation that had awakened his tongue when he told the Vaynot emissaries that he would not give up his bride and ordered them to depart. Mebet's son hoped that this desperation, and the bravery which he would probably show in battle, would save him and somewhat cleanse him. However, neither the war nor their victory in it changed anything. Hadne had surpassed Hadko in desperation. The Blizzard Man understood this. He felt his spirit dying within him, and if nothing were done, then with time he himself would die.

One month after the war, Hadko disappeared, along with one draft reindeer, a sled, and Voipel. Mebet had not yet returned from a big hunt.

"Where did your husband go off to?" Yadne asked the bride.

"He didn't tell me."

"And he took the sled," his mother said to herself. "Why did he need a big sled?"

Hadne sighed deeply and stretched blissfully. "Maybe he just wants to catch a lot of small fowl…" she said.

Yadne did not like this remark, but she let it pass and only thought to herself that they could now forget that little square-faced doll who, out of fear, had lost her power of speech, for Hadne had turned into an ordinary woman.

That day, when the sun was high, Mebet returned and also asked about his son. He accepted his wife's answer calmly, just like all the other answers he had ever heard. He was tired, and so were his dogs and reindeer. Enormous pieces of elk meat were stacked on his sled, under a sniff skin that smelled of blood. Despite his fatigue, Mebet began to carry the meat to his storehouse some distance from the camp. The Gods' Favorite brought the last piece back with him:

"Put this in the pot," he told the women. "There's no room for it in the storehouse. What need have we of any more hunting?"

That winter, Mebet's family lived contentedly without ever once worrying about food and never short of anything.

Yet the reason that Hadko had disappeared so suddenly and with such secrecy was something bigger than a hunt. Mebet's heir had set off to perform a great feat of heroism. A great feat would bring healing to his soul, save his life, and end his suffering. So fired up was he that he drove his reindeer on mercilessly, though he had no idea where he was going. When the reindeer, which were not keen to die of exhaustion, stopped to rest, thoughts flickered in Hadko's mind.

They were not sad, these thoughts. Hadko lacked real familiarity with women and not only on account of his youth. Rather, for people of the taiga, a woman's soul is a much less interesting subject than some new traps. But he knew one simple thing: he could get through to his woman with a gift. He needed to perform a wondrous feat, something that no one had ever seen or heard of before, and this would melt Hadne's heart like a handful of snow in a boiling pot, and all his sense of guilt would be utterly forgotten.

In fact, the Blizzard Man was not thinking so much as dreaming. When he himself realized that, his dreams turned back into mere thoughts, and Mebet's son again felt at a loss, his anguish returned. He suddenly became aware that he did not know what this wondrous feat should be. He would not win Hadne back with merely heaps of game. He could set traps and then visit other clans and trade his catch for embroidered clothing and jewelry wrought from yellow metal. But springtime furs were not considered lovely and they were not highly valued, and so even if multitudes of fox and sable fell into his traps, he still would not be able to purchase something truly amazing with their faded and ragged furs. And not every clan was rich in fine objects and embroidered clothing. Among the clans where both were abundant, he might kill for them or, worse yet, steal them away, but that is not how Hadko wanted to do things. His gift had to be a pure and honest one.

The four of them – one unhappy man, the reindeer, and the dog – stood there in the middle of the taiga and did not budge. The sun was high, as high as it could ever rise in late winter. The air was clear and the wind still. There was frozen silence, and only trace echoes of some vague movement descended upon them. There was no one around, only the taiga, and Hadko decided to surrender to its authority, to submit to its will – he had no other choice. He did not regret taking such a reckless approach.

He unloaded the sled and got down to setting up a temporary camp. After spending some time on this, he took Voipel along and went off to hunt, though only to get food for the next day. They still had some food stocked for the evening, though little remained, foolishly little. By sundown Hadko had caught two black grouse. He gave one to Voipel and hid the other one in the sled for himself.

The next morning, his work began. Mebet's heir set out traps, followed tracks to the beast that had left them, returned to his camp, and upon the next sunrise he set out to do the same thing all over again. This went on day after day. Three times Hadko came across an elk's track, but he never managed to reach it: the tracks were too old now, and besides, an elk was not the prey which the Blizzard Man needed.

At every sunset a shadow fell across his heart. The taiga seemed to be toying with him, but in order to fully enjoy its authority over him, it did not let him die of starvation and it left him with some pittance: once a scrawny, sorry-looking fox wandered into his trap, and soon thereafter Voipel came back carrying a live hare in his jaws. The taiga sent him petty fowl, and each evening he turned their plucked bodies on a skewer over the fire… The taiga was silent.

Hadko moved camp several times. The snow, though it thawed on the surface, would freeze overnight to a hard crust, and therefore the reindeer would be forced to pick the trees around Hadko's shelter clean of bark. Less and less were joy and fearsomeness seen in Voipel's huge and otherworldly eyes.

Sometimes as Hadko looked at the curved knife which his father had given him, he would recall the great hunt he had undertaken to gather a bride-price, and he would reflect on the vicissitudes of fate. He thought about how every catch involves not just strength and skill, but also the mercy of those powers which govern all living things. His father believed in himself alone and had no need of any other faith. But there were no other men like his father, just like there were no deeper pitfalls than the one that he, Mebet's son, had fallen into. Now every other person in this world surely found things better, easier, than he did.

When his father was not around, Hadko felt a strong desire to act the same way as other people: they perform sacrifices, speak certain words, prepare for the hunt. They do the same when something very important happens in their lives. But the Blizzard Man did not know the necessary words, he did not know how a sacrifice should be performed. His father had not taught him, and what Hadko had seen among other people was nearly forgotten now. Sometimes he felt that the feeling of powerlessness that occasionally fell upon him was a consequence of precisely this lack of the right words. At night he would look up at the stars and at the white blot smeared across the sky, and he would recall the story his mother had told him: long ago, people of every tribe and clan in the taiga had pursued an animal, chased it into the sky, and no longer did they walk any path on earth but kept chasing it up there, and will keep on chasing it forever. And the beast they stalked was a wondrous one, such as no longer exist on our earth.

Hadko would look up at that streak across the sky until his neck hurt, trying to identify people or the animal in it, and he did not even notice how his lips would murmur words that were not the right ones, merely human words:

"Hey, you, up there in the sky, send me the animal. Send me the animal, please. I really need an animal and you, sky people, can help me, give me that animal. I would be forever grateful to you. I will look up into the sky and thank you every night. Please, sky people, send me the animal. Provide an animal for my Hadne, or I will die of my grief. Sky people, hear me, please, send me an animal…"

He would look up and murmur, and the white streak and all the bright stars around it would twinkle and gradually fade into morning.

One morning Hadko moved camp, about half a day's journey from his previous site. Voipel had gone far in front of him, but the dog returned at midday – he was running at full speed, his eyes burning with excitement for the hunt.

Hadko understood that Voipel had found a den, and with his nose the great dog had sniffed out that single current of warm air that passed through the tiny hole in a bank of snow, a hole so small it was barely visible…

Mebet's son hurried after Voipel. He had never hunted after a bear before, let alone on his own and unaided. Without quite understanding what was happening to him, Hadko felt a rapturous awe before those mysterious people in the sky whom he had asked yesterday for an animal – he had not properly prayed but simply asked, like a miserably poor man asks a stranger for just a little help to survive and the stranger refuses him… The people in the sky had listened to Mebet's son and on the very next day they provided him a chance for success. After long and endless days when the taiga had left Hadko frustrated, worn his patience thin, and laughed at his grief, the den which Voipel had found seemed miraculous…

A bear slain by a lone hunter – even if it is an emaciated and sluggish bear in early spring, represents a real gift, a great feat. Hadko would slay this bear and bring Hadne its skin, its claws, its head on a big tray made from white metal, and then his suffering would end, his guilt would be assuaged. The Blizzard Man would become a hero, and a hero cannot be guilty of anything. Hadko would either slay this prey or fall prey to it.

Thus he thought to himself as his skis whirred under him.

Voipel, so fearless, so clever, served as his guide – he showed his master that the den was nearby. It was a hill from which little wisps of steam issued almost imperceptibly.

Hadko did as his father had taught him – he chopped down a long, thin pine, removed its branches, and sharpened it to a point. With this goad he would awake the bear and, after waiting for the furious beast to burst forth from its den, he would meet it with the iron blade of his spear.

The blood was pounding in his temples, but there was no fear. Voipel sniffed the bank of snow on all sides, as if he wanted to make sure once more that the beast which their luck had brought them, was still there – that it was sleeping and not thinking about what soon awaited it.

The dog was no longer moving around agitatedly. The memory of numerous similar hunts with his old master had put him now entirely at Hadko's disposal. He patiently waited for Mebet's son to finish his work and be ready.

Finally, Hadko appeared with his spear and the long, sharpened pine. At the place he assumed the entrance to the den to be, he cleared out a small area, trod the snow down, and set his spear beside him, so that he could immediately grab the weapon once the bear charged out in its mortal embrace. To fight a roused bear singlehandedly consisted of only a single motion. If the hunter missed with that single motion or if it came too late, then he would no longer get a second try.

Hadko took in a few brief and greedy lungfuls of air and then breathed out slowly. Voipel stood nearby and seemed to be waiting breathlessly.

The Blizzard Man took the sharpened pine and poked the bank of snow with it a few times. He then came closer, made a few more jabs. The sharpened tree passed through empty space and ultimately came up against something hard. But the hunter's hands could tell that it was not the beast's body. He had seen dens before and knew that they were not chums, where everything is right there to see. Before blindly reaching through to the bear, his goad would strike repeatedly against a stone, a clod of earth, the roots of a tree… Hadko frantically wielded the sharpened trunk, but his hands never felt it come to rest against the soft object he sought. A thought passed through his mind: had he erred in taking the white wisps issuing from the snowbank for the sleeping bear's breathing? But this thought quickly passed because it would have been impossible to fool Voipel.

Finally, Hadko's hand felt something different, neither tree, nor stone, nor frozen earth. After he tried to make sure that he had reached the right place, he took several steps back before striking the blow, and after a brief forward dash he stabbed with the pine and then froze, listening closely to the den. No sound came, however.

He stepped back and got ready for the next strike, and he suddenly noticed that Voipel had disappeared. An instant later – before Hadko even had time to be astonished – Voipel barked, and this time it was the threatening bark with which the dog would greet his foes.

Voipel then fell silent, and in this brief interval of silence a sound reached Hadko's ears which he had almost forgotten and which he least expected to hear in the deep taiga: a human voice. Hadko could not make out the words – and they were words – but he knew that more than one person was speaking. Voipel barked again and so Mebet's son did not hear the momentaneous twang of a bowstring. The arrow loudly struck a tree not far away from him.

Still no sound came from the bear's den. Hadko turned and saw a man standing on a height, then another man, and three more followed. The men were armed; two held long, sharpened pines just like Hadko had made. These men had come to kill the bear.

The men were about half a bow's shot away, their voices would carry well through the quiet, still air. But the men nevertheless decided to come closer – apparently they wanted a closer look at whomever had beaten them to the den. They were just as surprised as Hadko was. Their bows did not silence Voipel, who barked ever more fiercely. However, the dog did not attack these newcomers: he caught a whiff of conflict and awaited his master's decision.

One of the men walked slightly ahead of the others and Hadko heard his words:

"These are our hunting grounds. Identify yourself, so that we know who we are dealing with."

Hadko did not answer. He could now make out the men's faces, and they were unknown faces. He realized that he had broken the law.

"Why won't you answer?" the man asked. "We are of the Ivsha tribe."

These were forest dwellers of the same tribe which Hadko's father had shamed long before he was born. They spoke in a different fashion, in a slight whisper, and this served as a marker of their clan. This encounter nearly repeated the one which had taken place long ago: Ivsha men again, five of them, only instead of a deer they were dealing with a bear, and now Mebet's son stood in for Mebet.

"Stay silent if you'd like," the man went on. "Even without an answer, it's clear that you are a scoundrel and a thief. We could kill you and your dog right now from where we stand."

The courage which Hadko had gathered inside him for killing the bear now had to be turned towards these men. He realized what position he was in: the first arrow had been sent only to distract Hadko from his criminal undertaking – hunting in territory that belonged to others. The man had not lied when he said that they could kill him on the spot.

"I am Hadko, son of Mebet of the tribe of Vela."

No reply to that came right away, which was no surprise for Mebet's heir, for the fame of his all-powerful father had spread across the land. For the Ivsha, Mebet's fame was their long-ago shame.

"Mebet's son?" the man shouted, astonished, nearly overjoyed. "What luck! You take after your father in what you get up to, though you don't look much like him. Hold on, we won't kill you right away. We'd like to get a closer look at you."

All five of them threw their bows over their backs and began to come down from the height. As soon as they had taken their first steps, Voipel fell silent and darted over to his master: he knew where he needed to be at the moment of greatest danger and so he waited several paces away from Hadko. The Ivsha men approached, showing with their calm and composure that the lives of Hadko and his dog were entirely in their hands. The worst thing of all was that Hadko had left his bow on the sled. He had done that on purpose, so that in the one single motion that was the slaying of a bear, not a single thing would get in his way. His sled was several hundred feet away; Hadko had tied his draft reindeer securely to a tree.

Voipel's barking had subsided to a low growl. The Ivsha men came closer. The Blizzard Man could see the smiles on their faces, and he began to back away.

"Trying to run away?" the same man asked with a laugh. "Don't want to talk to us?" His comrades laughed with him.

Hadko was not fazed by this contemptuous laughter. He needed his bow, otherwise he and Voipel would die right then and there. He was no longer thinking about the hunt. Mebet's son flung his sharpened pine away and grabbed his spear. The iron blade in his hands wiped the smiles from the Ivsha men's faces. Two of them reached behind them for their bows, though to preserve their dignity they did this slowly.

That was their mistake… Like a rock dropping from a height, Voipel fell on the foremost Ivsha man, knocked him off his feet, and with a single motion the dog tore off the man's face which an instant before had worn a smile at the thought of humiliating Mebet's son.

Hadko leaped into action immediately after Voipel. He struck one at one of the Ivsha men, and though he missed with the blade and only knocked the man over the head with the butt of the spear, his opponent fell, stunned. The three other men, armed only with bows and long knives, jumped aside and prepared to shoot their arrows. But before they could bring their arrows to their bowstrings, Voipel rushed towards them, and his master right after him. The man with the savaged face was howling with pain. Hadko jabbed at one of the bowmen with his spear in an attempt to knock the weapon from the man's hand and impale him on the blade.

This was nevertheless an unequal bout. An arrow came to rest in Voipel's back and the dog thrashed, dripping blood. Somehow Hadko suddenly found his face in the snow, with the enemy pressing down on him and the blade of a knife at his throat. Mebet's son could see nothing from where he lay. The man on his back wheezed angrily.

"Finish off the dog," the man shouted to someone.

"Alright. The mutt broke my bowstring."

"Take my spear and finish the dog off."

There was no reply. Somewhere nearby Voipel gave a hoarse but nevertheless fearsome bark.

"Finish it off with my spear," the voice above Hadko said again. "What, you afraid?"

"Shut up."

Footsteps crunched over the snow. Voipel repelled his death by snapping furiously.

"The damned dog broke my bowstring."

The man sitting on Hadko's back laughed. The man with the savaged face was no longer crying out, he had grown terribly quiet. What the other three men were doing, Mebet's son had no idea. He was amazed to find that the thought of his imminent death did not alarm him, and he waited for the men to turn him over on his back.

A growl seemed to issue forth from under the earth and grew louder.

"The bear's den!" someone cried.

Only now did the Ivsha men notice that this skirmish had taken place right next to the sleeping beast. But it was too late, the bear's roar, ever louder, came closer to the surface. Suddenly the knife at Hadko's throat and the pressure on his back disappeared. He rolled over and saw how the bank of snow had come to life. Huge chunks of snow went flying in a cloud of icy dust.

The beast stepped forth from its den like a huge, shaggy boulder and swept snow aside with its snout. It then rose up on its hind legs and shook the taiga with its voice of bestial wrath...

The man with the savaged face once more helped his kinsmen – the bear went straight for him and while it was busy tearing the soft flesh apart furiously with its claws, the four other Ivsha men fled back the way they come.

Hadko too ran, without quite understanding how his legs had stood up of their own accord and carried him down the slope. He stopped running only when he reached the sled. The bear's roar resounded across the taiga and the reindeer were tearing at the reins. Hadko grabbed their antlers with both hands and held the reindeer fast for a long time, until their master's authority overpowered their sense of fear. Soon Voipel arrived, a black-feathered arrow lodged in his back. Hadko suddenly remembered that he had left his spear behind, the spear with the wide and long blade of shiny metal which his father had given him after the great hunt.

The terrible emptiness in his hands made him think only of that cherished weapon. The Blizzard Man fell to the snow. The bear's roar reached him – the beast was singing its song of victory over the humans it had put to flight.

Just a little while longer and the bear itself would have awoken. For a whole month or more the creature, emaciated after its long hibernation, would roam the slopes with ravenous hunger, waiting for the taiga to return to life and provide a bunch of young grass or even some prey – prey in just as weakened a state as the bear was. But the bear, awakened so early, found a bright side to this turn of fate: the men who had come to kill it, in fact rescued it from its tormenting springtime hunger and perhaps even saved its life by leaving some meat for it...

Hadko reflected on this, and his thoughts were as clear as those of a doomed man. The roar swept through the taiga and became ever louder. The beast was inflamed with fury and gladness which drove away the remnants of its slumber. No longer would the bear sleep, it had come back to life for good. It would not die, like some of its kin had died when they were unable to find sufficient nutrition in autumn or a suitable den, or if they were awakened before the onset of the severe frost – by spring only their bones would remain.

It made no sense for Hadko to wait until he could go back for the spear. Hadko was not worried about the prospect of his father's mockery and humiliation when he made it back to their camp (if indeed he ever made it back), and similarly he was not concerned about what Hadne would say. He was amazed at how calm and composed he felt. Mebet's son was young and knew that this was how the soul gathers strength before great trials…

Voipel lay on the snow, no longer able to stand on his legs. Hadko went up to him and, unafraid of the dog's fangs, he ripped the arrow out of his back with one sharp motion. The dog did not utter a sound, only sighed heavily. The two of them, Hadko and Voipel, collapsed onto the sled and began to make their way downhill.

The evening before, as Hadko had looked up at the white streak across the sky, he was still unaware that he had learned to pray. But on this evening of the following day, he learned to curse. Mebet's son cursed the people, representing all of the taiga's tribes and clans, who had chased the beast into the sky. He cursed them for laughing at him and for his misfortune. The sky said nothing in reply, and the more terrible that Hadko's words were, the clearer the bottomless void over his head became, the brighter the stars shone, and in the white streak the more distinct the outlines of people's arms, legs, weapons, and the body of an enormous beast like no other…

Hadko had directed his curses at the sky, and now the sky had come to life for him.

And Hadko himself came to life for the sky. That is why the story of Mebet's son does not end here, in the foreign territory of the Ivsha clan. The taiga sent him a miracle…

On the way back, Hadko decided to check the traps he had set several days before, though he did not expect to have caught anything good and he did not want to go on with this inglorious hunt. He was simply hungry and he hoped that the traps would provide him with a bird, a hare, or some other stupid little animal, for only a very stupid animal would fall into the trap of a man whom the sky had mocked.

Hadko found no birds or hares in his traps. But one snare, which he had set hastily and carelessly out of a looming sense of hopelessness, gifted him one sable. Just one sable.

But the sable was white, of the kind that people in the taiga had not seen for generations and spoke of as a true wonder.

The dead sable seemed to be asleep. Neither on the snare nor on the animal itself was there any trace of struggle before death…

The Vaynot tribe from which Hadne came, had the custom of sewing an arctic foxskin to the top of their coats, for which they were dubbed the "white-necked ones". The whiteness and the richness of the fur testified to the family's rank and the hunter's skill. A heavy, shining winter fur from an arctic fox was a mark of the very best people, and there were only a few of them around.

Hadne would wear on her shoulders not an arctic fox but a white sable. Among all human beings, there would never be a woman quite like the Blizzard Woman.

Mebet was unaware of his son's miraculous catch. He took Hadko's return after many days of hunting as a disappointment, because Hadko came back with signs of a violent struggle on his face, a bare sled, and a half-dead dog.

"Where is your spear?"

"Back in the taiga," Hadko replied coolly. He did not even try to explain.

"You stupid wolverine…" Mebet saw the suffering in his son and despised him for it. "What, your wife hasn't been nice to you?"

Hadko said nothing.

"You stupid wolverine," Mebet repeated and then walked away.

The cherished sable warmed Hadko's breast under his coat – it was there that he had hidden his catch, his last chance to save himself. He realized that he now had to take a step that would decide everything, and it had to be done, like a confrontation with a bear, in one single motion. The best thing would be to give Hadne the gift in such a way that no one else would see. In that way, when she reappeared before the others, it would be as one transformed by the miraculous thing on her shoulders. Then Hadko's mother and father would see what kind of a man he was.

Hadne was nearby, doing women's work. She came out of the chum several times to bring firewood in, and she was talking with Yadne about some matter or another.

When Hadko arrived home after an absence of many days, his mother wearily chided him for having gone off without telling anyone. Hadko's wife had bowed to him when they met, but Hadko knew she did this only so that her ambivalence about him would not be so glaringly obvious.

Hadne came out of the chum with a large birchbark pitcher for carrying water. She set off for the river, but then for some reason she hesitated. Hadko suddenly felt that she was tarrying because she expected something from him, and now Hadko had to gather his strength and step forth…

She was already walking down to the riverbank, and Mebet's son, who had to force himself to move as if his legs had grown rooted to the spot, set off after his wife. They were merely a few dozen steps apart when Hadne disappeared into a white hollow near the river. For an instant Hadko lost sight of her, and suddenly doubt set in, like a pack of savage dogs falling on him and tearing him apart.

Perhaps some supernatural power had placed the white sable into his trap merely for the sake of further mockery, one more joke played on him? If the desperation Hadne felt had been strong enough to make her shoot her own kin, then it would certainly suffice to cast scorn on his gift. Things would be worse still if she accepted it, if it amazed those close to her and drew the envy of others, but she nevertheless maintained the same lack of passion for Hadko, the same quiet dislike and refusal to forgive him. She would then turn the wonder that Hadko caught into something merely ordinary, however beautiful it might be – she had the power to do that.

Hadko was overcome by terror. He stopped, like a man who has stepped into a swamp freezes and feels how he is sinking into the quagmire, but he then found the strength to move forward. He gathered himself, shoved all evil thoughts aside, and ran towards the river.

She was near the riverbank. A brittle layer of refrozen water had clogged a hole cut into the ice. Hadne was using a short iron-tipped poker to break through it.

Hadko ran up to his wife and stopped several paces away. He was breathing heavily from the exertion and his inner turmoil. Hadne only saw to her business at the river and did not even turn around at the sound of his footsteps.

"Hadne," he called.

She did not answer.

"Hadne!" he shouted with all his might.

His shout resounded across the taiga and a few black birds flew out of the trees.

The Blizzard Woman turned. Hadko walked right up to her and, with shaking hands, he took the sable out from under his coat.

"Give me your hands… Give me your hands!"

Hadne unfolded her little palms, flushed red. Hadko laid the sable on them.

"This… This is for you. I caught this for you."

Hadko did not know what he should say. Any words would seem inane.

The magnificent fur glimmered in Hadne's hands. She looked down at it, yet she said nothing.

"Forgive me," Hadko said.

A black veil was lifted and Mebet's son seemed to get a close look at her face for the very first time, but he could not tell what this face was expressing.

Hadne turned completely around and swung her arm. The white sable went flying from her hands and fell into the middle of the river. A black bird, one of those which had been circling above the river, slipped away over the snow with the glimmering little miracle in its talons and then disappeared.

Hadne grabbed the poker and burned Hadko's neck with its ice-cold iron tip. Now he could see her face clearly, more clearly than ever before in all this time. Her lips quivered, tears rolled down her cheeks, her shining black eyes seemed huge – this was how everything which she had lived through and which her pride had stifled, now swirled in her and sought to burst forth from her overflowing heart: anger, resentment, and stinging self-pity.

In this brief moment when Hadne stood there with the iron-tipped poker at the throat of the husband she never asked for, the life which she had lived so far separated from her and fell away like a dry skin. Time swept past like a heavy sigh.

"You are strong. You are stronger than your father," she said in a low voice.

Her grip relaxed, the poker slid out of her hands and fell into the snow. Hadko said nothing in reply: he did not understand her words, and in fact he could no longer see anything – some force was bearing them away together over the snow-covered ice sheltered by the high riverbank…

That is how Hadne of the tribe of Vaynot became the true wife of Hadko, son of Mebet.

SEVSER IS BORN

Spring fell upon the taiga. With a crackling, surging water broke the weakened ice apart, the numbed spines of the rivers were straightened. The snow melted, yellow streams washed down the slopes, the earth swelled with humidity.

Hadne's belly was heavy, too. She turned cranky, lost her old liveliness and pride. She tried to keep away from other people; she sat inside and shed tears over her sewing. The men were rarely home: the herd required a great deal of attention. In addition, the big hunting and fishing would soon begin, so that a new food stockpile could be created for the winter.

The people of the taiga are not accustomed to going easy on pregnant women, but Yadne's compassion for her daughter-in-law freed the latter from the hardest work. Yadne alone did the work of two, and in Hadne's tears she could see the fear that the expectant mother felt before her first time giving birth. However, what Mebet's wife suspected was only a part of the truth – Yadne learned the whole truth on a day when her husband and son had left on a long journey and did not return to the camp for the night. Yadne was deeply worried by what she learned. In her weakened state, Hadne was suddenly reminded of her own tribe, she wept and murmured to herself mournfully about "mama and papa," as if she did not even remember the war…

Yadne tried to comfort her daughter-in-law, but it did not help. The pregnant woman was not open to any suggestions. Hadne madly insisted on her own feelings. Yadne hid her daughter-in-law's state from the men as best she could, and especially from Mebet. But hiding the truth from Hadko proved impossible. All the time that Hadko spent at home, he spent with Hadne. Hadko was himself concerned; like his mother, he hoped that it would all pass, but ultimately he realized that it was no use fooling himself. In a woman like Hadne, no desire, whim, or passion would ever just fade away.

In the morning, when they were tying a load down on the sled before going out to visit the herd, Hadko ventured to ask Mebet:

"Hadne is afraid to give birth without her parents' forgiveness and blessing. Father, we need to make peace with the Vaynot clan."

Mebet was tying their tent down at that moment and he froze, the rope still taut in his hands. He was not a man easy to surprise, but this time he was truly astonished. The Gods' Favorite thought that he had misheard his son and asked him to repeat what he had said.

Hadko did so. "We need to make peace with the Vaynots."

The taut strap in Mebet's hand slackened. His gaze rested somewhere off in the middle of the sled. The Gods' Favorite stood thus for some time, while he mentally went over the few things he knew about other human beings. He stopped without finding any answers, and he said:

"I have allowed you a great deal and forbidden you little, so that I could raise you with a sense of freedom," he said. "But now listen to me closely and do what I say, or else. Among the people of the taiga and the tundra there is no man who could truly do me ill. Now I see that there is one such person: you. They call me the Gods' Favorite because there is nothing I cannot manage. But they are wrong, there is one thing I am incapable of: I cannot regret what has been done, let alone repent of it. The day when that happens will be my last. Mebet will die, and he will die before his body stops moving. Remember this, don't ever forget it."

He jerked his hand so intensely that the strap squeaked and the poles of their tent crunched like bird bones.

"In any event you would be repenting in my name," Mebet went on. "Don't do that. Otherwise I will cast you out and you will become a vagabond like that Makhako."

A cold shiver ran down Hadko's back. "And Hadne? You would cast her out too?" he asked.

Mebet did not answer, he only tightened the strap and carefully, without hurrying, attached it to the sled. Then he walked off towards the storehouse. He returned shortly thereafter with something like a bearskin in his hands, an old felted hide. Mebet threw this item down at his son's feet. When Hadko examined it, he saw it was human hair.

"This is the skin of that man whom the Vaynots sent to scout out my preparations for war. They grew very worried when he went missing. I caught him the day before Nyaruy arrived at our camp, not far from here, and I scalped him. His body I hid under a fallen tree. They had no reason to get upset at that, the traditions of war allow playing such tricks. They could have done the same with you…" Now Mebet's haughty good spirits returned. "All the same, if your wife convinces you to visit her kinsmen, take this scalp along. They would be happy to receive such a gift."

Without breaking eye contact with his father, Hadko took the scalp and put it into the deerskin pouch at his belt.

The smile vanished from Mebet's face. "You do what I tell you, or else," he repeated. "Come on, we've got a lot of work today."

When Hadne saw her kinsman's scalp, she stopped crying and bringing up her mama and papa. Summer passed, and by autumn she was already walking like a duck and complaining about how unbearably heavy her belly was.

"You will have a grandson," Yadne said to Mebet.

Mebet smiled. He had been thinking the same thing.

The heavy belly accurately reflected her term – one night in the month of burbot-fish Hadne gave birth to a boy.

At that time Hadko had gone upriver to set a net for the last catch before the winter. He hurried home, but he arrived too late: his son had already been born in his absence.

Just like Mebet had gone to visit his wife in the unclean chum of a woman giving birth, now he entered his daughter-in-law's chum and looked around. Hadne, exhausted, hung limply from the straps (in those days, women gave birth standing up and, for support, they were tied to the crossing of the tent-like dwelling's structural beams). At her feet, a baby sluggishly moved its arms and legs like an autumn spider. The child lay there in silence, without demanding what a newborn ordinarily demands in his first moments of life.

Mebet's wife ran into the chum, helped her daughter-in-law get out of the straps, and laid her down on the furs. Yadne picked the baby up and gave him to his mother. But his mouth had not yet found her breast when Mebet said:

"Stop. Wait. Don't feed him until I return."

He went out and hurried to his storehouse. There he cut a thin piece of meat from a freshly slain reindeer and then returned to the unclean chum. The baby erupted into crying just a short distance from his mother's breast. The noise grew ever louder but Mebet slowed down, as if he was trying to determine how loud a voice his grandson would have. When the crying was already piercingly loud, like the whistling of an arrow, the Gods' Favorite carefully opened the baby's tiny hand and placed the meat in it. The baby froze, uncertain as to what he would go for first, his mother's breast or the meat. Finally, he turned away from Hadne's breast and dug into the meat. A red stream flowed down his round cheeks still wet from the waters of birth. His jaws moved as he stared up into empty space with eyes as bright as a leaf in springtime. The first thing he had consumed in his life was not his mother's milk but the blood of a reindeer.

There, in the chum deemed unclean, the prophecy of so many years ago now came true: Mebet's heart was broken.

They named the child Sevser, "Light-Eyed One." He became the first human being that Mebet could not imagine a life without.

Initially the Gods' Favorite was not yet conscious of this, for all great changes start off imperceptibly. His grandson, as Mebet had guessed from the first moments of the child's life, did not take after his father Hadko in either the latter's dark and shining eyes or in his wide cheekbones. After Sevser's birth Mebet did not initially know what kind of man he would grow up to be; no one could know that yet. But something told the Gods' Favorite that his grandson was like himself, with the same light-colored eyes and light-colored hair, totally unlike anyone else in the taiga, as if accidentally left behind by some long-forgotten foreign people passing through this region.

Mebet still retained his strength, and his fortune had not set on him like the summer sun, but he was no longer the same man he was before. How this happened, no one knew. Just like no mortal knew which of the gods had ordained things so that one person could not live without another.

Hadko was proud of his son and protected him like the greatest of treasures. Throughout the centuries, death had found the taiga peoples' infants to be easy pickings. Death could come with the child's first breath of cold air, it could come from a number of illnesses brought by outsiders; from hunger when its mother's breast came to resemble an empty deerskin sack; from unsanitary food; from other ills that loomed at every step; or often death could strike for no visible reason at all. Consequently, the death of an infant child was not considered a major tragedy. Babies would be buried in the hollow of a tree so that the infant's soul would not pass to the spirits of the underworld. And in order to cheat death, women bore as many children as they could.

Mebet himself could no longer remember how many times he had sent his wife into the forest to find a suitable hollow of a tree. Of their children – and until Hadko, Yadne had bore only girls – just one had lived to the age of three. Then hard times came: somehow, probably from the direction of the Selkup people, sickness entered their country. Reindeer began to die and animals left the taiga. Mebet's strength and luck were subjected to a severe trial. He was instantly reduced to penury, but he bore this change of fate easily, and with the same otherworldly smile he managed to wrangle fate and wrestle it, like a skittish reindeer, down to the ground.

In this fraught time, something unprecedented happened: Mebet spoke with a man of the Nevasyada clan, Yezanga by name (which means "Caught In The Trap"), who had a five-year-old son. They agreed on an arranged marriage. Yezanga was much poorer than Mebet, almost destitute, but this was no barrier to their agreement.

The tradition held that the two children would be named man and wife, and the father of the underage groom would pay the bride-price in installments until the bride turned fourteen years old, the age of childbearing…

Mebet no longer remembered what a bride-price he demanded – perhaps it was forty reindeer, or perhaps less. But his daughter died at the age of three, and afterwards he had no other daughters and the agreement was annulled. This was a painful story, and the Gods' Favorite tried not to look back on it; by his old age, he had completely forgotten it.

However, to everyone's great surprise, Mebet cared for light-eyed Sevser like a treasure. Mebet's fear that his grandson might share the fate of the other infants seemed to be the first fear that had ever struck his heart. During large migrations of their herd and household, Mebet set up a little house on the women's sled as the Selkup people do: a wooden box covered in deerskin and kept warm with furs inside. He ordered Hadne not to take the child out of this shelter unless it were truly necessary, especially in the season of severe cold. Mebet also sought to protect his daughter-in-law, he would not allow her to do the most grueling of the women's work, which now fell almost entirely on Yadne. The latter did not complain, however, as she was amazed and pleased at this change in Mebet.

Hadko made a cradle for his son. It was a box constructed from thick, boiled birchbark. He laid it with furs and filled it with white down. This made the Gods' Favorite jealous, and so Mebet made a second cradle of seasoned larch, brought it inside, and told the women:

"This one will be stronger. It will be good when we migrate the herd."

Once Mebet watched as Sevser, left alone in the chum, knocked his cradle over, crawled forth from it on his hands and knees towards a bucket of water, took the dipper hanging on the bucket, drank, hung the dipper back in its place, and then crawled back to his cradle. However, he proved unable to lift the cradle and so he burst into loud and insistent crying. At this time, Sevser was slightly older than four months old. He was not yet able to walk, and his speech consisted of solely the beginnings of a few words which only his mother, and perhaps Mebet, were able to make sense of.

At the age of six months, the light-eyed child once more amazed the family:

"Look here, kid," Mebet said as he drew something from a sack: it was a small wooden board with a long loop from a whole reindeer tendon. Mebet held the board with one hand and pulled on the loop with the other – the board gave off a thin whine like a draft of wind. This was *vylka*, an age-old children's toy among the peoples of the taiga and tundra. The little board sang in Mebet's hands and his grandson, who initially could not make sense of what was going on, goggled. The baby grabbed the board and burst into laughter. It sounded just like Mebet's laughter.

By the age of two, when Sevser's fingers were strong enough to tightly grip something he liked and would not let go, Mebet made him a bow. It was a real bow, from birch and larch glued together with fish glue, and with a bowstring of elk sinew. The Gods' Favorite made a few small but real arrows with white feathers and bone tips. He took his grandson's hand and, just like he had once placed a piece of raw meat therein, he now gave Sevser the bow.

"Grip it with all your fingers, kid, and hold on tight," he said.

His grandson picked at the feather at the end of the arrow.

"No, not like that, grab the end of the arrow with your fingers… Now raise the bow and hold it out right in front of you. Pull the bowstring as hard as you can. Keep it at your right cheek, or better yet, at your ear. Pull… Now shoot!"

The arrow plopped down only a few inches from Sevser. His first bow-shot had gone no farther than spitting distance. But it was still a shot, and Mebet was elated.

The others were hardly able to recognize the head of their household anymore, but they readily indulged his newfound passion. Sevser became the little treasure of the family. Within those two years between Sevser's birth and the first time he ever shot an arrow, Hadne had given birth to another child, a girl, but the baby lived little more than a week: her coming into the world and leaving it passed nearly without a trace.

Mebet and Hadko would go hunting and their catch was rich. Sables and arctic foxes came falling into their traps, and they could look forward to a good stockpile for the future. One day the Gods' Favorite returned from hunting, walked into the chum, and saw only two people there: Yadne and his grandson. He asked where Hadko and Hadne were.

"They went off this morning," his wife replied. "They promised to be back before sunset."

"What did they go off for?"

"They didn't tell me. They just got ready quickly and left…"

Mebet felt a sense of foreboding, but he did not show it. Soon, after his catch had been safely placed in the storehouse, he got down to his favorite pastime: teaching Sevser how to shoot.

He spent the rest of the day at this and as sunset came, he heard the barking of dogs and the rustling of sled runners. His son and daughter had returned. Mebet stepped outside. Hadko and Hadne were untying the straps on a sled laden with furs and sacks, but these were not the family's own things.

Hadko did not wait for his father to ask, he said:

"Hadne's parents are very old. They are asking us to forget the past and they want our families to live in peace and harmony, as families should. They have sent gifts for you and all of us as a peace offering. Really good gifts, new coats for you and mama. Ski skins, ivory, and a lot of other good stuff. We need to answer them in the same way with some worthy gifts…"

Anger came over Mebet's heart like a black storm cloud – his son had done precisely what should not have been done. Hadko's words had been spoken calmly and courageously, as if what had happened was something good. Hadne stood next to her husband and said nothing. Mebet had no doubt that she was the cause of all this. This little woman had never forgotten her wish, and the scalp of her kinsman had done nothing to dissuade her from her plan, it only delayed its execution. And such a calm and composed speech by his son, as if Hadko had forgotten his father's words, "Do what I tell you, or else."

Hadko and Hadne felt that together they created a distinct force of their own and they were no longer afraid of Mebet. "We need to think about what gifts we can send them in return," Hadko said.

Mebet's anger was at a boiling point. He wanted to remind them that they already had a gift for the Vaynot clan: their scout's scalp. Hadko had forgotten about that? Had he forgotten that he would be cast out and no longer have a home of his own?

But Mebet did not manage to utter these words, because he suddenly felt a slight jab in his left calf. He turned and saw that the flap over the chum's entrance had been thrown back, and his grandson was standing there, laughing, with the bow in his hands. The arrow with its bone tip had flown several paces and struck the Gods' Favorite in the leg.

All of Mebet's rage melted away, leaving nothing behind. He said nothing to his son.

HADKO'S DEATH

Hadko was twenty years old then. In his twenty-first year, Hadko died.

Whether due to the envy of his father's glory, or the memory of how he had fled from the awakened bear, Hadko tried his luck once more: to slay a bear in single combat, bring it to the bear feast, and be recognized as a hero among the people.

He found a bear's den, awoke the beast, but in the one single movement on which everything depended, he missed. Hadko was not standing at the right distance, and therefore his spear did not plunge into the bear but only grazed the animal's hide. The bear stood on its hind legs, embraced the Blizzard Man, and ravaged his back with its claws. The beast then left the dead body untouched; it merely left its abode behind and disappeared into the taiga.

It was Voipel which brought this terrible news home. The dog returned alone and covered in blood – the bear had nearly broken him – and all night long he howled into the darkness. The women wept and hoped for a miracle. Only Mebet was free of any doubt or hope. Inside, he understood what had happened to his son, even if he was ignorant of the details, which now counted for nothing. Everyone was aware of one thing, however: in a sticky patch of blood on the dog's back, Mebet found a clump of bear fur with a lot of dull white hairs. "A gray bear, an old one," he thought to himself.

The next morning Voipel led his old master to the bear's den and there the Gods' Favorite reconstructed what exactly had gone down.

Neither the bear itself, nor other animals or birds had touched Hadko's body. It still lay there, slightly dusted with the morning snow. The bear's claws had torn through his deerskin coat like thin fabric, and his gleaming white rib bones now stood visible. Hadko lay facedown, with one leg outstretched and the other folded under him. When Mebet turned his son over, he saw that the dead hands gripped the wood of the spear, and the right hand rested against the wide blade. Mebet guessed that when the bear had surged forth, Hadko's spear had betrayed him, the wood slipped in his hands.

On the spot where the showdown had taken place, Mebet found clumps of bear fur. They had come without reindeer, alone, with a small sled. Mebet laid his son on the sled, covered him with a skin, and began to head back home. Voipel, who was still breathing heavily, sadly followed the sled.

The funeral rites were usually held on the third day, but traditional custom demanded that a bit of downy fox fur be held to the deceased's nose – the person might have suddenly come back to life and the down would tremble at his faint breath. But Hadko was buried the very next morning, for it would have been foolish to believe that life could ever return to this ravaged body.

Hadko's mother was unable to weep for her son, instead she was totally dumbstruck. Mebet too was silent. The light-eyed child poked at his dead father's nose and laughed. Hadne took the child into the other chum and then secluded herself – she did not even come out for the funeral, when Mebet used straps to haul a hollowed trough containing Hadko's body up to the top of an enormous larch not far from their camp. This was the same larch where the bones of Hadne's swiftly-forgotten daughter had reposed.

The first nights were hard ones. Yadne regained her speech, but she ceaselessly muttered something and Mebet was unable to sleep. Mebet had never been troubled by insomnia, but now he was unable to catch a wink. At sundown Voipel would start to howl and would not let up until the moon vanished from the sky. Voipel's howling was long and drawn out. Each night the din grew ever more piercing, an assault on the ears, and eventually Mebet's patience was at an end.

Mebet armed himself with a strap and stepped out of the chum, intent on lashing the suffering dog over the back to make him shut up, but an unexpected sight caused the strap to fall from his hands. Voipel was not alone, Hadne was sitting next to him – the dog and the woman howled together, they howled at the moon, at the white smear across the sky, and at the countless twinkling stars.

Mebet decided that he would simply endure the noise and not say a word to Hadne.

His thoughts turned to the gray bear. It became his obsession.

What the Gods' Favorite felt in his heart after his son's death could not be called mourning. Hadko had been a good hunter, a brave warrior, but he had proven to be the only person capable of truly doing ill to Mebet. Hadko had gone to make amends in Mebet's name, and only the intervention of Sevser, whom Mebet adored, saved Hadko from the retribution which his father had promised.

But something else was worse still: his son had had the audacity to violate his father's prohibition, to transgress against what Mebet felt was paramount. This meant that Mebet's strength was not limitless as he had thought. His son had lost his battle against the bear, but Hadko had proved the victor in the confrontation with his father, who had no equals in the taiga or the tundra. For his grandson's sake, Mebet tolerated his impudent son and held off on his revenge, but now the thought of the defeat inflicted by his son was especially clear in his mind. Mebet had never thought about death and what lasting impact he might make, but Sevser's birth had made him muse on these things. He had even brooded on the idea of waiting until his grandson was grown up and then leaving everything he had to him, and not to Hadko. He would shrug off any thoughts of his son, for such evil should not go unpunished, and a threat that is never carried out serves only as a mark of weakness and humiliation.

Hadko's death had opened the way to the idea that Sevser would grow up to be a man just like Mebet, and he would continue the latter's legacy through time.

The Gods' Favorite suddenly remembered that he had gray hair now. He was aware of this, of course, but now his heart felt a strange pang at the thought of old age.

People die, they leave this world, like his own son had left it, but how much time was still apportioned to him? Would his own time come earlier than Sever would be able to confidently hold a weapon in his hands, support a family, and live the way he wanted to, like his grandfather had done?

Mebet continued to believe in his good luck, but thoughts of death stole upon him like an illness and began to flourish. He did not notice how he was gradually overcome with concern about his time left, the same care which spurs people to be cautious and makes them cowardly. He sensed this change in himself and it made him angry. He had turned into a mere human being, as mysterious gods had once sculpted out of white clay…

Suddenly Mebet saw a way out of this. He realized that the most important thing in his life now was that gray bear which had killed his son. He wanted to find that bear, whatever the cost. Even if the bear had made its lair in hell itself, he would find and kill that bear. He would kill it, take its strength, and live to a good old age.

It was not for his son that the Gods' Favorite was taking revenge. Rather, he was setting things straight for himself.

THE SHADOW DANCE

Mebet spent the rest of the winter and the following spring, summer, and autumn searching for the bear, to the point that he himself became an animal. He searched for the bear's tracks in every fallen leaf, every bit of fur left on a tree trunk, in the air and in the sounds around him. He spent days in the taiga with eyes peeled, and before the onset of the severe cold, he found the bear.

By this time the bear had already settled in to hibernate – whatever beast did not hibernate already was wandering around emaciated and awaiting its own death, for the harsh frost would eat away at its paws and its claws would crumble like a dry twig. Yet sometimes fate was kind to those late in hibernating and would provide them with some good prey and a suitable den.

The gray bear proved to be one example. Mebet came upon the half-eaten remains of a young elk – in the clotted blood on the ground, which was now frozen solid, he saw small clumps of brown fur with a dull gray tinge and he knew that he was now close to his quarry. The snowfall might have hidden the tracks, but the bear's lair was around here somewhere…

Mebet had found traces of the bear earlier, but only now did he feel that his search was over. Hadko had died exactly one year before, and the Gods' Favorite suddenly felt that the bear had purposely evaded him, in order to await precisely this anniversary.

He found the den. Voipel could not have failed to find it. For him, the entire taiga fell silent, all smells vanished except one: a warm, musty smell that drifted from a snowbank along with white puffs of steam. From far away Mebet could see that the snowdrift over the lair had still not completely settled, as if the bear had only yesterday made its lair there and it had not yet fallen deeply asleep.

At sunset the Gods' Favorite made a great big fire and pitched his camp not far from the cave. He did all this as if he was teasing the gray bear and warning it of what it could expect the next day.

At dawn Mebet began to prepare for the showdown. He cut an enormous stake from a larch tree and set sharp iron points at its ends. He inspected his spear and trampled the ground flat at the site of the looming battle. Voipel, who was nearly petrified from the suspense, waited for his time to act…

This was the strangest hunt of Mebet's life, like no other he had ever experienced. With his first jab into the lair with the wooden pike, he knew he had hit the beast, and when he pulled the pike back out, he saw that it was bloody and the iron tip was missing – it had lodged in the bear's hide. Mebet thrust the pike a second time and then cast it away, grabbed his spear, and prepared to meet his foe.

The lair rumbled and a distant, resounding roar reached Mebet's ears. The hunter gathered himself and waited for the moment when the snow would fly aside. The beast was taking its time. Mebet's hand again reached for the pike, but now the bear stuck its head out of the snowbank…

The bear came forth from its den like a man emerges from his dwelling in the morning – angrily and reluctantly. It stood on all four legs with his head low and it seemed to look somewhere past the hunter, past the dog, and past its own death. Mebet waited for the bear to become engaged and pounce; he could not strike now at the bear's head, for no iron would withstand the impact with a bear's skull. Yet the bear hesitated and sat doglike on its hind legs.

The bear was white over nearly half of its body, and it was huge – the paws, each as large as a shaman's drum, were crowned with claws that resembled curved knives. The creature's lower lip hung low, revealing yellow teeth, and its eyes were deeply set in its immense skull as if pushed back by its bear dotage. The bear seemed even bigger than the snowbank from which it had emerged.

The beast neither attacked nor seized the opportunity to run away, and this annoyed Mebet. He waited for his opponent to make the first move.

The bear lifted its head up, loudly breathed in the frosty air, and then gave a long and heavy roar. This roar was the bear's last, for the Gods' Favorite sprung into action, thrust his spear into the bear's upper chest, into the unprotected area around its throat, and with all his might he slashed with the iron blade down through the bear's entrails. The bear, as if inviting him to dance, waved its paws over its head, and then collapsed quietly and docile onto its side. Mebet pulled his spear free, decapitated the bear with his next swing, and then he stepped backward and fell onto his back.

This hunt had left him in a stupor – he could not understand what had happened to him, all thoughts and words had vanished from his mind. This daze did not last for long, however, for in his heart some space had now been made for celebration. This was not a celebration of avenging Hadko. The first thing that came over Mebet was a quiet, blissful awareness of what had been done. Something major, something truly important. The gray bear had been killed, and by doing this the Gods' Favorite had set things right in the world, righter than they had ever been before. He, Mebet, again saw himself as the sole man to truly live the way he wanted. If there was some power that directed the lives of men, then it must have been subject to his, Mebet's, will. He stood higher than what people call kindness or cruelty, because whatever action the Gods' Favorite took, his good fortune never set on him like the summer sun. He was free of any fear of his destiny because he himself was his destiny.

Just as he had planned, the light-eyed Sevser – and not his son, who had been impudent and too concerned with what other human beings and the gods might think – would serve to carry on his legacy.

The day was a marvelous one. The sun shone on the snow. No wind blew to trouble the world, to blur the clear and distinct shadows, dark-blue, of the trees, the man, his dog, and the defeated bear. Light came pouring down, just as joy flooded into Mebet's heart. A thought came to him, a particularly amusing one: to hold the bear feast right here. For him alone. There was no need to seek out his peers to arrange wrestling, archery competitions, reindeer races, jumping over sleds, or other silly entertainments. After all, Mebet had never had true peers even before. There was no need for esteemed and venerable elders with whom the victorious hunters, triumphantly and in full view of the others, would dine on the bear's head, for Mebet himself was both hunter and elder.

Let there be, he thought, only three guests, three witnesses: the sun, the taiga, and the shadows. The Gods' Favorite would perform for them his victory dance, and then he would haul the bear's head away. Mebet alone was the feast.

Mebet raised his arms to the sky, took the first step, and his body surrendered to dancing.

Mebet's shadow moved in tandem with him, its dance became ever more violent and it moved like a raging deity with many arms…

The Gods' Favorite had hardly abandoned his body to his emotions when something astonishing happened: his shadow stopped its dance, dropped its arms and walked away from him. Mebet stopped and threw up his arms, but the shadow moved several more steps away and, its head bent, sat down in the snow.

Mebet was soaked with sweat. He threw back the hood of his coat. The shadow put its hood up and huddled there as if it had got cold.

Mebet walked towards the shadow, but the shadow stood up, walked away from Mebet, stopped, and leaned against the wide trunk of a birch…

A voice came from nowhere in particular: "Mebet, can you recognize your own death?"

It was not death itself, only death's messenger, who visits a person shortly before the day when he must leave this world. Everyone in the taiga knew that a person's shadow would never deceive him.

"Can you recognize your own death, Mebet?"

He turned – it was the gray bear's head that was speaking.

"Who are you?"

"Strange that you would ask. After all, you slew me today." The voice fell silent and said nothing for a long time. Then it asked, "Are you afraid?"

"No," the Gods' Favorite replied and then suddenly cried out. He cried like an infant suddenly plunging from the warm environment of the womb into the alien world of men.

Only now did it hit Mebet that all his life, the gods had been watching him, and finally they were taking their revenge by doing to Mebet what they would do to any ordinary person. Worse yet, they had sent the messenger in the very hour of Mebet's triumph, on a day when it would be unthinkable that a person would die.

"You are afraid," the bear said.

"How much time do I have left?"

"I don't know," the bear said. "Only the Mother knows that. Sending people into the world and taking them back is something that only she decides. But one way or the other, you have little time left. Never has a man whose shadow has abandoned him lived until the next new moon."

The Gods' Favorite thought back to the night before the hunt and the enormous, impressive moon that had just waxed to its full size. That meant that Mebet had no more than five to seven moons left.

Pain pierced his heart. He remembered his grandson, his little light-eyed treasure. Sevser was still little, so little that a dog seemed bigger to him than a reindeer. He was not yet firm on his feet, and he only had enough strength to shoot an arrow a mere spitting distance away. He would be left all alone, with two defenseless women, one of which was old now and nearly worthless to others.

Mebet's death would be celebrated by everyone who had ever envied him, who had harbored resentment against him, who had doubted in the gods and their justice. Sevser would then become easy pickings for anyone looking to take revenge.

Even if Hadne, still young and beautiful, were mercifully accepted back in her old family, even if someone else married her and got all that Mebet had left behind, either way his household would not escape the fate of people who had lost a home of their own. Sevser's early years would be marked by the ignominious lot of a foster child.

Mebet had not maintained ties with his kinsmen, the others of the Vela clan, for many years now. They were no different than any other people, and they would probably be the first to seize anything that Mebet left behind.

"I cannot die now," the Gods' Favorite said.

The bear did not reply.

"Not now," Mebet said.

"Follow your shadow," the head told him. "It will lead you to a Sanctuary where the Old One lives. He is kind. Ask him for enough life as would be necessary to finish your affairs and leave this world calmly. The Old One will intercede for you before the Mother. He will not refuse anyone whose request is righteous and worth holding death off for. Go now. Hurry, the new moon is coming soon…"

"Why are you helping me? I slew you."

"Hurry."

The gray lids closed over the dull eyes. The head sighed and said no more.

THE SANCTUARY

Mebet's guide led him to a distant sanctuary which he had heard about but never visited. Initially Mebet was afraid that he would never catch up with his shadow or, on the contrary, that the shadow would move slowly and Mebet would never manage to arrive before the new moon came and his time was up. The shadow however proved a good guide, it moved at the same pace Mebet did, and it even tried to help him of its own accord – it was the first to rise when Mebet had stopped to rest.

The shadow also left tracks, though these were convex marks in the snow, not impressions. These tracks grew ever less visible with each day, and Mebet understood that he was running out of time. He rushed on with little thought for himself, at so frantic a pace that the skin lining his right ski began to come off. The tracks helped Mebet to keep up with his shadow when clouds obscured the sun or when snow fell. At night his guide paced not far from the campfire.

During these days Voipel followed the tracks left by his master and the latter's guide, and he tried to stay out of the way.

The moon shone bright and therefore they would continue their journey during the night as well. At dawn on the fourth day Mebet's shadow stopped and flung its arms out to indicate a place further below them. There, in a flat white space, a patch of round black forest stood that resembled a chum. The trees towards the middle of the circle rose ever higher, and the tip of the pyramid was crowned by three enormous larches. Mebet's incorporeal guide turned to him, pointed again to the sanctuary, and then vanished. The shadow's work was done.

The white field in which the small forest stood stretched on infinitely towards the limits of the world and, beyond them, the place where eternal cold reigned.

Mebet of the tribe of Vela walked towards his future, which had begun long before his birth. That is why the Old One did not ask his name, for the Old One already knew. He met his visitor at the edge of the small forest.

The Old One was none other than the gray bear.

"You have not come too late," he said. "You were lucky, as you always are: there is a raging blizzard right on your heels."

Mebet did not turn around, he already believed these words.

"You wish to ask me for more life to live? Why should you need it?"

"My son Hadko died while hunting. He was killed by a…" Mebet hesitated.

"He was killed by me, you want to say," the Old Man interrupted. "Yes, I killed your son. And then you killed me. Go on."

Why is he asking even me this, thought Mebet, but he nevertheless repeated what he had said besides the bear's den. "Hadko died, and now I will die. The women are unable to hunt, and my grandson is still a small child. My family will not survive without someone to provide for them. Don't let me die now."

The Old One rose, his lips stretched, and his eyes shone. Mebet felt that the Old One was smiling at him.

"You see, what you say is very simple, something any human being would say. How old is your grandson?"

"It is his fifth winter."

"And for how long do you want to put your death off?"

"Allow me to live until my grandson grows up and becomes a man. I will teach him everything that I know, and then I can die in peace."

Now the Old One was no longer smiling. Rather, he was laughing low and hoarsely, his entire massive body shaking. "Truly you are a lucky man, Mebet. Only a man who is truly fortunate could allow himself such audacity. Everyone in the taiga and in the tundra knows that here, at the sanctuary, a person can only keep death away for two or three days, and he cannot hope for more. The Mother is good, but she does not like to waive her own rules. She gives only a brief time, only long enough for people to think of how kind she is and to tell others about it. Therefore, people come to me only seldom, and then either out of strict necessity – for a few days to witness the birth of an heir or to exact revenge – or out of cowardice… You are asking for an entire lifespan to live. A whole new life, Mebet!

The Old One gave a long laugh and when his laughter had abated, he said, "But I think you will receive that new life nonetheless." He rose, went over to a dark corner, and then quickly returned. From his claws hung a bundle of wooden slats that were held together with a thin strap.

"There are eleven slats here, that means eleven years. Each flat has eleven notches, those are the eleven months of the year. I believe this will be enough time for your son to become a man and a true hunter. Take them, these are yours now."

Mebet reached out to take the bundle, stuffed the slats under his coat, gave a short bow, and then turned to leave. But there was nowhere to go – he saw before him only a white abyss bereft of earth, sky, sun, or stars. Behind him he heard the Old One's chuckle, a hoarse sound nearly like a cough.

"You are a child. A man-child, or rather already an old-man-child. A spoiled and silly infant who has not even left the cradle," the Old One bellowed. "You see, Mebet, you are essentially dead, but you behave the same way as before, as if you were still alive and your good fortune had not set on you like the summer sun. A mere child…"

Mebet shuddered within and he snapped out of his daze. He bowed low to the Old One. "Forgive me, I have been disrespectful. I have not thanked you properly…"

"I don't need your thanks. I know that you have not even thought about where this generosity comes from."

Mebet looked foolish, like all human beings. He asked, "Where does this generosity come from?"

"The life which you have lived is not your own."

"I don't understand," Mebet said.

"Of course, you could not understand. After all, everything was conceived and executed before you were even born." The Old One rose on his hind legs. On his chest Mebet could see clots of dried blood that hung necklace-like and were tangled up with fur. "It was we who called you… Let's go, the Mother wants to see you."

THE MOTHER

They walked through ghostly pines into the heart of the sanctuary, where in a cave overgrown with ghostly leaves, the roots of trees, and grass, Mother awaited. Mebet heard her voice before he saw her.

"You have come, child," the voice said. "You are different now, not like your heavenly reflection at all. Still, I can recognize something in you."

"Who are you?" Mebet asked.

"I am the one who gives life with one hand, and takes it away with the other."

Before him, the Mother revealed herself in a frozen cloud of water that swayed and changed color. He saw the figure of a woman within the water.

"Now you, child, stand before me. Few have been accorded this grace. But you are one of the few. Especially considering that it was I who wished to see you. They told me that you have asked for a long life before you? Even here you know no limits." Mebet could hear gentle mockery in her voice. "But I am unhappy with you, child, very unhappy. The longer you have lived, the more you have upset me."

Mebet hung his head. He was not accustomed to having to justify himself, and moreover he had no understanding of what guilt was.

Mother seemed to guess at his thoughts. "Yes, yes, it was I who made it so that the heavy burden of guilt never tormented you, your memories or desires never troubled you. I willed it thus. People call you the Gods' Favorite. They are wrong in that, though not very. You should have been called my favorite, the Mother's favorite. But in the world of men that sounds almost meaningless, for every mother – or nearly so – loves her child. How then did you stand apart? Even you don't know this, let alone other people. For them, let it be that you remain the Gods' Favorite. After all, I had no part in coining that name for you. Do you understand what I am saying, child?"

"No," Mebet said dejectedly.

"Then I will explain everything from the very beginning. Sit down, we are in no hurry. Time does not exist here."

MEBET'S BIRTH

Mother began her tale.

"I must confess, I was not the first one to see you. It would be silly to say that it was your mother or the midwife either who laid eyes on you first. No, was Ulgen, the god of the Upper World, who first saw you. The gods know what tedium is, and Ulgen is probably more familiar with it than anyone else. Just like the gods of the middle world, he dwells among people, but among a completely different sort of people: those who are fated to be born. They soar in space, they float over him like pale, indistinct shadows, because their lives have not yet been determined. Even when their destiny is determined, these shadows do not grow any clearer, because their being is still weak. They plunge down, still so gray and indistinct. In the unclean chum of the birth-giver they come into the world, cry out, and carry on after their ancestors for many generations. In the same way they will be riven with passions: greed, guilt, envy, yearning for what they have lost, unrequited love – everything that human beings are tormented by. None of them will find a way out, no one has the strength to break free of the fetters of their own weakness. That is why the earth is as gray as the heavens.

Occasionally I would ask, "What's new in the heavens, Ulgen?"

He would answer, "Same as on the earth: nothing."

Eventually I stopped asking, as I would always hear the same reply. Humankind streamed through me and my heart did not settle on any one person. I readily gave life, and took it away even more easily. Their sacrifices, prayers, and spells bored me...

But once the god above said to me, "I see a shadow different from the others. I can see everything: the arms, the legs, fingers, the hair on his head. I can see his alien stature. That was you, child. My heart settled on you."

Then I told the god above, "Oh, Ulgen, give him to me."

"This is a bright soul! You remember what a bright soul is," he said warily.

But still I was insistent and I coaxed Ulgen out of his worries with sweet words. "Give him to me right now, so that none of the other gods find out about him and send him into the world with other lives. I swear that I will keep what you have done for me a secret."

Ulgen did as I requested, and thus you were born. Do you know why I chose precisely you? Inside you there was a strength, such as none of those who besmirched the heavens with their shadows ever had. Strength is given from on high, it is engendered in the heavens above Ulgen. These heavens are inaccessible to human beings and even to many gods and spirits. There was a time when great heroes descended from these heavens to the earth. But the more strength they were endowed with, the more terrible their lives were. They fought with monsters, and when the monsters were all wiped out, they fought other men for the sake of some tribe or another, and they always died. People magnified them, wrote paeans to them, even called them gods, but those people became no better nor stronger themselves.

Then a time came when I saw you… If I had only hesitated and failed to act, then you too would have got some monster to fight, or an attack of a foreign tribe and a glorious death instead of material rewards. But I did not wish a glorious death for you. I wanted to see what it would be like if a man were happy from the moment he was born until the very end of his days. You possessed a great strength. That strength could easily satisfy any desire, and thus you never suffered. Your young heart sought glory, and you had your fill of glory. Your body demanded love, and you immediately received it. In the end, you became almost ambivalent to the things people kill each other over. I was glad. The gods had not managed to write your fate in stone, and this saved you from an untimely death or torments, for after all, everyone who stands above other people and leads them eventually suffers. While you were nearly still a baby you had learned what others learn only after many years of indoctrination and beatings, and so I could keep your infant soul safe from insults, humiliation, and hidden revenge. I let you be born among a humble family, so that your abilities would be ascribed to the kindness of the gods and not viewed as simply part of the glory of your clan. And then rumors claimed that I had swallowed up your father, I drowned him in a swamp. Maybe you know who your father was?

"I don't remember him," Mebet said.

"A pathetic, bald, and short little man, rather like old Pyak. It was I who asked Yenka of the swamp to take him. And when fame as the Gods' Favorite already ran ahead of your sled, rumors arose that your mother had lain with one of the gods. Now do you understand how much I loved you?"

"I do," the Gods' Favorite replied.

"But that is not all. As soon as a new human being appears in the middle world, evil bubbles up and demands its tribute. The spirits which bring illness, madness, hunger, poor hunting, the spirits of terror, revenge, and malediction – they all demanded that you be given to them. They howled, screamed, and wriggled with impatience to get ahold of your body and soul. But I would not let them get to you: and when I could no longer restrain their hunger, I bought them off. Do you know how I did that? I gave them your children, whose bones you laid to rest in the hollows of trees. I gave them your foes whom you defeated, and your kin who fell ill and died. I told them, 'Eat, gnaw on this, on whatever is around Mebet, but don't you touch Mebet himself.' Because I was waiting. Do you know what I was waiting for? No, you could not even guess.

"In the end, I had to buy them off with your son, Hadko. This Old One of mine tore him apart, and then I let him be slain in turn. That was the last action I took. But even after that, you did not understand what I expected from you. I expected gratitude. A sacrifice made by you would have been sweet incense to me, and not that acrid smoke which gray humanity seeks to appease me with. You alone were worth more than all of them, and Mother's heart fell on you. You did not understand that – you did not even want to understand. You entered into the unclean chum, you did not deign to commemorate me with even a clump of fur from the prey that fell to you. You never had to throw your mittens down at your wife's feet, you never experienced shame or humiliation, because good fortune followed with you like your shadow. But you credited yourself for all of this, for all of your strength, and so you made Mother very sad, ungrateful child…"

"Was it you who gave me strength, or did that come from on high?" Mebet was emboldened to ask, though guardedly.

The water churned and turned red:

"What use would your strength be, you whelp, if it weren't for my help? Even great heroes have been ravaged by diseases that turned them into a bag of bones. Bilget, who confronted an entire army alone, let himself be struck through the heart by the enemy's arrows, because his heart was already broken. You, too, would have rotted like grass. A person's strength is mere wind. It would have been just as easy for this Old One to kill you like you slew him. But that was not my wish, and so now you stand here before me. Your son died, and I have nothing left to buy the spirits off with. Listen to how they are howling with hunger for you, just listen!"

Mother fell silent and the pines stopped rustling. Even the light splashing of the water ceased. In the stillness, Mebet heard a drawn-out and nearly plaintive sound, like an old dog abandoned by its owner and now whimpering from hunger and self-pity. The baying went on, resonated in his ears, and became ever more oppressive. Soon Mebet could no longer see, as if a huge, fiery, and crushing boulder had fallen over his mind. With his head in his hands he dropped to his knees, then tumbled backward. He had only enough strength to hoarsely whisper, "Enough…"

At once everything was quiet again. The darkness was lifted from his eyes and the weight from his mind.

Mother and the Old One said nothing. Mebet rose and began to brush his clothes off, as if he had been lying on leaves and needles, but there were no leaves or needles.

"That is an echo," the Old One said. "Only an echo of the voices…"

Mebet did not reply.

The Mother asked once more:

"So you are asking to go back, into the world?"

"Yes," the Old One answered for him. "He is asking to go back. He is asking for a lot…"

"You spoiled child," the water sighed as it turned a pale lilac color. "How much time are you asking for? Three days, is that enough time for you to reach your camp and die at home?"

"He is asking for a lot," the Old One repeated. "He wants to live until his grandson…"

"His grandson…" the Mother's voiced echoed.

"Until his grandson can live on his own and do everything that a grown man must do."

"His grandson," the water uttered the words again. "Light-eyed Sevser, my gift to you…" The melodious voice suddenly turned grave. "My last gift to you, the last thing that I will ever send you. You, on whom my heart fell! I sent him so that I could awaken your ungrateful heart, but it remains asleep. You considered yourself a god and took your grandson to be the continuation of your godlike legacy. But you are a mortal man, only a man, a plaything for the spirits and food for worms. Even here you have not remembered me!"

Mebet fell to his knees. "I swear that I will bring you a sacrifice. I will bring the greatest of sacrifices in return for all you have done for me." His words were full of fear such as he had never felt before in his life, true fear.

"Now you are speaking like a mortal man," the Mother said. Mebet was baffled, he was uncertain whether this voice held sorrow or the gloating of the strong over the weak.

Mebet felt empty within. He searched for some remaining strength so that he could speak up again, but he said nothing and continued to kneel. The Mother and the Old One were also silent. Finally, words rose up in Mebet's heart, strange and unfamiliar ones. Like hot steam, words of adoration burst forth from him:

"Oh, great one without beginning or end, almighty, infinitely good, compassionate one… Mother of the morning… Mother of the living…"

As Mebet spoke, the image of the woman in the waters became ever clearer.

"Forgive me," he said. "I do not know how to pray. I had no one to teach me the words. I lost my mother when I was very small. Who could have told me that all things came from you? That for everything I am obliged to you?"

"Don't lie to me. This is not something that one must learn, for after all, you are already praying. It was merely your pride that did not let you utter these words before. Your mother thanked the gods for you the best she could, and you, child, saw that. She did not know who exactly to thank, and therefore she prayed to all of the supernatural powers, good or evil, me included. Your mother was a simple woman and she knew nothing of spells, magical dances, and secret lore. But she was grateful, do you understand? Grateful. Know that of all prayers, it is prayers of thanksgiving which reach the heavens first. But people invoke the gods when things are going badly: they fall on their knees like you have done and they ask for their troubles to disappear. Human beings are an ungrateful lot, and you most of all. Tell me, has gratitude welled in your heart even once?"

Mebet bowed even lower. All his life he had been grateful only to himself, that was the pure and simple truth.

"I know why you won't answer," Mother said. "Your heart has never been troubled. It was I who wished that for you. It is hard to expect gratitude from a man if he has never known unhappiness. At the moment when my heart fell on you, I was not thinking that you are just a mere ordinary human being. You see, even the gods make mistakes. You were predestined by those on high – I stole you from them. I don't know if Ulgen kept his promise to never speak of you to those who dwell in the heavens above him. Now that no longer matters: you are not dead yet, but you are no longer in the middle world. And believe me, child, it would be better to never return there…"

Mebet felt that something was stinging his eyes. He put his hands over his face, and a hot stream trickled through his clenched fingers.

"Those are tears," the Mother said dolefully. "Now you are an ordinary mortal man, like everyone else."

"The Old One gave me life to live…"

The waters took on a very slight scarlet tinge, a sign of bewilderment and looming anger. Before the Mother could ask, the Old One spoke up:

"Yes, that is true. I gave him life, eleven years, just enough so that Sevser would be able to take over supporting his family, let them grow old in safety, and keep the clan going. Don't be angry."

Suddenly Mebet watched as the bear's hide fell away, revealing the same crippled old man whom he had met thirty years before at the bear feast. A sled lined with skins stood nearby.

"I told you, young 'un, that there is no heart which has never been broken. Help me get onto my sled."

The old man disappeared, as did the sled, and the gray bear again stood in front of Mebet.

"You yourself ordered him to be summoned," he told the Mother. "Mebet, show her how much life I gave you to live."

The Gods' Favorite took the bundle of slats out from under his coat. In a flash the slats were dangling from the Old One's claws.

"People claim that the gods are unjust, that they shower blessings on some and are harsh to others," the bear said. "Let us finish the hunt, if we have already started it. We will be just."

"What have you done?" the Mother said quietly, without fury. "Do you have any idea what awaits him?"

"I do." The Old One turned sadly to Mebet and sat doglike on his haunches, just like on the day when he had come out from the den and met its death. Some time passed before he spoke again. "People liken the world to their own dwellings. But the world is not a chum that one can enter and leave and always throw back the same flap. You were brought here by your shadow, you followed it and arrived at the sanctuary. You cannot return by the same way. Now these," the bundle of slats swung from the Old One's claws, "you will have to carry through eleven chums. In actuality, they are not like the dwellings of human beings at all. They are invisible. You will make your way on your skis and your dog will run alongside you, and it will seem like you are moving across the same earth as always. But this will be a different earth, not even an earth at all. You must pass through eleven spaces which are the border between the world of human beings and the world of gods. They are known as the chums of atonement. Inside them dwell those things of man, good or bad, for which the person did not manage to achieve redemption while he lived and breathed upon the earth. Things good or ill that are not atoned for, know this. You have done good or ill, Mebet, and let people judge you for that. But you were called the Gods' Favorite only because we preserved you."

"If you want to go back," the Mother now took the Old One's words up, "you will face a great battle, because no longer are we capable of buying the hungry spirits off. Do you hear me? They are howling in anticipation of being able to feast on you. The Rekken are howling, the spirits of woe, who everywhere and always have run after your sled, followed you on migrations, but never were able to enjoy you. The Koy which bring illness are calling for you, they curse your good health. The Navi are crying, the spirits of vengeance weep – all those who wanted to have you but never could. Your path back to mankind lies through their territory, and on this road we will no longer be with you. Think on that, child…"

"Have you cursed me?" Mebet asked.

"No. I love you even now, and I do not wish for you to suffer. If you wanted to leave the world now, without these trials, that would come as greater comfort to me. After all, I was the one who chose you. But human beings die, and sooner or later this must happen to you as well. So it has been since the creation of the world, and even I am not capable of changing that. Do not think that the gods are all-powerful."

"You will face a great battle," the Old One repeated the Mother's words. "The greatest and most severe of all battles, for you will be fighting for your very self. With you, you will have only your weapons, your dog, and yourself. You can no longer trust in your good fortune like a summer sun that never sets, and whether you prove victorious is in the hands of fate. Think carefully about this, Mebet, before you decide to fight such a battle…"

It is said that a stone is happier than a tree, a tree is happier than an animal, but man is the most unhappy of all and it would have been better if he were never born. But Mebet had been born and, after living a life as the Gods' Favorite, he chose now the life of an ordinary man, for he was already an ordinary man through and through, and he was pained with fear for himself and those close to him.

"When the reindeer is sent with the mark of war," Mebet said, "it would be shameful to refuse it and foolish to hide. I thank you, great ones, for your favor and generosity. I choose to fight this battle."

He bowed down to the ground to show his respect for Mother and the Old One. But the Mother had already vanished – in place of the wall of turbulent waters, there stood a row of pines, so dense that the trees seemed to have grown together. The pines extended infinitely into the murky distance. Only the Mother's voice remained:

"Don't think to yourself that the gods are all-powerful. Farewell, child…"

Mebet picked up his spear and threw his quiver with its white arrows over his back. Voipel, who had been somewhere far off all this time, now came up and lied down at his master's feet.

The Old One turned. "Come, I will see you off." He put the strap holding the wooden slats around his neck, slowly rose on his four legs, and walked ahead along the rows of pines. His gray hide rolled on his enormous old body.

The three of them moved through the murk of the pines without saying anything. Only the moon-colored snow seemed to whisper something under their feet.

The rows of pines narrowed and soon there was no room for the three of them to walk abreast. The Old One stopped and gave Mebet the eleven years of his life. "You have probably heard that when people wish each other ill, they say 'May your fish traps stand empty, may you end up on the Path of Thunder.'"

"I have heard that said, though never to me."

"You too will walk this path, you and your dog. Try not to stray from it, otherwise you will meet your end. No one in that world or this will ever find you again."

"I will not stray from the path."

"Don't say that. What is coming will be extremely difficult for you. And truth be told, I am not convinced that you will arrive home with all of these," the Old One tapped a claw on the bundle in Mebet's hands. "There are battles where neither strength, nor smarts, nor bravery will lead to victory. You can buy your way out of those cases only with these. Maybe you won't make it with eleven, but only nine or seven… Maybe you'll be left with only a single year, and that would be better than nothing. Know your strength – it would be better to be crafty than to be proud."

The Old One turned to leave. "There," he pointed a paw into the darkness which loomed beyond the trees, "they will try to take everything from you. Everything we gave you. Remember that."

The Old One vanished, and at once a strong ray of silver light struck Mebet's face. In the place where the light was shining from, the pines ended and the Path of Thunder began with its invisible chums along the way.

THE PATH OF THUNDER

Though people think the spirits to be bodiless powers, they take on bodies at the border between the worlds. Anyone who sets foot on the Path of Thunder ought to keep this in mind. Weapons here must be wielded in a different way or they might not be any use at all, and the same holds for conventional techniques of war. Conventional approaches assume that any battle consists of wounding the bodies of one's foes, whether it be an animal or a man. But those who dwell along the Path of Thunder have bodies quite different from earthly beings, and therefore encountering them brings the traveler on the path one more foe, bodiless but powerful, which hounds him from his first step to his last. That additional foe is ignorance, not knowing how to kill one's attackers. The places on their bodies where a fatal blow could be struck, are not the same as for a human being or an animal. Moreover, the beings dwelling within one chum are different from those living in the next chum, and from all the others. Therefore, the traveler's ignorance turns into perplexity, then into fear, and finally into terror and insanity.

There is only one way to prove victorious. This is to turn away from yourself, to forgot how other people and you yourself have been accustomed to seeing you over all the years of your earthly life. To traverse the entire Path of Thunder from beginning to end is only possible for one whose strength lies not so much in boldness and skill with a weapon, as in the ability to change, to become a different person each time, to overcome one's previous self. If the traveler lacks this skill, terror will destroy him at the very start of his journey.

All these things are what awaited Mebet.

When the silver light struck the Gods' Favorite, he took several steps towards it, then turned to look behind him. The pines were no longer there, and instead of the patch of forest there was a gaping white emptiness.

The sanctuary had stood at the edge of the worlds, the taiga ended at it. But this was no earthly boundary, where the forest gives way to the tundra and the trees grow ever fewer at each day of the journey, as if they intentionally seek to vanish entirely as they approach the dark, icy limits of the world.

Where the Path of Thunder ran, there were neither trees, nor banks of snow concealing frozen swamps. There was only an endless white expanse, as if it had been polished by a lone long wind. There was however no wind, nor any sun, only an even milky-white light that came from no particular direction. The cold air did not hurt Mebet's face. Only the snow was real and it creaked under his skis almost like in the taiga.

The path itself, which was barely visible, stood out not by its snow being trampled down, but rather by its color: a grayish blue. Mebet moved over the colored snow, and he made his way forward for what seemed to him to be a long time. Anticipation of looming danger wriggled in his heart like a cold, slippery worm. His heart was no longer capable of beating at the same calm and even rhythm as in his former life.

THE FIRST CHUM: THE KOY

A whistle came, first thin and far off, as if a blizzard was playing an evil tune over the ragged skins with which the poor make their chums. The sound then grew to an intolerable and piercing volume, which caused Mebet to drop his spear, crouch down, and put his hands over his ears. The single whistling split into two, into three, and ultimately into a vast number. A dark cloud rose in the sky that dissolved into myriad individual dots which came flying towards the Gods' Favorite.

These were the Koy, the spirits of illness, birds with the heads of snakes. Among the spirits they hated Mebet more vehemently than any others. They had gnashed their teeth and seethed with rage at the Gods' Favorite, but they had never been able to get their claws on him. They hungered for Mebet like for no other man. That he remained alive and well drove them into a frenzy. The Koy had never got ahold of his heart, nor his liver, nor his muscles and innards. They had never pierced through him in the form of toothache, swelling of the gums, sores, abscesses, ulcers, or that disease where it seems that hot sand is being poured onto one's eyes. Now the Koy wanted to seize all that they considered theirs.

Mebet fell and pressed his face to the ground. If it were not for the double layer of skins that was his overcoat, the snake-headed ones would have torn his spine from him. Voipel caught the black birds as they flew and flung their torn heads away, which then slithered over the ground like hissing ropes. Once headless, the Koy flew away, but others appeared in their stead. Mebet could see this once he managed to rise to his feet. He swung his spear at the black birds, but nearly every blow met only empty air, and if he managed to fell one of the snake-headed creatures, others would attack his back, his arms, his face. He was soon covered in blood and his strength was leaving him.

"Run!"

Mebet started at hearing this cry.

"Run, save yourself, we won't be able to overcome them."

It was Voipel who spoke.

"Run!"

"Run? Run where?!" Mebet asked. Running away from a foe was something that he had never known before.

"I would sooner rip your throat out myself than let them have you! Run!"

The Gods' Favorite ran, with no thought of shame. Behind him Voipel raged, and the dog with his last strength broke free of the cloud of snake-headed creatures. The air above their heads was black, and soon this cloud was no longer chasing man and dog from behind, but rather it had completely enveloped the two and was getting ready to devour them completely.

"Throw them one of the years you were given!" Voipel cried.

"No!"

"Then no point trying to move on, we'll never make it to the next chum, they will tear us apart here and now."

"I can't see any chum. Where is it?" Mebet cried.

"It is still far from here, but if you throw them at least one year, then we'll make it there safely."

"I don't want to throw them one of my years…"

A snake-headed creature dug into Mebet's cheek and he howled with pain. He grabbed the bird by its black body and flung it away, but its wriggling neck with its tiny toothy head remained attached to his face.

"You are a foolish man, and you will die a foolish death," Voipel growled. "Heed my words now, just as I have obeyed you."

Mebet flung the snake into the snow and drew forth the bundle of wooden slats.

"Throw it away from you as far as you can," the dog cried.

Mebet swung his arm and threw.

The Koy stopped their mad flight and froze in mid-air, only to then come together in a massive hissing ball and rush to where the year granted to Mebet had fallen. The space around man and dog was now clear and they ran forward…

The Koy seemed to have forgotten about them, so busy were they mauling the wooden slat, and killing one another while doing so. When they had reduced the slat to mere fibers of wood thinner than a thread, they remembered their previous victim and set off after him.

Voipel ran with every last bit of strength. Suddenly he stopped and lay down, as if he had fallen dead. "It's over," the dog sighed. "They won't be able to get to us now."

Mebet was barely able to stay on his feet. He looked and saw that the snake-headed creatures were flying right at him, cutting through the air with a piercing whistle, but they had hardly flown a few feet before they began to fall and crumble to dust, as if a wall of utterly transparent and adamantine ice stood in their way.

Then everything disappeared and silence fell.

Thus the Gods' Favorite had passed through the first invisible chum. Another ten remained ahead of him, and ten more years of the life he had been granted. Mebet looked at his bundle sadly.

"Ten, that is a bit more than nine," Voipel said, "and a lot more than nothing."

"You're right," his master replied and hid the bundle under his coat, which was now as ragged as if it had been purposely smeared with blood and thrown to dogs for them to tear it apart. Mebet was drenched under his clothes, more from blood than from sweat. Mebet was unable to feel even amazement at the fact that Voipel could talk. He only said, "I hear that dogs on the earth, Voipel, can see the spirits as clearly as anything else."

"That is the truth. Only on the earth, my nose serves as my eyes. Therefore, I can smell people, animals, and trees better than I can see them. Listen to what I say, master. It will help you. After all, here I am still your dog and I still serve you."

Mebet collapsed to the snow.

"Rest a bit," Voipel said. "My heart can smell that the next battle will be an easier one. Do you see those two stripes on the snow, like two narrow ropes? Those are tracks made by skis."

"Skis?"

"Yes, the skis of the Rekken are small, slightly smaller than they themselves are."

THE SECOND CHUM: THE REKKEN

The Rekken are dwarfs with flat faces, bowlegs, and ugly narrow eyes. Just like human beings, they erect their chums using struts, but these are made from the bones of birds or fish. They make skis and line them with mouse fur. They possess copper kettles and other such utensils. These dwarfs are armed with tiny bows and with tiny spears whose blades are no longer than a needle. The Rekken carry weapons not so much for hunting (for the same mice for their skins to line skis, or for chipmunks to make fur boots and coats) as to wage war against one another.

For them the greatest joy is to erect their chums in a human dwelling – in the owners' bed, in the cradle, or on the runners or sleds, and to follow these humans on their migrations and make trouble for them. These dwarfs feed on misfortune like the heavenly gods find the waters of the sweet, invisible Surya delectable. Because there are fewer human beings around than Rekken, they constantly fight one another, and they are not able to enter into every chum. Their wars appear to be senseless, because they are spirits and thus unable to kill each other, but they are completely capable of driving a rival away from a full place. The vanquished will go hungry, for which reason they possess greater anger but – fortunately for human beings – less strength. The most that the defeated dwarfs are capable of doing is making a hole in a deerskin, tipping a pot full of food over into the fire, or sparking an argument between a young woman and her mother-in-law.

But when the Rekken managed to settle among a human family, things will go badly indeed for the latter. Sorrows and failures will follow them wherever they go.

The dwarfs had looked into Mebet's camp. Without regret, the Mother had given them two of her darling's daughters and one of his granddaughters, because she thought this would suffice to make the spirits leave Mebet alone once and for all. That is how things happened – the Rekken could only lick their lips, for the man from the tribe of Vela remained as enticing a feast as he was an inaccessible one. Moreover, they were terrified of Voipel, who would snap at their vile faces with his fangs, though the people around only assumed that the dog was amusing himself by trying to catch insects.

Mebet made his way through the chum of the Rekken without obstacle.

He only saw that on the snow, half a bow's flight away, there were lines that resembled strings of black beads – the dwarfs had come out in ranks to watch from a distance this man whom they had never got their hands on. The sight of the massive gray dog forbade them from coming any closer lest he attack.

"Things seem quiet here, but we shouldn't stop to sleep," Voipel warned his master. "Otherwise they will cut the soles off your boots or tear your clothes to rags."

The dog stopped and barked. The black strips vanished at once.

"Without you I would be as good as dead."

Voipel did not reply to this praise. Only eventually he said, "In life there are many things that dogs have no part in, only people. A time will come when I will not be able to help you in any way."

THE THIRD CHUM: THE SPIRITS OF RESENTMENT

In the third chum, Mebet was met by the spirits of the owners of lands where he had hunted and killed animals that did not belong to him. The man of the clan of Vela must have sinned greatly, because an uncountable number of spirits came out against him. An army of them appeared before the man and the dog but said nothing. Finally, three lame ones came out of the ranks – they had the faces of the Ivsha men, the same men Mebet had shot in the foot with his arrows while laughing and saying, "Let us reach an agreement, kinsmen. You leave me my quarry, and I will let you keep your lives." Two more stood behind them, the men who had got scared and ran away. Mebet could see the faces of his foes as if through muddy and uneven ice.

"Why do you call us kinsmen? We are of the Ivsha, but you are of the Vela," one of the lame ones finally asked.

Mebet briefly hesitated and then replied, "All men in the taiga are kin." He tried to be cordial, because he felt a strange sensation within: this was shame.

The spirits however took his gentle speech for cowardice. "You aren't the same person you were before," one of them said with relish. "You no longer stand as stately, you are no longer so proud, and your coat is ragged. Did you get attacked by dogs?"

The ranks of spirits shook with laughter.

"For the animals which you killed in others' territory, you should have been punished, severely punished. But clearly some supernatural force has shielded you from justice. It is not our fault, Mebet, that you have gone unpunished so far. But now everything must be set right. How will you redeem yourself?"

"I have a herd, a large herd. Take from it as many animals as you think right."

"You speak of right. But over there," the spirit pointed a finger somewhere over Mebet's head, "over there you thought that your might made right. And now, it seems to us that your might was never yours at all."

Laughter again briefly passed through the crowd.

"Foolish man," the lame one went on. "What would we need your herd for? We are spirits, the spirits of resentment. We care little for the animal which you stole from us, and even our wounded feet concern us little, though they did hurt. You forced us to endure humiliation, to be ashamed to look our women in the eye, and to feel uneasy among our fellow men and constantly expect mockery. How will you redeem yourself for that?"

As soon as the spirit had uttered these last words, the crowd came to life:

"How will you atone for our shame?"

"For the laughter behind our backs?"

"For the curses our elders showered us with?"

"I got a beating for it!"

"My neighbors made fun of me…"

"…they asked, don't your feet hurt, you cowards?"

The cries became ever louder and more frequent. A thick cloud of anger rose over the offended spirits. They shook their spears and bows.

"Yes, the right of the strong," the spirit in front said. "But that is over there." He again pointed above Mebet's head. "Here things are different. Know, Mebet, that the one who proves the weaker will suffer. And you must suffer now!"

The spirit raised his spear and prepared to fight. "We know what you're hiding under your coat. Give it to us!"

The other spirits followed him in readying their weapons and moving towards Mebet. The Gods' Favorite raised his spear, stood with legs spread and firmly pressed to the snow, so that he could withstand the first charge. In his heart he understood that he could not expect to win. He knew that, unlike in times past, he could hold his own against an entire army. He did not give in to cowardice, but he had forgotten his pride.

"How many years must I give you?" he shouted to his attackers.

"All of them. Give us all of them and go to hell! There is a place for you there. There you will see how much the weak suffer."

The man and the dog stood together. A growl rumbled inside Voipel, and then suddenly it stopped. "Mangi!" Voipel said under his breath, and then he took a deep breath and called out with all his might. "Mangi!"

This startled the army of spirits, and then they stood frozen. Only a few of them turned to look, and then they saw something.

Voipel's cry had been directed at a raging cloud of snow in which the enormous antlers of an elk moved. The cloud grew closer and it was difficult to determine if it was an animal or its ghost. The snow and the vague outlines of the beast swept forward like a hurricane.

"Mangi, he's coming, he's coming!"

In its trail another cloud appeared, even larger than the first. Through the white whirlwind one could make out the outlines of an enormous hunter. The giant swung his arms as he rushed forward.

The spirit army's ranks crumbled, and they dropped their weapons as they fled. In their mad flight they knocked one another aside or stepped on the skis of those in front of them.

"Stop, don't move," Voipel said.

The cloud swept towards them and Mebet's burning face was dusted with snow.

Mangi was the god of good hunting, a giant with the body of a man and the head of a bear who forever chased an elk. As for whether some power had willed his appearance here, Mebet did not know.

Mangi got angry whenever people mistreated an animal. People hurting one another did not concern him, however. The giant chased the elk, he had chased it since the beginning of time and he broke off his pursuit only when a crime against the equilibrium of life in the world proved stronger than his passion for the hunt.

Voipel knew that his master ought to fear the wrath of this god, inasmuch as Mebet's sins against voiceless creatures were many. Mebet had not only caught animals in other clans' hunting grounds, he had also often killed animals unnecessarily, left a mortally wounded creature to rot, shot at pregnant females and swans, and once he killed an alpha reindeer and dispersed the whole herd. He had done it all, especially in his youth.

The cloud grew closer, the features of a giant with a bear's head appeared through the snowy haze. The Gods' Favorite prepared to meet this trial.

Voipel however told his master, "Stay where you are and wait." The dog then cried, "Greetings, Mangi! I wish you a good hunt. I am Voipel, king of the dogs of the taiga."

The giant gave a bear-like roar, but to Mebet his voice did not sound angry. Mangi knew the name and face of every animal, and he immediately recognized this dog who had been named after the fierce north wind.

"Don't lay a hand on my master, I beg you."

The god stood motionless, as if he were deep in thought.

"The elk is getting away," Voipel cried again. "A good hunt is better than revenge. Don't hurt my master. He is ignorant, like all humans."

Mangi was capable of speaking, but he cared little for human speech and therefore he did not utter a word in reply. He looked up at the sky, drew a deep breath, and with a loud roar he rushed off towards where the rolling cloud with the elk antlers was disappearing to.

A few words from the great dog had outweighed all the sins of the great man.

The spirits of resentment, on the other hand, had no one who could intercede for them. They were clearly in the wrong with regard to Mangi, and so they had turned to flee and they had forgotten all about getting their revenge.

As the spirits ran, they shouted at Mebet, "Don't think you're safe! There are many, many spirits like us ahead of you…"

THE THREE LARGE CHUMS

The white veil was lifted to reveal a pack of gray phantasms. They ran in the distance at a dead, leaden pace without coming near the man and his dog.

"Who are they?" Mebet asked.

"I don't know," Voipel replied. "I can only see wolves, or something like wolves."

Mebet stopped, and the pack stopped, too. The man and his dog continued walking, and so did the pack. Mebet's legs felt unbearably heavy after so much walking. He had long since lost track of time on his journey because the Path of Thunder knew neither day nor night, neither sunrise nor sunset, no sun, moon, stars, or aurora.

Mebet had begun to feel truly alarmed. All this time, he kept his spear at the ready as he walked. Voipel never took his eyes off the enemy, though the enemy never attacked. This constant state of anxiety wore Mebet down more than fatigue. At first he felt comforted by the hope that he might inadvertently make it through – he would cross the boundaries of this chum without losing anything or getting involved in a skirmish. But he could see no boundaries, and his alarm only grew. Mebet stopped and asked Voipel:

"Can you see where this chum ends?"

Voipel slowed his step. "It has already ended," the dog sighed.

"Why didn't you tell me?"

"Forgive me, master," Voipel again heaved a guilty sigh. "The border was so inconspicuous that I thought I only imagined it. Either I'm tired from walking, or I'm getting old and it's time for you to get rid of me. But now I understand: there was a boundary, we crossed it and are now in a different chum. But what this chum is like, I have no idea, and I don't know the spirits here."

"Why aren't they attacking?" Mebet asked.

"They look like wolves, and the way they hunt is like wolves. A lynx hidden in a tree will pounce on its prey and quickly kill it. A bear can break its prey's spine with a swing of its paw. But wolves, when an animal is too big for any one member of the pack to take down, will pursue the prey without hurrying, until its legs fail it. You know the feeling yourself. When a pack sees that an elk is totally exhausted and can no longer raise its legs to kick, then they attack and tear it to pieces. These spirits must be waiting for the same chance. They won't attack as long as they can see that our legs are strong, even if we aren't moving so fast. You strike them as a big catch."

"Then we will attack them," Mebet said resolutely.

"You shouldn't do that," the dog said, but Mebet seemed not to be listening. He raised his weapon and walked towards the gray mass. With a heavy heart, but nevertheless obedient to his master, Voipel hastened after Mebet.

Mebet's heart was aflame with fury. He moved faster and faster, then broke out into a run. Soon he could already make out the spirits' features, sharp snouts like those of earthly wolves but shorter.

Voipel and Mebet approached, and suddenly the pack stopped moving. The gray mass froze and erupted into myriad ears pointing up, suggesting tension. When the man and his dog had nearly come up against the pack, a mere spear's distance away, the wolves rose and, without any especial hurry, backed away. Mebet perked up to see them retreat and he forgot all about his fatigue.

"They're running away. They're afraid of us. Let's get them!"

"It's not worth it," Voipel wheezed, but again his master was not listening.

Mebet never did catch up with the gray mass. He could see the spirits before him, but he never reached them. Tired, he sat down on the snow, and immediately the pack sat down, at the same distance they had maintained before.

"Let's go back, master," Voipel said. "We have gone too far off the path. We'll never catch these spirits. My nose can sense that we wouldn't be able to get away from them. We need to find the end of this chum."

Mebet agreed. "You're right. Let's look for it. Maybe something would happen, that would be better."

"That would be easier."

"Quite right…"

It was not a single pack but three: the spirits of Melancholy, Despair, and Fear.

Each of these lived in their own chum, but their invisible dwellings merged into a single space divided by borders that could barely be made out, for melancholy, despair, and fear always coexist. They give rise to one another, they stem from one another, and they resemble one another like one wolf resembles another. They live and hunt as wolves do: they lure some people into pitfalls and they starve others into surrendering. Every man knows the way they hunt: the spirits pursue you from the time you reach the age of reason until your dying day. They chase you, and if you show weakness, they tear you into pieces.

No one knows where these spirits came from, and only a few people have had the great fortune of never once encountering them. Never in Mebet's life had the pack approached him, and now the spirits wanted to take their fair share from him. They wanted his flesh, they wanted his very life.

But here, on the Path of Thunder, the man and the dog saw them as only wolves. They expected from the pack of spirits the same thing they would expect from any ordinary pack on earth.

The spirits of the three wolf chums wore Mebet down. When he could no longer bear to run, his legs had seemingly turned to stone and his body could barely hold on, the pack stopped and let out a howl. The sound sapped Mebet's strength, as if his blood were being sucked out with a straw. He melted like snow in the sun; his energy drained away like water leaks from a container with a hole in it. He writhed and collapsed like a body from which the bones had been removed…

There was no trace of Mebet's former fury, anger, or hope, and he no longer had the energy to raise his spear. Mebet fell, and no longer did he think about the Path of Thunder, his family, the life that had been granted him. He thought of nothing, he saw nothing and felt nothing, besides his own suffering. He wanted to howl like the pack of wolflike spirits was howling. He tried to cry out, but his weakened chest could push only a dry, barely audible sound through his throat. His tongue had become no more than the inert clapper of a bell. A shudder passed through his body, and his hand of his own accord drew the bundle of years granted him from under his coat and flung it into the snow.

As soon as his hand had let go of the bundle, the howling stopped.

Mebet was still in the grip of pain, but he found the strength again to stand up and walk. He stood up and walked like a man half-dead, without even knowing where. Voipel picked up the bundle so that he could return it to his master, but as soon as Mebet laid hold of the years of life given to him, the howling began anew and the Gods' Favorite fell down again.

The dog tried to stuff the bundle under Mebet's coat, but Mebet fought him off with whatever energy he could muster. He wriggled like a snake, he pressed his face into the snow, and from his mouth a feeble cry issued, "Get it away from me, dog. Get those damned slats away from me. Don't touch me, dog. Don't you try to give me those slats…"

The extra years given to Mebet had come to torment him, just like life itself is torture for those who are ravaged by melancholy, who are worn down by fear, and who give in to despair.

Mebet was no longer crying out. He lay on the snow with no desire to ever rise again. Now three wolves separated from the pack and came rushing towards him.

"They're coming for your extra years, I suppose," Voipel said, and he took the strap around the bundle in his teeth. "Let them just try to take them. On the earth I tore wolves apart, and I will do the same here."

"You listen here, dog," Mebet said. "If you don't give them that bundle, may you be cursed. For a dog there is nothing worse than the curses of a human being. But even if you fight them off and try to give those slats back to me, I won't take them. If I die, if you die, if everyone dies, I don't care. There's no use fighting them, it's not worth it."

Voipel could see that his master was telling the truth and so the dog did not bother arguing with him. It would be silly to try to save the life of a man for whom living had become torment. He walked slightly away from Mebet, laid the bundle down on the snow, and then went back up to his master and lay down next to him. The dog waited for the pack's emissaries to come and take what they wanted.

Three spirits on long and springy legs ran up, picked the bundle up, and then headed back to their pack. They did not even glance at Mebet, as if the years granted him were something they had found alongside the road and could legally take as theirs.

"I'm going to sleep," Mebet said. "Just sleep. You sleep too."

Voipel lay down at his master's feet.

Mebet slept for a long time, and he might have never awoken at all, but he felt a gentle but insistent hand nudging him by the shoulder. With effort the Gods' Favorite opened his eyes, and the first thing he saw was an open hand holding the strap around the bundle of granted years. Mebet started at the sight. He could not tell who the hand belonged to, it seemed to loom out of empty space; he could only vaguely see the outlines of a man wearing a coat.

"Take these," the voice said. "You lost them and I picked them up. Don't lose them again."

Again Mebet shuddered. He reached out to take the bundle, but his fingers would not obey him and the years slipped from his hand. They fell down into the snow and clattered against one another. The bundle continued to lay there.

Mebet suddenly realized that once he had touched these precious wooden slats, he felt no pain, nor could he hear the howling.

"Who are you?"

"A spirit." The speaker paused, but then, as if he anticipated Mebet's question, he said, "I have known these creatures for a long time. They came and gave me your years themselves."

"Did you order them to do that? Can you really order them around?"

"No. But there, back in the world, I encountered them many times. I fought with them and won. Or nearly won. They remember that and they even preserve some fear of me."

"Is there really anyone capable of winning against them?"

"I don't know, probably. As for me, I died at just the right time; if it hadn't been for that bear, they would have defeated me in some other battle. A timely death is a good thing, a person's life does not seem unfairly short. You, the living, cannot understand this well, or at all."

Mebet's heart was pounding in his chest. "Who are you?" he cried.

"I am Hadko, your son. You would hardly recognize me, my appearance is still vague, because I died only recently. But I think that when we meet again here on the other side, you will easily recognize me. But the time is not yet ripe. Hello, father."

Mebet was so amazed that he was unable to return his son's greeting, but Hadko did not reproach him for it. After a long silence, Mebet regained his composure and said, "Son, I killed that bear, I got revenge for…"

The Blizzard Man gently interrupted him. "You don't have to tell me, I know. Better you tell me about my son, is he well? My mother? My wife?"

"They are all well. They miss you."

"They shouldn't. Don't let them worry about me, nothing bad has happened to me here. Tell them that when you arrive back at home."

Mebet was choked with tears and his voice faltered. "I will. If I ever make it home. These chums are tough. They are my reckoning for how I lived my life…"

"Don't blame yourself," Hadko said. His voice was calm and untroubled. "Every man must atone for his life, either after his death, or while he is still there, on the earth."

"Did you have to atone?"

"I suppose I did. But I don't know what will happen to me in the future. My fate has still not been decided up there," Hadko pointed upwards. "Not enough time has passed yet. But I think the gods were kind to me in that they took my life at a happy time. I had a son, a beautiful wife, and the hunting was good. My love had started off evilly, but ultimately it had been cleansed of evil. I ceased being enemies with anyone, I established a firm peace with other people. Doesn't that count for something? I even went to kill that last bear so that I could be even happier, but perhaps that was going too far. There was one thing that puzzled me, though. I don't know who willed it – though it was undoubtedly a blessing – that I could overcome the fear I felt deep inside me: the fear of you. I was no longer afraid, I wasn't sullen whenever I saw you, but I still knew that we would inevitably come to blows. Not now but much later, when my son, your grandson, was already grown. I had guessed that you intended to make him your heir instead of me…"

Mebet was grieved. "You guessed correctly."

Hadko went on as if he had not heard him. "But praised be the gods who allowed me to die at a good time. They saved me from strife with my own father."

"Would you have raised a weapon against me?"

"For a man to deny his own son his birthright, and for a son to raise a weapon against his own father – could there be a more horrible fate? Anyone who claimed that they knew how to resolve this state of affairs would be a fool. I was wise enough not to solve this conundrum before the right time came. Time gave me some respite, and my thoughts turned to other things, though I knew that you are not a man who can forgive and forget insults. But I will tell you just one thing: I would have done everything I could to stay alive, even if you had sought my death. But as you can see, the gods decided differently, and so it doesn't make sense to talk about this."

"Can you forgive me, son?"

"You don't need my forgiveness."

Mebet hung his head. He felt a soreness again in his heart, as if the pack of wolflike spirits had returned and resumed their howling.

"No, you can't," he said, his voice like that of a doomed man. "You can't forgive me."

"Believe me, father, I do not speak these words out of anger or the old resentment. I left my anger and resentment behind there and they will never return to me. There is no stone, tree, bird, or animal that needs forgiveness, only man needs it. He is farthest of all from truth, he alone knows what suffering is. He alone longs for forgiveness and vindication. But you are not a man like everyone else, that is clear as day. It was not by your own decision that you became the person you are, because becoming such a person is beyond the power of any man. If anyone needs forgiveness, it is whoever made you the favorite of the gods."

"I know. I'll tell you…"

"No need. It won't change anything. Save your strength, father, don't waste time thinking about things that aren't important. Now, when you have become an ordinary human being like everyone else, you have done nothing wrong. You are suffering now, and much suffering awaits ahead. I know that each of these wooden slats represents a year of living in the world. You yourself agreed to suffer, so that my son, light-eyed Sevser, my mother, and my wife would not become destitute and not fall victim to others. So, you don't need my forgiveness. Whatever you have done, you are already forgiven. Just go on, please, and don't go off the path. Gather whatever strength is within you, and just go. You, Voipel, my brother, true friend, helper, and servant: help your master as best you can. Get up, Mebet, it's time. I think they will summon me soon, and before I hear the voice from on high, I want to see you walking on. Then my heart will be at peace."

Mebet got up and took his spear and the bundle of years granted to him. He stood firm on his feet and felt a new wind.

"Go on," Hadko insisted.

"Will we ever see each other again, son?"

"That is not for us to decide."

Mebet suddenly felt that his dead son's appearance grew clearer for an instant, and his son was smiling.

"I might not have the same eyes and wide cheekbones as you," Hadko said, "but I think that you are not the only favorite of the gods. Farewell."

"Wait," Mebet cried. "Don't leave. I promise to accept anything I could bear, or even anything I couldn't, but just tell me one thing. Is it true that along with each man's birth, his own measure of suffering is born as well? And if that's true, who is responsible for such evil?"

Hadko's spirit floated in the air, became flat, and fluttered like a mournful flag of war in a heavy wind. "If I were the last man left alive, then the gods might reveal that truth to me," he said. "But I am not, and I don't know. But I believe that at the end of time, if not earlier, this will all be revealed. Right now, the important thing is for you to move on. Go, father. Don't waste your energy thinking about things whose time hasn't come yet. Take care of yourself."

After Hadko's spirit said this, he vanished.

THE SEVENTH CHUM: THE DEAD ARMY

A man, short, hunched, and quiet, walked behind Mebet. He did not approach Mebet, he did not try to catch up with him or speak to him, but he stopped when Mebet stopped, and he appeared to be waiting for something.

"Who are you and why are you following me?"

The man did not respond, he only covered his face with the sleeve of his threadbare coat that was obviously too large for him. He possessed no weapon.

"What do you want?" Mebet asked again, though he did not feel like he was in any danger.

Finally, the man uncovered his face, which was just as blurry as the other inhabitants of this zone. In order to recognize a man here, one would have had to know him well in life. But Mebet did not know this fellow, though he had undoubtedly met him somewhere.

The man shifted from one foot to the other, as if he was gathering the courage to speak, and finally he asked, "Do you have a comb?"

This struck Mebet not so much as a stupid question as a strange one. "Why would I need such a thing?" he replied. "After all, I'm not a woman."

"Pity," the man heaved a heavy and bitter sigh. "A real pity that you don't have a comb. My hair really hurts me. I heard that if I combed it, especially with a silver comb or one from walrus ivory, it wouldn't hurt so much."

From the deerskin bag on his belt he drew a head of hair with the skin still on it and showed it to Mebet. "See? It hurts, but I don't have anything to comb it with…"

The Gods' Favorite shuddered – this was the same Vaynot scout whom he had scalped, and then killed and hid under a fallen tree. Mebet still recognized him, though he had seen the man only for a brief time. Tracking the scout and killing him had not posed a challenge, and plus this young man was hardly a formidable opponent. Catching him, killing him, and hiding the body all took place within a short while. After the marvelous victory over the Vaynot fighters, this minor episode in the fighting remained in his memory only as the simple satisfaction at a job well done.

But now the memory stood front and center in Mebet's mind and it pained him. The young man guessed at his thoughts:

"You did it all so easily," he said, and his blurry face twitched with something resembling a smile. "Where did you learn to do such a thing? I wish I could do something like that. Don't worry, I'm not asking anything from you. Just a comb, but you don't have one."

The young man pulled the hood of his coat down to reveal the bare bone of his skull.

"I don't even hold it against you. After all, it was all under the rules of war. If things were reversed, I would have scalped you. If I could have reached that high, I mean. You're awfully tall." He laughed at his own joke, but then sadness quickly caught hold of him. "It's a pity." He was silent for a time after that, but then he perked up and said, "But I'm happy. You know why? I'm happy that I didn't even cry out when you scalped me. I behaved like a real warrior. Don't you agree?"

"Yes, you behaved like a real warrior," Mebet said dully, almost dejectedly. "Only a real, experienced warrior could have withstood that pain like you did. Though you are quite young. What's your name?"

His interlocutor did not seem to hear the question. He went on, "Did you ever tell anyone that I behaved like a real warrior? Tell them. That's what really matters to me."

Mebet realized that the sole thing that he could *not* say to this man was the truth. But the Gods' Favorite could not lie. He fell silent for a moment as he tried to choose the right words. "Only I witnessed your bravery. Besides me, no one else knows about it."

The young man wilted and nearly cried. "A pity," he said. "I asked them to let me be a scout, because I wanted everyone to know: I might have been an orphan, I might have been taken in by others because I didn't have my own home, but I had smarts, I could help them. Maybe even better than their own guys." He then put the hair back into his bag and turned to go.

"Wait, don't go," Mebet cried. "I will go back to the world and tell everyone of your bravery. What is your name?"

"Do you really mean it?"

"Yes. Unless, of course, I never make it to the end of this path."

"I will help you. We'll go together, I'll vouch for you to my kinsmen, they are waiting up ahead. There's a lot of people there."

They walked on together, and the young scout told of his life. They had called him Susoy, which means "Weakling."

"They gave me a bad name," Susoy said, "and the worst thing is that it's not true. How could I be a weakling if I chop wood, haul sleds around, and I can wrangle reindeer? But for those guys I was always Susoy. That's why I asked to scout out your camp, so that they would start calling me by some other name. Something nice, something that would impress people."

The kinsmen to whom the young scout referred, turned out to be the Vaynot host which Mebet had annihilated. At its head stood Nyaruy, the one who could not bear the shame and so killed himself.

The commander was sitting on the snow with his legs crossed, and he seemed to be singing something to himself, swaying to the rhythm of the words:

"Could one man really stand against a whole army?" he asked no one in particular, and then he went on to answer himself: "No, he could not. But Mebet, his son, and another one – a woman – defeated me. Me, who never led my clan to a loss, who never experienced defeat. Could such a thing really happen? No, it couldn't. The elk is mighty, but what would happen if it stood alone against a whole pack of wolves? The bear is fearsome when it is brought forth from its lair, but it would inevitably die if the hunters are many, brave, and standing in the right place. I, Nyaruy, went forth against the tattooed Tungus, against the Enets, the Selkups, the Arins, the Nganasan. Against other tribes and clans who sought after our lands. I led men with weapons when we sought after the lands of others. I went out against forces two and three times larger than my own, and never did my clan experience defeat. Because the god of war loved me. And he gave me, Nyaruy, not only boldness but impeccable knowledge of how to plan the attack, and how to assign my men in accordance with their abilities and their strength. But Mebet, his son, and a woman won against my host, a whole host of brave men. How could that be? How did I miscalculate? Why did I send out a stupid boy as a scout, and not a man with experience? Why did I give into the fear that cowards feel? Why did I succumb to the foolishness of fools, the greed of the greedy? How could I have walked right into the trap?"

Forked Arrow raised his head as if he sought from the emptiness some reply, some excuse for him. "I did everything properly, after all. As a scout, I sent out someone who the enemy would least suspect, someone who looked like a wandering simpleton. I went to the enemy's camp myself so that I could beat him to the attack. I did not allow cowardice or greed, and I should have won, because I did not violate the laws of war and my god of war should have helped me this time, too. But Mebet won. It was a bitter loss. Tell me,

Mebet, how could you, who scoff at all laws and even stooped to take advantage of a woman's betrayal – how could you win? Why wasn't it me who won, the man who ensured that his clan never suffered defeat? Why did the god of war send me this strange battle and abandon me? I raise the tent-flap and look at my life like I would look into a well-lit chum where everything is there to see, but I can't see any reason that I should have made my god angry. Maybe you could tell me?"

"The gods are not all-powerful," Mebet said. "Just like humans, their desires are all mixed up and they make mistakes. I know this now, Nyaruy. Don't be hard on yourself, don't feel guilty. For you everything is past now."

"No," Nyaruy replied. "No," he repeated firmly and bitterly. "It is not past. I feel that this is only the beginning of the great torments, which will stretch on forever like the frozen tundra. The good warrior is the one whose soul is pure, white like snow, and whose thoughts are simple. And who had already slain his main enemy – doubt – at the start of his path, when he first took a weapon into his hands. Only in that way can he not be afraid of death. I served my clan and I had no doubt as to the justice of my job. A warrior loyal to his clan is guilty of nothing. But now something is gnawing at me: I think about whether I was in the right. I even think, what is right? I think on this and I struggle with doubt, and that is the greatest trial for a warrior. It is better to suffer any wound from an iron blade, than this torment. How can I rid myself of all these memories?"

"I feel for you. Don't wonder about how you angered your god. You could not have won anyway, you were a mere plaything."

"A plaything?"

"Yes. Like children find bits of wood or stone that look like a reindeer or a dog, and they amuse themselves with these. You were the same amusement, you and your people."

"Who were you then?"

"The same as you, a mere plaything, just of a different sort."

"A different sort?"

"Mother Earth made me into her toy, so that she could amuse herself by watching a human being who was capable of everything and untouched by human sorrows. It is only for that reason that you could not beat me."

"Does that mean it's true when they say that you are descended from the gods?"

"We all come from the gods. It is by their will that we appear in this world, and it is by their will we live our lives and we pass away. The only way that I'm different is because the Mother's heart fell on me. That was her doing, not mine. Her whim lifted me higher than other people, and her whim made me fall."

"Fall…" Nyaruy repeated pensively. "Tell me, is the Mother good?"

"I don't know. She is not a human being, so why should she be good or evil? The Mother is a divinity and she acts as a divinity does."

"But why did her heart fall on you? Are other people really so unworthy?"

"I couldn't tell you. No one could. The gods play with human beings and become enraged at them if they don't respond with gratitude to the gods' own mistakes."

"What are you walking this path for?" Forked Arrow asked. He did not ask where Mebet was bound, because he already knew that Mebet wished to return to the world and live on.

"I need to live until my grandson becomes a man, otherwise my family will perish."

"Strange. You never showed any concern for other people before, whether they were strangers or your own family. Remember Yadne…"

"I remember Yadne. It is for her sake that I am going back along this path. I must come to know the grief which was meant for me, but inflicted on others."

"Like me?"

"Like you. The Mother clearly wanted to make me into nearly a god, but all the same she got an ordinary human being like everyone else. My concern for my family is drawing me back, and so great is its power that I have agreed to pay my dues. The fun which I had at others' expense is now turning into suffering, my conscience will burn me, and like others I will tremble for my life. Now justice is being done, and it is in your power, Nyaruy, to stop me. After all, it would be impossible for one man to stand against a whole army, especially with such a skilled commander as you."

"You are right, it would be impossible."

"I know that you were placed here to seize the bundle of years granted to me. If you take them from me, that will be what people call justice. Let it be so, but I want you to know that I will not surrender them without a fight. Otherwise, why should I return to the world?"

Nyaruy said nothing, nor did the army sitting behind him in ranks. Finally, he said, "Yes, now is the time for us to settle scores. But you don't know what god I have been praying to. No one knows, because his name cannot be uttered among men. He is the god of treaties, service, and justice. He is the patron of good wars. I may be dead, but I remain the same warrior who they called Forked Arrow. The shame which fell upon me continues to tear at my heart. I broke the laws of war and brought my army to your camp, because I thought that you were not so crazy as to confront me all alone."

"You acted sensibly," Mebet said.

"Although…" Nyaruy hesitated for a moment and then went on, "Now I know that a great ally was standing behind you, one greater than any army. But now things are different: I have armed men behind me, and you are alone, truly alone. Unleashing this army on you would simply mean murdering you. I don't want my god to think badly of me when he learns that I got revenge on you in such a cowardly and dishonorable way. I know how strong you are, and how even without the help of the gods you fought many. I must confess, I am amazed at how fate never made you the commander of an army. You have been a better man than me, better than many. But no matter. Back then you chose not to fight me one on one, and I think that it would be fair if you accept my challenge now. If you win, you can proceed further. No one would dare touch you."

Mebet bowed. "You are generous, Forked Arrow. Too generous."

Nyaruy was silent for a moment as he thought about what Mebet meant. Suddenly his face turned red and he jumped up. "Why 'too generous'? Are you trying to say that defeating me would be a mere trifling matter?"

"No, I didn't mean that."

"Then what did you mean?"

"Hear me out," Mebet said. "Now as warriors we are both reliant on fortune, and fortune is the whim of the gods. Especially in a duel."

"I agree."

"If suddenly your good fortune were overturned for merely an instant, I would inevitably kill you. I must do that."

"How could it be otherwise?" Nyaruy said in nearly a merry tone. "I would do the same if you made but a single wrong move. You are already dead, but I live on." He took a step towards Mebet and his chest under his chainmail heaved as he breathed with excitement. "You are not as I imagined you. You know what true nobleness is. Let us sit down and talk about true nobleness."

During his life Nyaruy had not grazed reindeer, caught fish, or hunted to feed his family, for he never had one. He only fought, and he lived off what booty he seized in war and what remuneration his kinsmen gave him for his leadership. He considered his lot in life to be the best possible one, and he developed a sophisticated understanding of military strategy. But Forked Arrow's personality was a simple one: he was as resentful as children are, and disingenuousness was foreign to him.

"Sit down, Mebet. We will talk about how one should act with true nobleness."

They sat down. At first Nyaruy spoke. He spoke for a long time and with great eloquence, something he was fond of. The Gods' Favorite listened and looked the commander directly in the eye. Nyaruy's visage grew clearer with every word he spoke, as if he were returning to the world of the living. Mebet held his gaze and saw that the other man was flattered by how closely he was listening. But in fact, the Gods' Favorite was struck by painful thoughts and Nyaruy's lofty speech only went in one ear and out the other. Mebet was not thinking about where exactly on these spirits' bodies a fatal blow could best be struck, though that is what should have been occupying his mind.

Rather, Mebet was beginning to understand the laws that governed the Path of Thunder. Nyaruy had died because he was a simple man who could not bear the shame of their war, and the entire weight of his clan's reversal had fallen on him. Now that was all redeemed, and that meant that Nyaruy was obviously stronger now. Another thought arose not from Mebet's conscious, but from somewhere deep inside him, and it pained him: to kill Forked Arrow, if luck were still on Mebet's side, struck him as something absurd, abhorrent. His victory in the confrontation would forever weigh on him.

Mebet knew a way out of this: it would be better to face off with a dozen of Nyaruy's warriors at once, or fight them individually one on one, as long as Mebet would not have to fight Nyaruy himself. But Mebet did not know how to communicate this thought to this man in armor who was as resentful as a child. He nevertheless decided to make an effort to do so. He sought to phrase it all in the right words so that chagrin and perplexity would not overcome him entirely, though he did not utter these words aloud.

THE GODS INTERFERE

Harmony is something that one rarely encounters among human societies, but there is no peace in the heavens either.

While Mebet was confronted by the dead army, Num, the god of the Upper Heaven, who beholds all time, who has no appearance, and who is surrounded by the Perfect Ones, suddenly said, "Where is Mebet?"

In this way he discovered the crime committed by the Mother, who had taken possession of this bright human soul before the supreme god could write his fate.

The question resounded across the heavens: "Where is Mebet… Where is Mebet… Where is Mebet…"

The god had directed his voice downward, and now the celestials answered him:

"Mebet isn't here…"

"Mebet isn't here…"

"Mebet isn't here…"

Their voices from below reached him. Num did not go looking for this lost man on the earth – he did not see human beings at all, because his eye did not condescend to gaze at the middle world. The god's mind told him that here, in the heavens, he ought to see the man who had been given the name Mebet and a bright destiny as would elevate a human being to the ranks of the Perfect Ones.

Num asked the god below him, "In your heaven, Ulgen, there should be a bright soul. Is he there?"

Ulgen immediately recalled the agreement he had made with the Mother. He was afraid, and he lied to play for time. "There have not been any bright souls here for a long time. Only gray ones. But now I see that one might be coming along."

Like a whirlwind, Ulgen descended to the border between the worlds, to where the Mother was. "Num is asking about Mebet, about the soul which you took from me. What should I tell him?"

The Mother had heard the voice of the faceless god. She turned transparent as if she were innocence itself, and she did not show the unease that she felt. "I release the souls which you give me into the world. You gave me that soul, and I let a human being be born from it. What more do you want from me?"

"You asked me for that particular soul yourself. I told you that it was a bright soul, that its destiny had not been written yet, and that the higher gods would be angry. But you begged me for it."

"I begged you? Why should I beg you for one soul, when from sunrise to sunset a torrent of them passes by me, either on their way to the world or out of it?"

Ulgen raged – the Mother tended to betray him thus. "The Faceless One may well punish me and I might end up among the spirits of the underworld, but you won't get away with this."

"Do not threaten me," came the voice from the waters.

"If you think that when he unleashes his wrath on us, you can just hide behind your woman's weakness and foolishness, you are wrong. He won't forgive you a second time. Think about that."

The Mother darkened and froze. Ulgen had dredged up some bad memories for her.

Long ago, back when the world was still being created, the Mother had been the wife of a god from one of the higher heavens, but she was seduced by the King of the Underworld. When the Mother's infidelity was discovered, she begged her husband for leniency, wailing and moaning. If the jealousy of her heavenly spouse had been any stronger, she would have been cast into hell. But the Mother successfully made her case, and she was mercifully placed at the border between the worlds instead. An eon passed, and many things had become different in the heavens and on the earth, in the spaces where the living and the dead dwell, but the Mother never returned to live alongside the other celestials. She realized that her path lay only downwards.

Nevertheless, she remained one of the gods, and therefore she spoke in a haughty tone to conceal her fear. "Yes, Mebet was my fancy, but now I have had enough of him. What should I care about his being fated for greatness?"

Ulgen could see through her prideful tone, he knew she was afraid. Now he now longer concealed his rage. "Do you understand what bright souls mean? There are very few such souls. So few that even the Faceless One knows their names."

"I know," the Mother replied. "No need for you to try to teach me the workings of heaven."

"It is through such bright souls that the will of the higher gods is implemented in the word; they are the tools of the gods. The designs of the higher gods are a mystery to us, but if you want to stand in their way, then save your haughtiness for hell."

The Mother said nothing to this. She could see the truth in Ulgen's threat.

With an almost cordial tone Ulgen said, "Good, I see that you can be reasonable." Then, "Where is Mebet?"

"He wants to return to the world. He is walking the Path of Thunder."

"Bring him back. Bring Mebet back no matter what it takes. Let him appear in my heaven as a bright soul again, let him be born and live out a destiny set by the higher gods. This way, we can hide our crime before it's too late. Hurry now, you who give birth to men."

The Mother's heart was anxious, but no longer about her own fate, rather about her favorite. She remembered how passionately she had desired to see one happy man on the earth, regardless of the toll on other people. She remembered how his heart was broken and how he had longed for a world where men suffer, and he agreed to take upon himself all the suffering he had never experienced before.

Ulgen snapped her out of her reverie. As he ascended to his heaven, he said again, "Hurry! I'll be waiting to hear from you."

The Mother took on the form of a silver loon and flew across the white sky over the Path of Thunder, where she caught sight of Mebet seated and facing the Vaynot host. Mebet and Nyaruy were speaking to one another. The loon did not descend to the ground but only hovered above their heads and spoke with the Mother's voice.

"Mebet," the Mother called. "Do you recognize me?"

"It's you!" an astonished Mebet said and leaped to his feet.

"Do you remember the oath you swore?"

"I do. I swore to make the greatest of sacrifices to you for all that you have done for me. I swear that I will do that on the very day when I arrive back in the world."

The loon landed on the ground with a fluttering of its wings. "You can fulfill your promise right now."

"Right now?"

"Yes, right now, Mebet, as quickly as possible."

The man of the tribe of Vela felt a vague alarm in his heart. "I don't understand what you mean. I haven't made it through all of the chums yet, and I don't know if I'll even be able to…"

"Forget about what is past. Forget about the chums, or the path, or the years that were granted to you. Things are different now. There have been changes in the heavens."

"Changes?"

"Yes, big changes. You must go back to the heaven of the future, back to Ulgen, and again become the bright soul which you once were. The Faceless One has plans for you. That will be the sacrifice offered to me which you swore to make. Keep your promise!"

Mebet's hand slackened and his weapon fell to the snow.

"Everything is for the best, child," the Mother went on. "You will be born anew, you will live those years all over again. You will grow up and become great among men, the sort of person who leads peoples, brings new knowledge into the world, or serves as a herald for the higher gods – that is what you are destined to be. Go back, child, and don't delay. I will send my messenger for you, a white-necked eagle. He will bear you away from these spirits, he will take you where you need to go."

"But what about my family?" Mebet asked. "What will happen to them while I am there in that heaven and waiting to be born?"

"It amazes me that after what I have just said, you are still asking about this," the Mother said.

"Will they die?"

"They are in the hands of fate. Maybe they will die, maybe they won't. You need to change your way of thinking. Don't be concerned about other people when the gods are concerned with you."

"I can't do that."

"You can't?"

Choked with emotion, Mebet repeated what he had said. "I can't. I can't help but think of the people I have left behind and who I'm trying to get back to. I will get back, no matter what it takes."

The loon flew up into the sky. It turned from its previous silver into the color of dark iron. "Suffering has never affected you. Who do you owe that to?"

"To you."

"Say it again, so I can hear it once more. Or perhaps some other gods had a part in your never experiencing sorrow, guilt, the pain of loss, and in ensuring that your good fortune never failed you?"

"No, you, only you."

"Do you remember your vow? Or do you want to add to your infamy the reputation of an oathbreaker?"

"No, I don't want that," he replied helplessly.

"Then I am glad," the loon said. "Await my messenger, the white-necked eagle." The Mother then vanished.

Soon thereafter, at some incredible height something huge was circling: an eagle was swerving down from the heavens towards the Path of Thunder in order to pick Mebet up. It took a long time for the eagle to land, so that its wings seemed to batter Mebet's weary soul.

Suddenly Nyaruy, who had said nothing all this time, spoke up. "People ask why I consider myself under the patronage of a god whose name is unknown to us. They say that his name was left behind by some foreign tribe that once visited our lands long ago. I am no adept in theology and I don't know; maybe that was the case. I don't even remember when I first heard that there is such a secret and powerful god who watches over wars. But I liked his name, and I remembered it. Once, when fighting took me to a land where the taiga is broken up into a multitude of lakes and it ends with the endless sea, I met strangers on an enormous boat covered in iron and sailing under sails just as huge. The men were clad in armor, but their war lay on the other side of the sea, while ours awaited us in the taiga, and we held no enmity towards one another. Those men confirmed that such a god really does exist, the god of treaties and justice and the patron of warriors.

"Then I asked, 'What commandments does this god set for warriors?' They answered, 'There is only one commandment: do what you must, and nothing bad will happen to you, either in this world or in the next. Only don't utter his name among men, otherwise he will turn away from you.' I had fought for many years, but I thought that never had such fine words come out of a man's mouth. I did what I must, and my god never abandoned me. And for that reason, although I knew what it was like to be worried, my heart never gave into boundless despair."

"Even on the day when you killed yourself?" Mebet asked.

"A commander who has lost his army in so foolish a manner, does not deserve to live. Otherwise, the shame and others' condemnation will eat him up worse than the most terrible disease. There, in your camp, the god saved me from a worse fate, he placed into my heart such a despair as would kill me quickly, like an arrow. He was just in doing that – after all, I had never violated the laws of war and I had done everything I should. He showed his mercy to me in doing that. The better I understand that, the lighter my heart feels. You claimed that the gods are toying with us and the whims of fate hang like a shadow over us and make us sore at heart. But everything is quite simple, Mebet: first think about what has to be done, and then listen to your heart – if they accord, then it is no accident, no mere whim of fate. The feeling that everything is arbitrary will vanish like fog vanishes in a single gust of wind. Then you will see whose hands rend you apart, and whose hands lead you towards the good – you will trust in it and feel at ease. Before that bird lands on the ground, allow me to ask you: what does your heart say?"

"It cannot speak."

Mebet looked up, and his expression was so poignant that it deeply touched Nyaruy, who just before had seemed quite composed. Nyaruy answered for Mebet: "It cannot speak, because it is weeping."

He asked no more questions of the Gods' Favorite. Forked Arrow stood up, went to his army, and ordered them not to rise or to use their weapons.

The wind beat down on them in waves. The eagle messenger grew closer to the ground and with its enormous wings it stirred up flurries of snow.

It landed half an arrow's flight from Mebet and then sat immobile, staring blankly somewhere off in the distance. It was a mere messenger.

"Mebet, Mebet," came a voice, the familiar voice of the Mother. "It is time. Leave your weapon, leave your dog, and get on the eagle's back. Try to nestle deep in its feathers so that the heavenly cold doesn't kill you. Hurry."

Mebet raised his spear, stood up straight, and gestured to Voipel. The dog came and lay down at his master's feet.

"Listen to me!" Mebet cried as loudly as he could. "Take your eagle away, no need for its wings to be burdened. I do not want to fly away."

The air resounded with his words, but the Mother hesitated in replying, and the heavenly messenger did not stir from its spot.

"Do you hear me?" the Gods' Favorite shouted even louder. "I will not fly to that heaven, I will not be born again, whether as a great man or a small one. I will make it through to the end of these chums and live out my allotted years."

The familiar voice again spoke up, but never had it sounded so terrible. "Food for worms, does your feeble mind understand who you are getting in the way of?"

"You said yourself that I must fight a difficult battle for my very self. I must see this battle through. Let your bird leave from here."

Space seemed to groan, and in this groan Mebet heard a curt command. The eagle took off into the sky and an instant later the Gods' Favorite saw it coming down on him like a massive rock with talons.

Mebet struck the first blow with his spear. The eagle made a second circle. The Gods' Favorite dived down and the messenger's talons scraped only snow. As the voice commanded, the eagle relentlessly aimed for its prey. On its third pass it got a glimmer of luck: one of its talons impaled Mebet's coat.

Again there came a cry, but this time it was not from above. Nyaruy had ordered his army into action and an instant later, Mebet was surrounded by a dome of shields and spears pointed upward. The eagle circled, its talons grabbed up men by the handful. Men then rained down upon the earth, but a moment later they stood in ranks again as a single iron body – their fall had not left them crippled.

The messenger showed neither anger nor annoyance at its failure to catch Mebet nor at the wounds inflicted on it, it only acted as it had been ordered to. The Mother, however, was furious. She soon realized that her doggedness was pointless.

There, in the heavens, Ulgen was burning with impatience. "Where is Mebet?" he asked constantly, which caused the Mother to fly into a rage that left her exhausted. In the end, the goddess said, "That creature does not want to become a bright soul again. He may die, but he will not ascended to the heavens."

"In that case," Ulgen said, "It would be better for us if Mebet disappeared completely. Let him be lost among the worlds, let him rot, turn to dust, if he does not wish to be born again upon the earth. We will be stubborn, you and I, and let the Faceless One consider Mebet his own mistake. When a new bright soul appears again – and that is bound to happen sooner or later – then let that one be Mebet."

Ulgen's words met with the Mother's tacit agreement, and these were her own last remarks, albeit unspoken, on the fate of the man from the clan of Vela.

The eagle noticed this silence, and so it flew away, though drops of gray blood from its wounded legs poured in a torrent upon the earth. Once it hit the snow, the drops turned into chunks of raw iron.

The army of spirits was battered but alive – if one can speak thus about the dead – and it gathered around its commander. Nyaruy celebrated their victory:

"You never know which war is yours," he told Mebet. "Now your war is our war. Thus my god has decided." Forked Arrow smiled, and smile in return flickered over Mebet's face.

Voipel came up to his master. "Hold off on the celebration. The eagle might have flown away, but we will still have to deal with the Mother's revenge. I don't know what awaits us in the next chum, but we need to get out of this one already."

"You have a wise dog," Nyaruy said to Mebet. "But in any case, it is senseless to try to run away from a battle. Does this chum end somewhere soon?"

"I don't know," Voipel replied. "I can't see the end of it."

"I will go with you."

The army assembled into formation, the experience of fighting had made the warriors' vague faces shine. Mebet could now recognize among them men whom he had once encountered in his past life.

They set off along the Path of Thunder, and to keep the conversation pleasant they concealed their anticipation of whatever new, unknown danger might soon reveal itself.

THE LAST BATTLE

The earth's innards rumbled, as if a huge beast had awoken and was steaming with rage.

Voipel sniffed the air. "Kin-Iki," he said. "The lord of death, rot, worms, and serpents is coming towards us."

Nyaruy turned pale. "To battle with death itself, can one aspire to anything greater? I thank you, good god of mine."

Doing away with Mebet and his dog, as well as the dead army which had taken on bodies at the border between the worlds – doing away with them so that no gods or spirits, let alone human beings, would ever find them again – was something only one being was capable of, namely Kin-Iki. The Mother had remembered this terrible god, who had after all been her longtime silent servant.

Neither Mebet, nor Nyaruy and his army were yet aware of this.

Kin-Iki, the god with a thousand mouths, a thousand empty eye sockets bereft of eyes, who in lieu of hands had six huge snakes and who exuded cold and the stench of all the graves of the earth, appeared before the army. He stood on a sled that was half hidden by a shield made from skulls. The sled did not move; it was not even harnessed to anything.

Nyaruy gave an abrupt shout and the dead army, their iron rattling, set off at a sprightly pace towards the enemy. As the warriors moved forward, a black and gleaming mass arose around the god of death as if from out of nowhere, and it began to expand. Soon it had grown huge and moved in strange waves that did not heave but rather crawled atop one another, and instead of splashing they heard the sickly sucking sound of a swamp. There was no one else around Kin-Iki. The Vaynot men stood up and froze in bewilderment, unable to see any enemy. They assumed that the god of death presided over some army, but his army was nowhere to be found.

"Is he really alone?" Nyaruy asked quietly, as if talking to himself.

"Isn't god of death already enough?" Mebet asked in reply.

The warriors might have stood there forever had a shout not come from somewhere in the ranks.

"What are we waiting for, commander? He's all alone. There's nothing to think about or be afraid of."

Several of his comrades were pushed aside as the man rushed forward. He wore a patched coat that was too big for him. It was Susoy, the young scout whose skull now lay bare. He shouted again, "Whoever isn't a coward, follow me!"

He let out a ragged cry, raised his spear with its chipped and rusty blade, and ran forth towards the god of death. The army began to surge forward, but Nyaruy ordered it to stop. "Get back here, you stupid whelp!" he shouted at Susoy, but the young scout was already far away.

As soon as Susoy ran up to the edge of the black lake, it sucked him in. The flat waves closed over him, and a moment later they spat forth his old coat. White bones, picked clean of all flesh, came tumbling out from the coat as if from a torn sack. The Vaynot host shuddered violently, like a reindeer that had been bitten by a dozen horseflies.

The shiny black lake was already drawing near them and it was not a lake at all, but rather a mass of worms as found in graves, Kin-Iki's great army that no one among the living could hope to defeat.

The mass came upon the Vaynot host. Forked Army's men met the worms. Unaware of how to fight them, they swung with their weapons, but it was soon obvious that the battle's outcome was already a foregone conclusion.

"Our task is to die in this world, too!" Nyaruy shouted to his men. He alone knew how this battle needed to be fought.

Mebet watched as the warriors' strength was drained from them. The men tried to raise their weapons, but their bodies could no longer obey them. They were no longer fighting the enemy, but they held their ground, so that they could give Mebet time to escape this chum before the worms destroyed them. This was Nyaruy's plan. The Vaynots surrounded the black lake in a dense formation in order to prevent it from reaching Mebet.

Forked Arrow and a few other warriors held out nearly to the end. They still had the strength to stand on their feet, but now they were falling one after the other. Mebet realized that this all represented a sacrifice for his sake.

The warriors fell one by one and the shiny, black abomination stripped them of flesh. The foul muck seeped through their chainmail and armor, under their iron bracers and greaves. The warriors screamed and were quickly silenced.

Nyaruy was the last man left. The wood of his spear had been reduced nearly to splinters. He held onto the wide end of the blade itself and swung with it, sending wiggling clumps of the slimy creatures flying down into the snow. But his end was near. The foe beneath his iron blade had begun to devour his flesh.

With every breath, the Vaynot commander exalted his secret god. "Oh, just god… Oh, just god…"

Mebet heard this and was stricken with inexplicable, unbearable grief. In front of his very eyes death was greedily gulping up the best of men. Nyaruy fell and stood up again, he stepped away in an attempt to block death from getting closer to the Gods' Favorite. Mebet grabbed him by the arm and tried to drag him away, but the commander pulled his arm away abruptly and shouted:

"Don't you dare, otherwise they'll crawl over you, too! Grab me one more time and I'll kill you myself."

"But you'll die," Mebet cried, but Nyaruy didn't seem to hear him.

Suddenly an idea struck Mebet. Why, why had he not done it earlier? He tore at the collar of his coat and took out the bundle. He took several of the years granted him and, without even looking down to see how many he held in his hand, he flung them in front of Nyaruy. The hissing mass of worms pounced and then immediately receded: the wooden slats were no longer to be seen. Nyaruy was shocked as he crawled back on his elbows away from the mass and he froze for an instant. Mebet stood with the bundle in his hands, his arm flung back in preparation to make another throw.

"What are you doing?" Nyaruy cried. "Stop this madness. This is death you're dealing with, it can devour thousands of years. What does it care for your pathetic little slats?"

Mebet's arm continued its motion… Nyaruy's strength had hit bottom, and the god whom he had served and trusted in unquestioningly, now gave his warrior the final order for what to do with his last breath.

Like a huge taimen fish pulled from a river flops furiously on the shore and sends the fisherman trying to wrestle it flying, Nyaruy swung and hit Mebet in the face with his iron gauntlet. Mebet's sight went dim and he was oblivious to whatever happened over the next several moments.

"It's better this way," Nyaruy said. "And that's what you get for being so sneaky and recruiting a woman to fight under you."

Forked Arrow knew exactly what he was doing: before the worms made it up to his face, he managed to smile and whisper the name one more time.

While Mebet was lying unconscious, Voipel ran up as from out of nowhere, sunk his teeth into the collar of his master's coat, and dragged him across the snow. The creeping black mass could not keep up. The Gods' Favorite came to when they were already out of the invisible chum, and they had reached a place where death could no longer reach them.

Nothing remained of the Vaynot army. Kin-Iki's servants had covered the last of the men, and when the black wave gradually receded, Mebet saw only the warriors' armor and white bones, stripped clean of flesh.

"Brother," Mebet whispered. "Brother…"

Of Nyaruy there was nothing left even for an arctic fox or mouse to pick at. The Gods' Favorite leaped up, flung the bundle of years down into the snow, and shouted to the featureless void above him:

"Hey, you up there, can you hear me? I bitterly regret neglecting you when I lived. I should have outright hated you, hated you with a passion. The games you play bring torment to human beings. Everything that you have created is torment, too. All you can ever think up is suffering and death. I despise your greatness, and I despise my own insignificance. It would be better to die and to rot than to be merely your plaything, or better yet not to be born at all. Hey, can you hear me? Is there anyone among you who knows how to tell good from evil, and send that good down as blessings? Is there anyone among you who grieves for Forked Arrow?"

He fell down, out of breath. The only answer that came was the dull, mute wind.

"There is no one good among you," he murmured. "I have no one to defend me. Humankind has no one to defend it. I curse your games and your intrigues."

Mebet's strength was spent. He wept, and his tears gave way to sleep. Voipel, however, had some energy left, and he used it to pick up the bundle of years and push it back under his master's coat.

Two invisible chums still lay ahead, and Mebet was now left with eight slats out of the original eleven.

THE WOMEN'S CHUM

Mebet did not know how long he had slept. He awoke when he felt a small, warm hand enter under his coat and stroke his chest. No one knows what he was dreaming right then, but it must have been something, because he did not immediately open his eyes. When he finally opened them, he was astonished.

Yadne was sitting several feet away from him, with the strap around the bundle dangling from her fingers. She was going through the slats, examining each one in turn. She did not look at Mebet.

"Yadne," he quietly called to her.

She looked up, briefly glanced at her husband, and then went back to keenly examining the slats. Mebet suddenly felt that this was not his present wife, but rather the girl whom he had once stolen from the Okotetta clan's camp and made the mother of his children.

"Yadne." He tried to rise, though he was still weak. "How did you get here?"

"I miss you," Yadne said. "What about you. Do you miss me?"

"I do."

"Do you miss me?" Yadne repeated. There was a trembling in her voice.

Mebet tried again to stand up, but he was unable – pain surged through his body. He suppressed a moan and tried not to show his pain. "I do miss you, Yadne. You're the reason why I'm here. Do you know what it is that you're holding there…?"

She cut him off. "Do you remember our children?"

"Yes, I remember."

"All of them?"

"All of them. Or almost all of them…"

"Do you remember how you buried them in the hollows of trees?"

"I remember."

"You didn't seem to grieve at all when you buried them."

Mebet was unable to respond to that right away.

"You don't have to answer," Yadne said. "I know that you didn't grieve." Her voice turned cold. "Do you remember how you set me out as bait while you were shooting off arrows all around me?"

"It was you who asked to do that."

"Yes, I did ask." A tear gleamed on Yadne's pale cheek. She wiped it away with an abrupt motion. "Do you do everything that a woman asks?"

She was silent for a moment. Mebet waited for her to go on, but he realized that here on the Path of Thunder he would have to endure everything.

"Don't answer that, no need to," his wife continued. "After all, I still remember how you hugged me. That has happened so rarely that I remember every single time. You only show affection when you want me to calm down. It bothers you if I'm upset, you find it annoying. It's the same way people calm a reindeer down before thrusting a knife into its heart."

"Yadne..."

"When you want to calm a woman down, you clasp her to yourself. When you want to calm a dog, you hit it with a stick. But you never beat me, though every man in the taiga does that to his wife!"

She jumped up and burst into insolent and vengeful laughter. "You never loved me. Never."

"I didn't love you. I love no one. But I protected you."

Yadne's anger only grew. "Do you remember Hadko? Your daughter-in-law was right, he proved stronger than you. He didn't fear you."

Mebet again tried to get to his feet, but Yadne jumped away, as if she were afraid to stand next to him.

"Listen to me, wife. Just listen," he tried to speak as gently as he could. "What you're holding there in your hands is eight years more of life that were granted to me. I don't know if you're a spirit, or an apparition, or the real-life Yadne, but believe me when I say that I will carry those through all my trials, and I will return to you. Eight years are a lot and our lives will not be like the way we lived before, not at all. I am no longer the Gods' Favorite, I will arrive back home as an ordinary human being like everyone else. Ordinary human pleasures will bring pleasure to me, too, and ordinary sorrows will make me sad as well. I will atone for all that I have done..." With shaking legs Mebet took his first two steps forward.

Yadne again shrank from him and let out a cry that did not sound like her at all. "For all you have done? How, I'd like to know, will you atone for even just one of the many things you have done?"

"What have I done?"

"You cut my head off!" Yadne shrieked. But it was no longer Mebet's wife. In her stead a swirling column of snow had appeared, and from it a completely different woman flew forth. It was the One-Eyed Witch.

She passed over Mebet's head and showered him with curses in a voice so loud that it drowned out Voipel's barking. "You cut my head off with your knife. You treated my head like a toy, something you could use to make fun of a simpleton. Then you kicked it away. How are you going to atone for that? How?" She shook the bundle.

Mebet grabbed his spear.

"Are you going to hunt me, Gods' Favorite? Where is your bow? How will you reach me?"

Mebet dropped his weapon and said, "You did evil, you nearly poisoned my son. You shouldn't forget that. But nevertheless, how much do you want in compensation for your head?"

The One-Eyed Witch hung in the air. The wind fluttered the ragged ribbons that adorned her coat, which was moreover decorated with the image of an elk.

"I shall forgive you for my head," she said. "But atone for something else."

"I don't understand what you mean."

"Let me remind you." The Witch soared up into the air. She made an arc across the sky, such a wide arc that she completely disappeared from view for a moment. When she returned, it was in another guise.

She now appeared as a pretty, white-faced girl of short stature, wearing a new coat that was embroidered with furs and beads. "Do you remember me now?" she said as she swept in a circle over Mebet's head, but not so fast that the Gods' Favorite could not get a good look at her and see that the Witch had once been a truly lovely woman.

"Of course, how could you remember me like this? But I'll remind you: at every feast I suppressed my embarrassment and walked in front of you so that you might see me. But how could you see me if you always had your nose up? You would have to be willing to look down at people from your great height."

She made one more circle and now was so close that Mebet could strike at her, but he did not move.

"I am a shaman's granddaughter and I had my path set out for me. But you ruined everything. Everything was ruined as soon as I laid eyes on you. That summer when you turned twenty and you first killed a bear, do you remember? No, you don't remember... After that feast, I thought of nothing else but being with you, winning you over! It wasn't just love, it was a matter of what would be right and fair. I am capable of commanding the spirits, while you are the greatest of men, the Gods' Favorite. The best would mate with the best, two powerful individuals would come together – isn't that how things should be? I dreamed that you would abduct me as you abducted other young women. I wore the best clothing, but you refused to look at it. I danced in front of you together with other girls, and you had eyes only for those other girls."

The Witch made another circle. "When it came time for my grandmother to die, and for me to take her place and cease to live like other people, cease to go to feasts or dance or dress up – I still refused to give you up. I went after you every way I knew how. I sent the spirits upon you, I performed magic in the bright chum and in the dark chum so that I might look into your heart and reveal your feelings there. I boiled herbs and uttered spells over them so powerful that trees would wither. I secretly placed enchantments on your weapons and sent you ailments, so that you might finally come to me after being hounded by sickness and poor hunting. But you never came. Some force stood between us – your heart was dark to me, the spirits always returned without success. The magic broths I prepared only cast a stench, the ailments I sent bounced off you like red nuts off iron, and your good fortune never wavered. But it got even worse!"

The Witch shrieked again. "It got even worse – everything seemed to be turned back against me. My talents as a shaman abandoned me, I became no different from anyone else. But I would have paid even that price for love if it weren't for something else, the worst thing of all. One day I woke up and I couldn't open my eye, this one, my right eye. No one could recognize me anymore, everyone thought that the previous girl had died, and a witch had come out of the taiga to replace her. I myself started a rumor that I had been born with only one eye. But look, look at what lovely eyes I once had!"

She brought her face nearer to Mebet's, and he saw two green islands on two sparkling floes of ice, framed by blindingly black lashes.

"You have suffered greatly," Mebet said.

"Yes, I have suffered. I forgive you for that, too."

The girl turned back into the hideous old woman that he knew. "Even when you came to kill me," she said. "You refused to hear me out. You only laughed and then you killed me."

"I came to kill the One-Eyed Witch. Tell me what you cannot forgive me for."

The Witch chortled as she circled. "In fact, I forgive you nothing. Nothing of what you have done to me. I cannot forgive the fact that that mousy, obedient creature from the clan of Okotetta got you instead. I cannot accept that your heart never knew that sickness which leads to madness, to transgression and death! You never suffered, so atone for that now! Now pay for that like I paid with my shamanic talents, my disfigurement, my head! Give up everything that you have, everything!"

As the Witch circled, she waved the bundle. "Here they are, your years, your pathetic little slats. Now they are mine, every last one of them. You will go to hell, and your stupid old lady can cut wood and haul sleds for other people. Let her and your daughter-in-law and grandson subsist on scraps, or rather on whatever is left after the dogs are fed first."

Thus the Witch circled, waving Mebet's life in front of her and drunk on the pleasure of venting the pain in her heart. As she whirled through the air, she seemed to no longer even notice the man and his dog, or how Mebet raised his spear and nearly sliced her belly open as her whirling came close to the ground.

"So, you want to hunt?" the Witch teased him. "Let's see what kind of hunter you are." She moved faster than he heard the sound of her voice, and it tormented Mebet to see how useless his weapon was. She continued to circle, constantly laughing, but suddenly Voipel leaped up and grabbed the bundle in his teeth.

The two of them – the Witch in the air and the dog on the snow – wrestled over the bundle. Mebet rushed to grab it. But now the Witch let out a whistle so sharp that the man and the dog were left stunned and a spasm passed through their bodies.

The Witch now made her exit. She did not hurry as she flew off, so that Mebet could get a long look at whose hands were still holding the years which had been granted to him.

They had come to the end of the tenth chum. Mebet was left with nothing under his coat.

"I guess I have nowhere to go now," he said.

Voipel walked up to his master and, instead of uttering a word in reply, he dropped a small splinter of wood down on the snow. His fangs had torn it from the slats. Mebet picked it up and stared at it blankly.

He weighed in his palm this remnant of the bundle. "How much life is this?" he asked himself.

"Show it to me," Voipel said.

Mebet held his palm out to the dog.

"If you could still see the notch on it, then it would have been a month," the dog said. "But this, I don't know. Maybe five days, maybe seven."

THE LAST CHUM: YEZANGA

Mebet sat down on the snow. He was no longer in any hurry to get anywhere, and his mind was blank. His dog was the only thing around. Suddenly the man spoke:

"Once, a long time ago, I heard a story about how the gods sculpted man out of clay, out of white clay which they had found on a riverbank. They sculpted arms, legs, a head, a torso. They sculpted every finger, every joint. With shiny pebbles they made eyes, and they used fish scales for the fingernails. Thin wisps of grass served for hair. Who those gods were, I don't know, nor do I know how they got the idea of sculpting with clay. But judging by the story, they put in a lot of effort. Then, if I am to believe what I heard, they went to some secret place where supposedly an Eternal Larch grew, and under the roots of this tree they dug down to a spring of living water. These gods had good intentions, because they filled whole containers with this water, so that man would have abundant life and never die at all.

"But clearly it was a long way to that spring, and while they were going there, other gods crawled up from under the earth. For their own amusement, these other gods befouled the clay figures and went off laughing. The good gods were unaware of this and so they poured the living water on the defiled bodies of clay and they too went off, pleased with their efforts. Thus, man resulted from something both groups had made for their own amusement. And then suddenly the gods, both the good ones and the evil ones, saw that nothing ended up as they intended. Ever since, they have been fighting over man, like foxes fight over carrion, and they refuse to share him.

"I couldn't take this story seriously, I just laughed. But now I look down at my hand and I think, whose is it? Is it mine or theirs? And the thoughts in my head, are they my own? And the desires in my heart, do they really come from me? Who does my good fortune really belong to? Do my sorrows make for someone else's triumph?"

Mebet laughed quietly to himself. "What sense does it make either to pray to the gods or curse them? To sacrifice to them or not to sacrifice? A sacrifice to one god would only offend another, and one can expect revenge to ensue. If one human being comes to feel a connection with another human being, then there is always someone around who wants to break that connection. What we call good and just never wins. On the contrary, it is humbled, while what we call evil and base is exalted. A man's life is always someone else's war, and whatever victory happens in it is never your own. The only thing that is your own are the defeats. Why are we fighting someone else's war? Tell me that, dear brother."

"I don't know," Voipel replied. "But you're right. When it's someone else's war, then the only thing that is yours is death. I am only a dog and I am not very familiar with the affairs of the gods; it matters little to me who makes my legs run, my tail wag, or my teeth to show themselves. I just walk along, wag my tail, or bare my teeth when there is need. But I will tell you what I do know. If enough water remains for only a single sip, then you should still drink it all. If you have only enough room to make a single step, then take that step. If your arms and legs still obey you, then you should walk on. You may well only have enough days to return home and die, but you must live out these few days. Perhaps there is some benefit in that which we don't know about. After we escaped the god of death himself, I think you have already experienced the greatest ill. I hardly think that some powerful entity awaits us in the last chum. Stand up."

Mebet rose and they walked on for a long time without encountering anyone on the path. They had lost track entirely of how much time had gone by when the tired man saw some dark shape looming in the distance.

"Those are trees," Voipel said. "That must be the way out back into the world, into the taiga. We're close."

The space around them began to change: the invariable emptiness gave way to jagged dead trees. The wind howled through their bare branches.

They continued walking and eventually they came across a man. He was sitting towards the bottom end of a fallen pine tree and swinging his legs. On his feet he wore threadbare boots, and he was singing some endless song known only to himself. When he saw the two wayfarers, he broke off his song.

"Greetings, Mebet," came his jubilant shout. "You've got a great dog there, I've always dreamed of having one like that. But where could I get a good dog from? After all, they're expensive. I've been expecting you and I'm glad to see you. Come, sit down beside me."

Mebet recognized the man and everything he had experienced across ten chums was forgotten, as if it had never existed at all. It was Yezanga who sat there in front of him.

Mebet had walked along the border between the worlds and the Path of Thunder had dredged up his old memories. He had gone over all the days of his long and now almost finished life, which he had lived the way he wanted and nearly without any hardships. Much seemed different to him now. Some of those things in his life had not even weighed on his conscience.

There had been times when he acted harshly, but that harshness was within the bounds of propriety. Nyaruy had, over the course of his life, killed more people than Mebet had ever killed beasts in hunting, and he had scalped more heads than Mebet had skinned animals. But that had been all dictated by Nyaruy's job as a warrior, and it never weighed on the man; the war leader's conscience remained clear.

Even the episode with that youth, the Vaynot clan's scout, never gave Mebet any pangs of guilt. The Gods' Favorite only regretted that no one on earth knew about the bravery with which that junior warrior had accepted his death. Mebet recalled all the young women he had abducted, but their families' grief had not lasted for long, and moreover, Mebet had never mistreated any of the girls.

What Mebet felt truly sorry for was that he had openly humiliated others. He had used his strength to bring other men low and that had given him pleasure. Now the pain which those humiliated men felt had now been transferred to him, and it tormented him greatly. But there had been many such days in his life, they all merged into a single long day in the life of the Gods' Favorite. Mebet wanted to return now to the taiga and so he accepted this pain as something which had long been coming to him.

Finally Mebet cursed the gods and the world which they had created for their own amusement. If he had not seen the gods with his own eyes, he would have been unable to believe in them at all. But he had seen them, and now after he had cursed them, he felt a foreboding, like the expectation of a looming battle. His curses had been sincere. The deaths of Nyaruy and his men had cut through an invisible line within him, and he still did not know where the border between good and evil is.

It was not even just Forked Arrow that Mebet was thinking about but himself, too. Even here, on the Path of Thunder, on the border between life and death, they had toyed with him. They had used a man who was nearly dead to play their evil games that had nothing to do with him, and they had won.

Mebet had gone back through his former life as if it were a string of beads. But as he did so, he had quietly lied to himself all the while, hoping that the Path of Thunder would not bring him face to face with that day that he had been loath to recall back on earth, and finally had nearly forgotten. But now the Path of Thunder had brought him here, and that day stood before him as his last trial before he could get back to the world. He was dealing with that same man in threadbare boots and a patched and filthy coat.

The man was sitting on the trunk, swinging his legs, and singing some words that only he understood. Mebet remembered how the man had been sitting just like that at his camp – singing and swinging his legs – on the day when the two of them had agreed to the betrothal of their children.

Yadne prepared a lavish meal for the occasion. She brought a reindeer leg into the chum, and as she walked past Mebet, she sarcastically whispered into her husband's ear, "Well, what a new relative you've found for us…"

Mebet had smiled at that. "You've got to accept him the way he is," he replied.

Yezanga, a poor man from the Nevasyada clan, was an object of ridicule. His very name meant "Caught In The Trap," in commemoration of an episode that the clans of the taiga long laughed over, and even the clans of the tundra as well.

Long ago Yezanga (who was known then by a different name) decided to find himself a wife. At a feast he laid eyes on a girl who was beautiful and wore a rich coat. He spent a long time staring at her and he pressed his way through the crowd in order to examine her from every side.

After he had got a good look at her, he nudged an acquaintance who was standing next to him. "What a beautiful girl," he said so loudly that everyone could hear him. "So beautiful. And she's got such good clothes. Her parents must be rich. I'd love to marry her, I would!"

The other young man burst out laughing. Not only was Yezanga poor, but his looks were plain, ridiculous even. He was short, bowlegged, and he did not walk so much as prance along. His cheekbones were so wide and his eyes so narrow, that one would think the gods had barely had enough skin to cover such a face. It was therefore difficult to tell when Yezanga was smiling and when he was not, though he tended to smile more than he was serious, and he was always thrilled to meet other people, as if they were relatives whom he had not seen for a long time. He never placed people into categories of great or small: he would speak to respected people the same way he spoke to children, or vice versa. He never walked anywhere without a song on his lips, though no one could ever tell what exactly he was singing.

"What are you singing there?" they would sometimes ask him. "Why don't you sing it to us."

"See that jay flying up there?" Yezanga pointed a finger at the sky. "I'm singing about it now."

Even then kinder people were saying that Yezanga was a fool, a useless man who would only bring grief to his family. (In fact, they were wrong: Yezanga was a good hunter and he knew how to take care of a herd.)

The other young man laughed, but secretly he had an idea. "So, go and marry her if you like her so much," he said.

"But would her family give her up?" Yezanga asked. "After all, I'm poor."

"No, they definitely wouldn't give her up," the other youth said. "That girl's from the Yaptik clan, I know her father. He owns more reindeer than you've got hairs on your head. You see how pretty she is? Her family would demand a huge bride-price for her. No, they wouldn't give her up to you."

Awkward young Yezanga was offended. "Why did you tell me to go and marry her, then? Are you just making fun of me?"

"I wouldn't dare make fun of you. I'll tell you what you should do: abduct her, and then later, in a year or so, go to her father and make peace. A lot of guys do it that way."

"I have never abducted a girl before…"

"You want me to help?"

"Would you help me?" Yezanga felt humiliated that he had to ask. "I'd really like to get me a pretty wife. I'd love her so much and never treat her badly. I'd only beat her once a year, or even less. So, you'll help me?"

The other young man arranged with his friends to play a trick on Yezanga. They told him that they would bring him to a chum where the young lady was waiting, and they would be nearby with their sleds so that Yezanga could spirit her away. In fact, what they really intended was to hide in the neighboring chum, armed with sticks, so that when the awkward young man went in abduct the bride, they would sneak in and give him a beating.

But Yezanga was destined to have a much greater joke played on him than his peers had planned.

He avoided their ambush by walking into the wrong chum. There the sister of the girl he admired was weaving a net from nettle fibers. She had already done a lot of weaving and now finished nets hung throughout the chum. Yezanga rushed towards the girl without even looking at what was in front of him. The girl shrieked and fended him off with one of the nets. The would-be abductor, terrified, flung his arms up, and in the end he had got so tangled in the netting that he could not move an arm or a leg.

The other young men had been waiting in a neighboring chum, sticks in hand and giggling to themselves, but Yezanga had not showed yet. They heard a shriek, then a shout, and finally the other girl calling for help. They ran to answer the call, saw what a mess there was in the chum, and then they began calling other people. A big crowd eventually ran up. The father of the family was the last to arrive.

"What are you doing here?" he asked.

"I wanted to abduct your daughter so I could get myself a wife," came tangled Yezanga's innocent reply. "But not this daughter, the other one."

The people gathered laughed heartily at that, but while they were laughing at the poor thief, the girl who had been weaving burst out crying.

She did not share her sister's beauty, nor did she take after her mother or father – no one knew where exactly she had got her looks from. She was just like Yezanga: wide-cheeked, bowlegged, and slightly hunchbacked. Consequently, the family did not give her any fine clothing or treat her with affection. When she heard the crowd mocking a man who had wanted to abduct her lovely sister, and had ended up with unlovely her instead, it drove her to tears.

When the crowd had laughed enough, the elder of the clan said, "I ought to give you a good thrashing. But I won't. Instead I'll give you one of my daughters, the one that you burst in on here. Go ahead, take her. You would be perfect for each other. Pay whatever you can as the bride-price."

The people gathered again laughed, while the girl wept.

"Well, obviously this is destiny," Yezanga said. "But please, help me get out of this net."

When he had spoken these words, the girl suddenly ceased her crying and began to free this ridiculous visitor from the net. Ever since then, he was known by his new name Yezanga, "Caught In The Trap."

Yezanga brought the girl to his camp and got a beating from his father for marrying without permission. The next day his father, with a great deal of cursing, chose five reindeer from their herd and drove them to the Yaptik clan's camp. A year later his father died, and Yezanga was left with his elderly mother and his young and homely wife. His wife bore him children, he never hurt her; he only beat her once a year or even less.

When Mebet heard the story of how Yezanga got married, he too laughed. Then, a year after this odd wedding, the awkward young man visited Mebet's own camp.

"Hello, Mebet!" Yezanga shouted, a broad smile across his face as if he had met a dear old friend. "You've got a real nice camp here. New skins on your chums. A lovely wife and kids..."

Mebet realized then that this odd fellow simply had the habit of praising whatever he happened to lay eyes on. Mebet's wife and two daughters were present on this occasion; his third daughter, a tiny infant, slept in her cradle in the chum. If Mebet's dogs had run up, Yezanga would have had some good words for them as well.

"Hello yourself," Mebet said, amused by this clumsy uninvited guest. "What brings you here?"

"I've come on important business, very important," Yezanga replied. He bent down and began frantically untying the straps on his skis. When this was done, he walked up to Mebet with his usual prancing gait. He came up so close to Mebet that the latter even took a step back.

"It's a good thing I've come for. Let me explain. I've got two daughters who have survived, and I've got one son who is growing up, he is five now. I ought to marry off my daughters, but I already hear people saying that a hunched wife can only produce hunched daughters, so what man would want to have them? And they're not hunched at all, that's nonsense. You can come yourself and see what fine daughters I have. One sings so beautifully, and the other..."

"What brings you here?" Mebet asked again, lest his guest prattle on for hours.

Yezanga was slightly embarrassed at this, and when he continued it was no longer quite as confidently. "What brings me here... I'm a poor man, I don't have a lot of reindeer. Last winter we nearly had to seek refuge with some other family. But the gods have been merciful and we're getting by. So, I got to thinking. The time will come when I ought to see my son married, and what bride-price could I pay? I thought about that, and I remembered Mebet! They say that you've got three daughters. This one here," he pointed to the daughter who could stand up straight, "how old is she?"

"Why does that matter to you?" Mebet asked. He could guess what Yezanga was getting at, though he could hardly believe it.

"Why? I want to arrange a union for my son and your daughter. An early betrothal. I don't have any other way of going about it, you see."

The custom of childhood betrothals was the refuge of poor men with few reindeer who were incapable of paying the whole bride-price at once. They would marry off their children aged three or five, or even their babies. Then, until the girl reached childbearing age, the boy's father would pay the bride-price in installments to the girl's father. It sometimes happened that the less than destitute resorted to such betrothals; this usually happened during hard times, when plague entered the taiga and swept through the herds and the chums, or when foreign tribes attacked and carried women off. At times like that, eligible brides got expensive, and their fathers would shamelessly demand a bride-price of a hundred reindeer or more. Plus skins, iron blades, clothing, copper kettles…

Mebet laughed so loud that his children shrunk away from him. "Wife," he called through his laughter. "Come here. They have come to make a match for your daughter. Come and see your new relative."

Yadne came out of the chum. The sleeves of her coat were rolled up, her arms were covered in fish blood and scales up to her elbows. She had overheard their conversation (Yezanga was incapable of speaking in anything but a loud voice) and fear struck her heart. Like any mother, she wanted a good, respectable match for her daughter. For that reason, she did not find Yezanga amusing, rather he was infuriating. Her fear competed with a faint hope that her husband, the Gods' Favorite, would not allow such a ridiculous and even shameful union to take place. But her hope was weak against her fear. She had already bore her fourth child; the first had died in childbirth, and the others had survived, but these were all daughters. Mebet had got increasingly upset at not having a son, and he was no longer trying to hide it. He told Yadne that he would steal himself another wife and send her away, since he didn't like it when there were a lot of women around in the camp. She knew that whatever Mebet decided, she would have no choice but to accept it.

But the worst thing of all, Yadne thought, was that the Gods' Favorite liked his jokes. "As you wish," she said blankly. Her reply did not satisfy her husband, and she immediately saw that her fears were justified.

"Great!" Mebet said and gave Yezanga a friendly clap on the shoulder. "What bride-price can you offer?"

"I'll send five reindeer over here right away," the visitor shouted and fidgeted with excitement. "Five at once! And I'll throw in two skins. No, three skins!"

Yadne said nothing to this.

"Lady," Yezanga shouted, "my son is a really good boy. He can sing, and dance, and he's already setting traps…"

"Did you hear that, woman?" Mebet laughed. "Five reindeer!"

"And more," Yezanga added.

"And more, you hear? If you bear me a daughter every year, we'll get rich on just her bride-price. There would be no more need for hunting. And I wouldn't need a son, either. Why would I?"

Yadne covered her face with a filthy hand and dived back under the tent flap. The sound of her crying reached them.

Yezanga was beaming. "That's fine, let your wife have a good cry. But she'll be happy later, you'll see."

The mirth suddenly vanished from Mebet's face. "Why have you come to me? Haven't you heard what kind of man I am? Or could you not find people on your level in the taiga?"

This left Yezanga feeling embarrassed. "Well, people say all kinds of things, so I don't listen to them, I see for myself. And you seem like a really great guy. A fine man. And again, you've got daughters…"

"This one here," Mebet pointed to his eldest daughter, "is three years old, nearly four. For her you will give me forty reindeer."

"Forty reindeer," Yezanga murmured. His face with its wide cheekbones grew long and now he stared wide-eyed. The number which Mebet had quoted was staggering and he could only repeat, "Forty reindeer, forty reindeer…"

The Gods' Favorite cut him off. "Forty reindeer for a daughter of Mebet is practically nothing."

"Practically nothing…" He looked into Mebet's blue eyes and said in a loud voice, "Forty then, alright. You're a great guy, a really great guy. I love people like that."

They shook hands, and thus the betrothal agreement was sealed between Mebet from the clan of Vela and Yezanga from the clan of Nevasyada.

Several days later, the father of the five-year-old future groom returned to the camp of the father to the three-year-old future bride. He brought five reindeer and two reindeer hides. He promised to give Mebet the same every year until he had paid the bride-price in full. They celebrated their agreement with a lavish meal. Yezanga ate his fill and, contended, he sat on a tree trunk and sang his songs while swinging his legs.

In the autumn of the same year, on the first day of snow, the three-year-old future bride somehow managed to climb to the top of a tall storehouse. She fell from it and struck her head on a sharp stone. Thus she died. How Yezanga learned of this was unclear, but already the next day he rushed to Mebet's camp and cried together with Yadne.

As he wept, he said, "Oh, I shouldn't cry. I shouldn't cry now. She's already crying a river and I'm just adding to it. I shouldn't cry…"

Mebet looked at Yezanga. This man is an idiot, he thought yet again, but this time it was not in anger. On the same day Mebet offered him his next daughter, who was little more than one year old. Yezanga agreed.

However, the death of Mebet's three-year-old daughter proved to be only the start of great hardships. A new plague swept through the taiga and brought death to both the chums and the herds. Mebet's own reindeer were practically unaffected by the illness, but by spring the plague had taken both of his remaining daughters. The Gods' Favorite was left childless.

Yezanga came and cried with Yadne again, and he was not driven away. The illness had decimated his own herd, which had already been a meager one. From among his household, the plague had taken only his elderly mother. His wife and children remained among the living, but now they faced hunger and starvation.

His wife wailed and Yezanga tried to comfort her. "We'll get by with some hunting," he said, but even he recognized how foolish this attempt to soothe her was. Men had clearly angered the gods, they had upset the spirits, for along with the plague the game in the taiga began to dwindle. There were ever fewer animals to catch, and the wolves proved more successful than people at hunting the remaining elks.

Yezanga's wife began to plead with him: Mebet no longer had any eligible brides, so let him return the five reindeer which he had received from them under the agreement.

"Come on!" Yezanga waved her suggestion away. "There's no going back on the agreement."

But his wife would not let up with her moaning, and she had a point that five reindeer would make up at least some kind of herd. Without it, they would perish.

"You said Mebet was a good man," she wailed. "Then even if it's going against custom, at least let him show some kindness and give us those five reindeer back."

Finally, Yezanga could not take any more of his wife's crying. He steeled himself and went to Mebet's camp. He looked like the nickname he had been given, he was inextricably bound up in his hardships with no escape.

Yezanga began speaking when he was still some distance away, but he could not manage to get to his point.

Mebet however understood everything at once. "You can't go back on the agreement, don't you know that?"

"I know, but…"

"So why are you here?"

"My wife pushed me to do it."

"Control your wife, then."

"Things are bad, Mebet, very bad... Five reindeer aren't a lot, but they would still make a herd. Maybe someone up there will be looking out for us, and if we manage to survive, we'll thank you..."

Mebet laughed. "Do you think I need any thanks from you or your hunchbacked wife?"

Yezanga swallowed the bitter lump in his throat and was already ready to leave, but he asked nevertheless, "Why don't you want to give me those reindeer back, Mebet? You don't want to go against custom?"

"I make my own custom."

"Just give them back," Yezanga pleaded. "I won't tell anybody."

The Gods' Favorite took this uninvited visitor by the shoulder – Yezanga barely came up to Mebet's chest – turned him around and gave him a slight push, which sent Yezanga flying several feet and nearly made him trip and fall into the snow.

"Don't ask me any more," Mebet said. "And don't come around here either. Our agreement is over."

The awkward man returned home empty-handed.

Yezanga was the father of a family and the same age as Mebet, but he still made no distinction between the big people and the humble ones, the strong and the lowly. For him, all people were equally good. Even when they had laughed at him when he got caught in that net, he harbored no resentment or desire for revenge. His grief now stemmed from the fact that he had hoped in vain for some mercy from this almost-relative, whose herd had almost survived the plague unscathed.

After that, things got even worse. His family ate their last reserves of food, and Yezanga only managed to bring small fowl back from hunting – a grouse, say – and sometimes he came back with nothing at all. By spring they were on the brink of starvation. His wife and child were weak and unsteady on their feet. They gave the last bit of food to their family's provider, so that he would have the strength to try his luck in the taiga, but eventually no last bit of food remained. They considered throwing themselves on the mercy of the wife's family, but her kin lived far away and they no longer had the strength to haul their sleds such a distance. Moreover, their kin might not take them in at all, as the wife's family was said to have lost over half of their herd from the plague.

One morning Yezanga's son did not wake up. The evening before he had asked for food, and after being unable to eat anything, he died in his sleep. After this, his wife developed a mad obsession with those five reindeer.

"If he wouldn't give us back five, then he could at least have given us one, just one. Then we could have butchered it, made soup, gnawed on the bones. Our son could have survived. Mebet got his revenge on us: now there's no longer any groom or any bride for that union."

Now a thought came into Yezanga's simple mind and humble heart: according to custom, the reindeer belonged to Mebet, but by rights they belonged to him. Because it would be right for a human being to live, but if he dies, what is right in that? What would right and wrong matter to a dead man? By rights, they would have survived with those five reindeer until summer and their son would not have died.

Once Yezanga began thinking about this, he could not put it out of his mind. In his heart he grumbled about it. He felt emboldened. Without telling his wife, he stumbled off one morning towards Mebet's camp. When he came up to it, he caught the dizzying sweet aroma that issued from Mebet's pots and carried across the taiga. In both chums, pots were boiling with meat. The Gods' Favorite was preparing to migrate his herd, and he had tasked Yadne with preparing a large amount of meat for the road. Strange though it may be, Mebet had listened to his wife for once and decided to pack up and move away from the lousy site they had been occupying.

Yezanga stumbled into the chum without even announcing his presence. He sat at the threshold. "My son died, Mebet," he said. "By spring we'll all be dead. Give me those reindeer back. By rights they belong to me."

He sat there in silence, awaiting what the master of the home would say. But it was Yadne who suddenly spoke up:

"Give him those reindeer, Mebet. We've got loads of food here, it's time to share it with people. Don't make things worse, just give him the reindeer. After all, we've got a lot."

Mebet rose. "Come on," he said to Yezanga. "I'll give you what belongs to you by rights." He pushed the visitor out of the chum.

They walked out of the camp. The awkward man stumbled after the Gods' Favorite, thinking that they were headed for the corral and there he would get his own reindeer back, the reindeer that would save him and his family.

Mebet had no intentions of giving the reindeer back, however. This was not out of respect for custom, but simply because he was loath to do so. He wanted to give Yezanga a thorough beating so that the latter would not dare come anywhere near his camp. This was the kind of heart that Mebet had – it could not sympathize with another's grief, like a happy man's heart could, rather it could only feel annoyance. The enormous woe that had fallen over the taiga only led to Mebet's enormous annoyance, and this had to be dealt with. And the annoyance was personified by Yezanga.

Mebet grabbed his almost-relative by the collar and threw him down into the snow. He kicked him in the stomach and watched how the man writhed. Just as gadflies swarm in the summer, the Gods' Favorite suddenly felt, he had to constantly deal with these ridiculous and weak creatures, who made pathetic sounds, constantly demanded things, and clung to their miserable lives, and were simply stupid, ugly, miserable, and capable only of infecting others with that same misery.

"So, by rights they're yours?"

"Mine…"

This ugly creature, with a face like a worm's, also wanted to keep living and teach him something about rights.

"By what right?"

Yezanga understood what awaited him.

"Don't kick me… I'll die… I'm so weak now…"

Mebet struck him once more; he had expected an answer to his question.

"Don't kick me, Mebet," Yezanga helplessly repeated. Then he suddenly whispered, "You'll die too, you see."

"Me?! I will die?" Mebet shouted the words, but he was now blind with rage. He was swallowed up for the first time in his life by a black hatred that left him insensate. He kicked Yezanga without hearing either the man's cries or his own grunts.

Mebet did not notice the moment when Yezanga ceased to cry out. He only returned to his senses when he felt like his legs were striking empty air. He stopped. No puffs of vapor came from Yezanga's mouth – Yezanga was dead.

He was the first and only person whom the Gods' Favorite killed needlessly, and out of an immense feeling of hatred within him. He had sacrificed Yezanga to his own eternally contended heart, in the same way as white reindeer are butchered to gratify the spirits.

The sacrifice was accepted with great appreciation. Mebet's heart was like a bird held fast by two enormous and strong hands. But as soon as Yezanga fell silent, the hands slackened, the bird fluttered forth and disappeared into the sky, again happy and free.

Later, when many years had passed since that day, Mebet seldom thought back on the man he had killed. He never forgot about Yezanga entirely, but he was often visited by the memory of how his heart had been set free. He never admitted this to anyone, and the very memory of it seemed rather ridiculous, but it gave him some secret and taboo satisfaction, which was especially strong in the first days and months after this sacrifice.

Mebet returned to his chum and deliberately put on a gloomy face, so that Yadne would not see the inexplicable joy he felt.

"Did you give him the reindeer back?" his wife asked him.

Her husband said nothing in reply. He only crawled under the furs and fell asleep. Yadne assumed that he had given them back, and she did not ask him about the reindeer again.

Thereafter, no one in the taiga heard any word of the man they had called Caught In The Trap. This did not come as any surprise, they simply assumed that he had fallen victim to the plague. Mebet never learned what happened to Yezanga's family, though rumor had it that the silly man's hunched wife had been sighted among some other clan. This news did not interest the Gods' Favorite, however.

Now that same silly man was sitting before him on the boundary between the worlds, in the last chum of the Path of Thunder. Deep down Mebet understood that it was in Yezanga's hands now whether he would be able to return to the world or not.

"Hello there," Mebet said blankly and sat down across from him.

"What are you doing?" Yezanga said, offended though still in lively spirits. "Sit down here next to me, let's talk." He moved over to make some room on the tree. "Otherwise I've got no one here to talk to. It's awfully boring to sit here alone."

Mebet however remained seated where he was. Some time went by without either of them saying anything. Suddenly the Gods' Favorite felt terrified, not due to any looming revenge, but rather out of expectation of some unpleasant surprise.

"Alright, then," Yezanga stopped swinging his legs. "You don't want to talk with me. That's a pity…"

"What should I talk about?" Mebet said helplessly.

Yezanga understood these words in his own way, however. "You really don't have anything to talk about? I've been sitting here for a long time now, and you've just arrived from over yonder. Tell me how the kids are, how's the wife, how's the herd. Good people always have something to talk about."

"I'm not a good person, Yezanga. I have never been a good person."

"Oh, hush now. Everyone is good, though it doesn't always work out."

"What you mean by that?"

"Oh," Yezanga exclaimed, "Now you and I are talking, even though you didn't want to at first. I mean that it doesn't always happen that they can be good, some hassle always gets in the way. You go hunting, and the wolves gobble up everything in your traps, so you get angry. It happened to me once that I fell down, broke a ski, and came home all wet. I don't know how I managed to survive. And my wife still hadn't cooked anything to eat. I cuffed her on the back of her head, wham! I went into the taiga a good man, and I came back a bad man. Where was there any chance of being a good person once I had got all wet and broke a ski? The same goes for everybody: they're good, but some lousy thing gets in the way."

Mebet listened to Yezanga. He began to feel confused. "Do you really think that?"

"Why would I lie?" Yezanga asked. The question had not embarrassed him. He continued, "There's only a short path from my brain to my tongue. And then to you. If you really want to know, I hold no grudge. You felt troubled, I was pestering you, so you got angry. But you are a good man."

"All this you're saying… You're mistaken."

"Maybe I am. I'm no genius." Yezanga suddenly hopped down onto the snow and stomped around a bit to stretch his stiff legs. "You need to get home," he said. "Let's go, I'll show you the way."

He said this without glancing at Mebet. With his prancing walk he set off ahead of Mebet, and now the Gods' Favorite trudged after the silly man.

Yezanga continued to sing his song and did not look back. He suddenly stopped, fell silent, and bent over as if some treacherous archer had hit him in the stomach. Still hunched, he turned, and Mebet no longer beheld Yezanga as he was formerly. The foolish man's face was now distorted and disfigured by suffering and he moaned terrifying words:

"Why did you kill me? What did you kill me for? Why? Why?" He spoke in an inhuman howl. "I wanted to live, I really wanted to live… Ever since I was born I just wanted to live. When I lived, I wanted to live. When I fell into poverty, I wanted to live. When you killed me, I wanted to live. Until the very last kick you gave me, I wanted to live. Can you understand that?!"

His eyes rolled back to show only the whites. His face became dead. Yezanga fell, he rolled on the ground and moaned. "I wanted to live. To live. To eat, drink, make love to my wife, fall asleep, sleep, and wake up. I wanted to sing and be silent. To talk and laugh. To go into my chum and step out of my chum. To spend time with my children. To hunt squirrels and catch fish. To look up at the stars. To warm myself by the fire. I wanted all that, I loved everything. Why did my simple little life bother you so much?" He leaped up and shouted into the sky, "Gods, why did my simple little life bother the Gods' Favorite? That is what I would have shouted if I could have shouted. But even that shout you refused me…"

The little splinter of wood which Voipel had torn from the bundle of years, Mebet was keeping in his little bag for tinder. He feel to his knees and undid the little strap around the bag. He searched for the splinter for a while, then he drew it forth with his fingernails and placed it on Yezanga's shaking palm.

"This is all I have left. It's several days. Five days or less. Just enough time to get back to my camp and die at home. I didn't accomplish what I set out for; my grandson, wife, and daughter-in-law will be left all alone…"

"Left all alone," Yezanga took his words up. "They will wander seeking shelter with others, or they will die from hunger. If they don't die, they can only hope for some leftover scraps thrown their way. They will face the same fate that my children and my dear hunched wife did. You don't know what happened to them?"

"No, I don't know about your children. I heard that your wife was spotted at some camp far away."

"She's here!" Yezanga barked angrily. "I saw her as the spirits of people streamed past me. I didn't see my children. They must be still there, in the world…"

Yezanga fell silent. The spasms that distorted his face abated. He went completely limp and seemed to have sunk into thought. He blinked frequently, as if his eyes stung with his welling grief, though Mebet saw no tears.

Mebet just stood there with his hand outstretched, and for a time he did not dare to break the other man's silence. "This is all that's left," he said quietly. "The gods gave, and the gods took away. Take this sliver of wood, maybe it will bring comfort to your soul." After a pause, he added, "And to mine, too."

Yezanga got up and took Mebet's hands in his own, though he refused the offering. "Is it not terrible to be a human being?" he asked. But it was not Yezanga's voice…

Here the story of how Mebet returned to the world of men by the Path of Thunder breaks off.

THE VISION

As soon as the one who had appeared to him under the guise of foolish Yezanga touched his hands, Mebet's vision was plunged into a dark-blue darkness. He could no longer feel the surrounding air on his body, all sound fell away into a silence as soft as deep moss. Yet Mebet still saw and heard, though not as human beings ordinarily do. The same voice, as if soundless yet commanding, said, "Look."

The darkness deepened, turned black and heavy. Clumps of it began to move in a circle, ever faster. They rushed about, flew, fought, and tore at each other to become one furious abyss. The abyss spun in a vortex, and a burst of light suddenly appeared at the bottom of the funnel. The light washed away the edges of the darkness, grew stronger and revealed water. A firmament emerged from the waters, and in the middle of it a green star flickered – it was the eternal tree. From the tree issued at first green streams thinner than a hair, and then greater flows and ultimately torrents spreading over the area around it, which had previously been only bare gray rock. The ground was covered with abundant and gleaming greenery – this was the world of the living, which men call the taiga. With a vantage point that was capable of seeing near and far, the great and the small, the visible and the invisible, Mebet gazed on a myriad of creatures that filled the world and lit it up with the flickering of countless hearths. Traces of their existence floated over the world first as a thin, gray smoke, and then grew blacker and plunged everything into darkness. Iron-skinned snakes came slithering out of the darkness, then came ghostly elks, wolverines, reindeer. Birds flew out that covered half the earth with the span of their wings. The birds plucked creatures from the earth and gulped them down – these were human beings. The rivers seethed, all who ever fell in battle rose again from the earth, raised their weapons and fought one another, continuing their wars that had never arrived at satisfaction.

Again, the bare gray rock advanced and caused the waters to surge up. An enormous serpent emerged from the water, and a wolf from the depths of the earth. The wolf defeated the serpent in brief single combat, then it went on to devour all living creatures, flinging bits of them away from its maws. But then a man came down from heaven, he battled the wolf and defeated it, though he too died. Subsequently a war began among all creatures remaining on the earth: beasts, men, spirits, gods. They fought one another, fell, died. The whole earth was strewn with bodies. Once more the earth quaked, the waters surged up, and the earth erupted from some inner turmoil and a thick smoke covered it. When the smoke settled, Mebet could see how the green covering the world began to disappear, like water on hot stones, and soon only a glimmering green star remained: the eternal tree. Then it too died out. The rocky land went black, was consumed by the waters and fell silent. The silence was shattered by an epic sound of thunder, and the remaining light disappeared, like milk poured out on the ground.

The echo of the thunder settled on the earth, silence followed, and time seemed to freeze.

Suddenly a sound so low it could barely be heard was born out of the darkness, a sound that was soft but commanding. Mebet watched as a small parcel of earth appeared out of the cold, dark waters, and on this land were human bones. Just as a tree in the brief spring season fills with sap and covers itself with leaves, flesh now grew over these bones, skin covered them, and they took on the appearance of a human being, in which Mebet recognized himself. The waters retreated.

This vision made his head spin.

"Mebet," a voice sounded in the heavens. "Mebet, can you hear me?"

"Who are you?" he asked.

"Do not ask that, for my name is ineffable. You were a bright soul in the heaven of the future, so listen. The world is fundamentally imperfect, and therefore man cannot avoid suffering. Everything will happen again: I will create the world, destroy it, and create it again until it takes on the form that I conceive in my heart. Until then, suffering will be the lot of every man. Do you understand?"

Mebet did not answer.

"Go and proclaim this," the voice continued. "Suffering encloses man in a cave and rolls a stone over the entrance. Man will bang his fists against the stone but be unable to leave. But that hand which frees him and rolls the stone away will be called mercy. Proclaim this mercy, you who remain alive by this mercy."

"How can I proclaim it, if I have only a few days left to live?"

"Don't be concerned with that," the voice said. "You must only listen, and don't think about how the news will strike the world. Do you understand me?"

"Yes?"

"Go. My son, my forsaken son…"

The voice was silent. A terrifying sound of thunder crashed over the world. The Path of Thunder vanished, and Mebet and his dog Voipel found themselves next to the cave where Mebet had killed the gray bear.

MEBET'S MORNING

Mebet returned to his camp on the third day after he had left it and set off into the taiga. His return represented victory, though he carried no proof of his triumph. He had not even taken a sled with him when he left; after all, his goal had not been to catch the bear and haul it back, but rather to kill the creature that had killed his son. His wife and daughter-in-law knew this and did not bother him with questions. Sevser however pestered his grandfather about why he had not brought the gray bear's head back, or at least the creature's paw.

Mebet smiled as he looked down on his light-haired grandson, but he did not utter a word in reply.

He ate a large portion of boiled reindeer and then laid down to sleep.

The Gods' Favorite awoke earlier than usual, took his ax, and headed for the taiga, though he did not go far. Yadne and Hadne sat at their sewing in the big chum and heard the iron strike against wood.

"Do we really not have enough firewood already?" Hadne asked.

"He knows what he's doing," Yadne replied.

He returned at sundown, and in his hands he held only the ax. The women were puzzled, but they did not try to satisfy their curiosity. They were only amazed to watch Mebet in unusually boisterous spirits as he played with his grandson.

The next morning he went into the taiga once more, and the women again heard the chopping of the ax. At midday Yadne stepped out of the chum and saw Mebet far off. He was using reins to haul something heavy from the forest, and the sight weighed heavily on her heart.

It was a hollowed log, of the sort in which the dead are placed. The Gods' Favorite had not been chopping wood but hewing this, and he had fashioned it from a whole larch trunk. He had not left it in the forest but was bringing it home, and this was intentional, for he had to show the women what task awaited them on the following day.

"Hadne, since she has good legs for walking," he told his wife, "will need to visit some of the kind people around and ask them to help her raise this up to the branches. You two wouldn't be able to manage this alone."

When his daughter-in-law came out of the chum, Mebet smiled wide and asked if she knew where some kind people lived in the vicinity.

"Everyone around us are kind people…" she replied. She still understood nothing of what was going on.

"Then hurry," Mebet said. "It would be best if they arrive by tomorrow evening, or the day after tomorrow during the day. I think that neither the spirits of the underworld nor the crows will get to me in the meantime."

He again harnessed himself to the hollowed log and hauled it back into the forest, to the same tree where Hadko's body had been laid to rest.

Yadne, in tears, followed her husband. Life with Mebet had taught her to simply accept anything that the Gods' Favorite did as something inevitable. Even this last thing she accepted without inquiring as to where it came from.

"Don't cry," Mebet said. "I'm not scared. And don't you be scared, either; don't allow yourself to be overcome with grief. You will be in no danger, I know that for sure. Go and prepare some more food. Hadne will bring some kind people here, and we must thank them for their help."

Yadne wept as she walked across the camp. She was incapable of doing anything – the meat slipped from her hands, she knocked the pot over, and boiling water doused the hearth. Hadne had to see to it all.

As Mebet patiently waited for the food, he spent time playing with his grandson, and then after dinner he crawled under the furs and fell asleep. Only grandfather and grandson slept that night. Yadne moaned, while Hadne sobbed as she held her grandson, with whom she slept in the same bed after they had lost Hadko.

Before dawn, when the moon was touching the tips of the black trees, Mebet got out of bed and said in a brisk voice as if he had never slept at all, "Here it is, the morning appointed for me."

As he stepped across the threshold, he turned and looked at his sleeping grandson, and then he went out. The light dusting of fresh snow crunched under his steps. Yadne needed time to collect herself. She stepped out of the chum and hurried after Mebet's tracks. She plunged into snow up to her knees. She noticed, though without astonishment, that the tracks that Mebet had left were not deep at all.

When Yadne caught up with her husband, he was already lying in the hollowed log. He had placed his arms along his sides and his face expressed peace. She cried out and shook Mebet by the shoulder, but he did not respond. Their daughter-in-law now came running up behind her. Hadne tore a tuft from the arctic fox fur on her collar and held it to Mebet's lips.

The fur did not tremble at any breath. Mebet was dead.

The time which Mebet had spent walking the Path of Thunder through its eleven chums of atonement, were not numbered among his days on earth. Consequently, both his wife and daughter-in-law counted that death had come for Mebet four days after he returned from hunting the gray bear. The same is believed by all who knew Mebet's life on earth. Such an error is entirely understandable, and there is little need to correct it, let alone reproach a person for it.

The reins cut into Hadne's hands and left them scarred. A white reindeer and Voipel helped her to pull Mebet's coffin up into the branches of a pine, the same tree where Hadko had been laid to rest a year before.

No kind people came from the vicinity.

Now both coffins rocked together in the branches. The Blizzard Woman was breathing heavily. Old Yadne wept, but her daughter-in-law had no time for tears. That morning she had something else on her mind than grief.

If a clan is left without its men, then women must take their place. Hadne became the head of Mebet's clan. Even when her son Sevser grew up and became a man, she remained the chief authority and would not cede that authority to anyone. She had the strength and intelligence to wield such.

No one dared lay a finger on the family of the late Gods' Favorite. The Blizzard Woman did not find a new husband; she did not even seek one. The sole time that any man came to court her, Hadne drove her suitor away with a spear. She did not want another husband after Hadko, and moreover she was not keen to yield her authority over the family to any outsider.

Yadne heeded Hadne in all things, like her daughter-in-law had once heeded her.

AFTERWORD BY SEVSER

Yadne was my grandmother, Hadne my mother. Now they are long since deceased, the wind has scattered their bones. May those bones rest in peace, may their souls rest in peace.

I, light-eyed Sevser, have told the story of my grandfather, Mebet the strong, whom people called the Gods' Favorite.

When he was still alive, I was still very small. What things I might have seen with my own eyes, I can no longer remember. But the story I have told here is the truth.

Mebet's journey along the Path of Thunder was revealed to me in a dream. I learned of it earlier than I learned the facts of my grandfather's earthly life. When I was still hardly able to utter any words and my mind could not yet make sense of what I saw, I dreamed of a tall man in a fine coat who walked over the snow. That dream came to me each night, and this went on year after year, until I had grown older and was capable of speaking intelligibly and intelligently. I told my grandmother of this dream that I kept having. Yadne did not take what I said seriously, but I was insistent, and then she asked me to describe how the man looked. I could describe him in fine detail, because I had seen the man every night and I knew him like the back of my hand.

Yadne was stunned, for she recognized her husband in this man. She asked me about the color of his hair and his eyes, the patterns embroidered on his clothing, his weapons. She asked me to describe the dog which ran alongside him. If I was unable to answer her questions right away, then I lay down to sleep, and when I woke up I could give her a perfect account. In the end, Yadne had no doubt that Mebet, her late husband, had settled into my dream world and was living a life that she knew nothing about. My grandmother in turn told my mother about all of this, and my mother was astonished.

I grew up and began to master the bow. I brought back my first catch – a small black capercaillie – but the man and his dog walking along a snowy path did not leave my dreams. They continue to dwell there to this day, when I am already old, and when none of the people who have figured in my account are still among the living. Therefore, as long as I still have breath, Mebet's story will not have arrived at its end, and I hasten to recount it to others, so that it does not vanish when I do.

In my childhood, the dog fascinated me more than the man. Voipel outlived his master by three years. When I played outside, he served as a reindeer and obediently bore me around, though he did growl when I hopped onto his elderly back with its old wounds. He went off into the taiga to die, as is the custom for dogs, when I had reached an age when I was already capable of remembering him. The dog who accompanied the man in my dreams was Voipel, I soon had no doubt about that.

When I was convinced that what I was seeing in my dreams was true, I began to pester Yadne and Hadne to tell me about Mebet's earthly life. They did so patiently, not only out of their love for me, but also because they believed my dreams to represent a manifestation from some higher power. It did not annoy them that they had to retell the same things many times, day after day, year after year. But here, too, something extraordinary happened, because in their memory the details became rougher, sparser, while my own memory grew ever more vivid. Thus, colors and smells appeared, I could distinguish voices and even feel heat and cold on my skin, wind, terror, and pain. Over the years my memory, like a tree branch, has been covered with frost in the autumn, and soon the frost has given way to snow. But the branch eventually bends under the weight, and suddenly the snow falls from it. Thus the story of my grandfather, who I do not even remember, came from my lips.

When I became a graybeard and I was left on my own, I met a man from a foreign land. His dress was not like ours and he arrived in the taiga from a country we knew nothing of. The details of his life were obscure, I learned only that his people had exiled him for some transgression which he avoided discussing even as he lived in my camp for several years and learned to speak Nenets. As a token of his gratitude for taking him in, feeding him, and treating him as my own kin, he taught me secret lore of his own people: how to set words and sounds down. He told me that words die just as animals and people do. "A word which you utter only to yourself will die with you," the man told me. "You don't have anyone living around you now, and if you have any stories which you want to outlive you, you must record them."

I replied that I did have such a story, and I told him everything which I had seen in my dreams and which I had heard about Mebet's earthly life. All this amazed the man just as much as it had once amazed my grandmother and my mother. He asked me to bring him a piece of reindeer skin and to fill a small cup with reindeer blood. He used his knife to sharpen the tip of a stick and he taught me signs – these were words that one could look upon. I learned quickly, though my wits were no longer as sharp as they had been in my younger days.

In the month when the sun rises no higher than a man's shoulder and cold sets in across the taiga, we almost never left the chum (only when nature called, or to chop wood; I had been fortunate with hunting in summer and autumn and I had stockpiled a great deal) and we dedicated ourselves to drawing these words on the deerskin. The foreigner was so taken with the story of my grandfather that he asked me to tell it again and again. He told me that we had to preserve it against oblivion so that other people could learn from it, too. I was very pleased by this. The events, which were jumbled together in my head, we set out in their proper order, as one makes a string of different-colored beads. We spent our time doing this until spring came.

When the snow began to give way and creep down from the slopes, the man disappeared. He stepped out of the chum one morning and I never saw him again. While he had been there with me in front of my very eyes, I had remembered his face and his name. Once the face disappeared, the name did, too: it was washed clean from my memory like the waters of springtime wash the leaves and needles from under the stones along the riverbank… May that man find peace if he is alive, may his bones and his soul rest in peace if he is dead. But it seems to me that the man was no human being at all. Who he was, I do not know, my heart accepts what my eyes cannot see and my mind cannot grasp. I thank you, gods. You have my eternal gratitude for being in my life and appearing to me so often in the guise of man or beast. Everything that exists in this world comes from you. Thus I am never alone, though I have had few visitors already for many years now.

Even death no longer seems so terrible now that I have the skin covered in signs made with reindeer blood. I am not afraid that it will vanish once I myself depart for the hereafter, that it might be burnt, might sink or vanish like any object might vanish. It does not worry me that among my tribespeople there is no one capable of thus preserving words on surfaces and reading there the stories that we should hear. Deep down, I feel sure that it is not my own will preserved there in the inscribed skin, it is not my own message. This will and this message are stronger than a human being's will and human words. Therefore, I feel at ease and I do not think it necessary to say anything more than what I have said.

I am worried about another thing, though not so worried that it keeps me awake at night. I know that after others discover my account, they will say that these words are all lies. Well, let them say that. To anyone who doubts, I could show them my old childhood bow with its rotting string, but why bother. Let time go by and eventually they will understand the same thing I do: there are no such things as lies. There is only truth. A lie is itself a truth, for it conceals the true desires of the liar. Is it not all the same whether a person speaks of what he saw with his own eyes, or what only existed in his mind? In the lives of animals, human beings, spirits, and gods, nothing exists independently of itself and arising only from itself. While a man is speaking the truth or only a fiction, he lives on, he does not vanish from this universe; neither in reality, nor in dreams, nor even after death will he vanish it. Everything in the world is a truth that interweaves things truly seen, traditions, speculations, life, and death. For whoever comprehends this, there is no great or small, no significant or insignificant – everything is one and all things serve one another. Therefore, believe in everything around you. Believe the friend whose path led him to you, believe the enemy who comes to kill you. Believe the swelling of the rivers and the receding of the waters. Believe truth and lies. Believe pain and pleasure. Believe dreams and reality. Even the mosquito that lands on your face, or the leaf that drops down on you, believe those things, too. They all come to you as messengers. Do not abruptly brush them off, for they will bring you nearer to the ultimate truth, and the ultimate truth will bring peace to your heart.

You might ask, "When will I reach that ultimate truth and when can I expect to find peace?" My answer is that you will hardly reach it, for it is hard to imagine anyone remaining totally unaffected by one of the countless passions. That is why people suffer, though this is suffering from blindness, not pain. It is not the person who lacks the ultimate truth who is blind, but rather the person who does not even go searching for it and who believes that everything in the world is arbitrary and meaningless.

Everything that surrounds you represents messengers from the gods, and they all bear the gods' will. But what gods, you might ask. How can you identify whose will, whose voice or sign is shown to you therein?

I will be brief: you will know these things when what has been destined comes to pass, and even then not right away. Then you – if you remain reasonable – will be able to distinguish the signs pointing to the good from those pointing to the ill. Such knowledge is the greatest of all, for it is the last understanding that comes to a man towards the end of his days. Therefore, delve deeper into what is happening within you.

Moreover, there is no especial wisdom in being able to distinguish between the gods. They move around the heavens like people move about earth, they change their names and their guises, but they remain the same gods, for all of them are – just like human beings – children of the Nameless One who created them.

You might ask how one could seek the mercy of the gods when there is no peace in the heavens, just as there is no peace on the earth. If the gods commit outrages and the lower heavens steal from the higher ones, then what could people do, for they are left with anxiety and the fear of the unknown?

I would say that you have a point there. The world is imperfect, but the will which made it is a benevolent will. Before our era there were floods that ravaged the earth and there were onslaughts of ice, and such things will happen after us as well. How many times the earth must perish before it is made perfect is something beyond human understanding. The human race will face disasters; reconcile yourself to these and accept them as a blessing, because the will of the One who created the gods, the stars, and the earth, who filled it with living beings and gave it over to man, is a benevolent will. It alone is the true good, it alone is worthy of love, and for the sake of growing nearer to it, human sufferings are never bereft of hope. Go and seek that will in the world, wherever you are.

I would like to convey one more thing to you: for the great destiny predestined for some men in the heavens to come to pass, it does not take an entire lifetime. Sometimes just as a few days or even hours before one's death, accepted calmly, will suffice.

Leo Tolstoy – Flight from Paradise
by Pavel Basinsky

Over a hundred years ago, something truly outrageous occurred at Yasnaya Polyana. Count Leo Tolstoy, a famous author aged eighty-two at the time, took off, destination unknown. Since then, the circumstances surrounding the writer's whereabouts during his final days and his eventual death have given rise to many myths and legends. In this book, popular Russian writer and reporter Pavel Basinsky delves into the archives and presents his interpretation of the situation prior to Leo Tolstoy's mysterious disappearance. Basinsky follows Leo Tolstoy throughout his life, right up to his final moments. Reconstructing the story from historical documents, he creates a visionary account of the events that led to the Tolstoys' family drama.

Flight from Paradise will be of particular interest to international researchers studying Leo Tolstoy's life and works, and is highly recommended to a broader audience worldwide.

Buy it > www.glagoslav.com

Nikolai Gumilev's Africa

Gumilev holds a unique position in the history of Russian poetry as a result of his profound involvement with Africa. He extensively wrote both poetry and prose on the culture of the continent in general and on Ethiopia (Abyssinia, as it was called in Gumilev's time) in particular. During his abbreviated lifetime Gumilev made four trips to Northern and Eastern Africa, the most extensive of which was a 1913 expedition to Abyssinia undertaken on assignment from the St. Petersburg Imperial Museum of Anthropology and Ethnography. During that trip Gumilev collected Ethiopian folklore and ethnographic objects, which, upon his return to St. Petersburg, he deposited at the Museum. He and his assistant Nikolai Sverchkov also made more than 200 photographs that offer a unique picture of the African country in the early part of the century.

This volume collects all of Gumilev's poetry and prose written about Africa for the first time as well as a number of the photographs that he and Nikolai Sverchkov took during their trip that give a fascinating view of that part of the world in the early twentieth century.

Buy it > www.glagoslav.com

Alpine Ballad
by Vasil Bykau

Towards the end of World War II, a Belarusian soldier and an Italian girl escape from a Nazi concentration camp. The soldier wonders if he should get rid of the girl; she is a burden and is slowing him down. However, he cannot bring himself to abandon her in the snowy wilderness. Somewhere along the way, the two develop feelings for each other, but their love is not destined to grow beyond the edge of the mountains. Yet their bond cannot be denied, and in the end it proves stronger than death itself.

From the master of psychological narrative whose firsthand experience with World War II enabled him to re-create the ordeal on pages of his books, *Alpine Ballad* is Vasil Bykau's most heartfelt story. Bykau sends a powerful message to his readers: human values can be extrapolated and in the context of war people can still uphold their humanity.

Buy it > www.glagoslav.com

Someone Else's Life
by Elena Dolgopyat

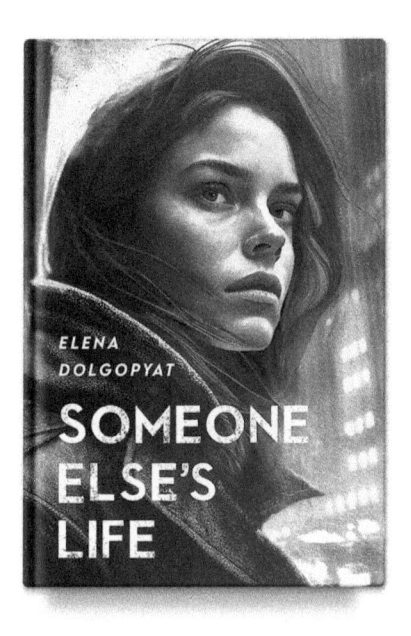

Elena Dolgopyat was born and raised in the USSR, trained as a computer programmer in a Soviet military facility, and retrained as a cinematographer post-perestroika. Fusing her diverse experiences with her own sensitivities and preoccupations, and weaving throughout a colourful thread of magic realism, she has produced an unsettling group of fifteen stories all concerned in some way with the theme of estrangement. Elena herself, in an interview given at the time of the book's launch, said, "Into each of these stories is woven the motif that one's life is 'alien'. It is as if you are separate from your own life and someone else is living it. You feel either that your own life is 'other', or you experience a yearning for a life you have not led, an envy for some other life." In his introduction to the collection, Leonid Yuzefovich writes, "Each of Elena Dolgopyat's stories … painfully stirs the soul with a sense of the fragility, the evanescence, even, of human existence … in her quiet voice, she is telling us of "the multicoloured underside of life". She is telling us of things that matter to us all."

Buy it > www.glagoslav.com

Glagoslav Publications Catalogue

- *The Time of Women* by Elena Chizhova
- *Andrei Tarkovsky: A Life on the Cross* by Lyudmila Boyadzhieva
- *Sin* by Zakhar Prilepin
- *Hardly Ever Otherwise* by Maria Matios
- *Khatyn* by Ales Adamovich
- *The Lost Button* by Irene Rozdobudko
- *Christened with Crosses* by Eduard Kochergin
- *The Vital Needs of the Dead* by Igor Sakhnovsky
- *The Sarabande of Sara's Band* by Larysa Denysenko
- *A Poet and Bin Laden* by Hamid Ismailov
- *Zo Gaat Dat in Rusland* (Dutch Edition) by Maria Konjoekova
- *Kobzar* by Taras Shevchenko
- *The Stone Bridge* by Alexander Terekhov
- *Moryak* by Lee Mandel
- *King Stakh's Wild Hunt* by Uladzimir Karatkevich
- *The Hawks of Peace* by Dmitry Rogozin
- *Harlequin's Costume* by Leonid Yuzefovich
- *Depeche Mode* by Serhii Zhadan
- *Groot Slem en Andere Verhalen* (Dutch Edition) by Leonid Andrejev
- *METRO 2033* (Dutch Edition) by Dmitry Glukhovsky
- *METRO 2034* (Dutch Edition) by Dmitry Glukhovsky
- *A Russian Story* by Eugenia Kononenko
- *Herstories, An Anthology of New Ukrainian Women Prose Writers*
- *The Battle of the Sexes Russian Style* by Nadezhda Ptushkina
- *A Book Without Photographs* by Sergey Shargunov
- *Down Among The Fishes* by Natalka Babina
- *disUNITY* by Anatoly Kudryavitsky
- *Sankya* by Zakhar Prilepin
- *Wolf Messing* by Tatiana Lungin
- *Good Stalin* by Victor Erofeyev
- *Solar Plexus* by Rustam Ibragimbekov
- *Don't Call me a Victim!* by Dina Yafasova
- *Poetin* (Dutch Edition) by Chris Hutchins and Alexander Korobko

- *A History of Belarus* by Lubov Bazan
- *Children's Fashion of the Russian Empire* by Alexander Vasiliev
- *Empire of Corruption: The Russian National Pastime* by Vladimir Soloviev
- *Heroes of the 90s: People and Money. The Modern History of Russian Capitalism* by Alexander Solovev, Vladislav Dorofeev and Valeria Bashkirova
- *Fifty Highlights from the Russian Literature* (Dutch Edition) by Maarten Tengbergen
- *Bajesvolk* (Dutch Edition) by Michail Chodorkovsky
- *Dagboek van Keizerin Alexandra* (Dutch Edition)
- *Myths about Russia* by Vladimir Medinskiy
- *Boris Yeltsin: The Decade that Shook the World* by Boris Minaev
- *A Man Of Change: A study of the political life of Boris Yeltsin*
- *Sberbank: The Rebirth of Russia's Financial Giant* by Evgeny Karasyuk
- *To Get Ukraine* by Oleksandr Shyshko
- *Asystole* by Oleg Pavlov
- *Gnedich* by Maria Rybakova
- *Marina Tsvetaeva: The Essential Poetry*
- *Multiple Personalities* by Tatyana Shcherbina
- *The Investigator* by Margarita Khemlin
- *The Exile* by Zinaida Tulub
- *Leo Tolstoy: Flight from Paradise* by Pavel Basinsky
- *Moscow in the 1930* by Natalia Gromova
- *Laurus* (Dutch edition) by Evgenij Vodolazkin
- *Prisoner* by Anna Nemzer
- *The Crime of Chernobyl: The Nuclear Goulag* by Wladimir Tchertkoff
- *Alpine Ballad* by Vasil Bykau
- *The Complete Correspondence of Hryhory Skovoroda*
- *The Tale of Aypi* by Ak Welsapar
- *Selected Poems* by Lydia Grigorieva
- *The Fantastic Worlds of Yuri Vynnychuk*
- *The Garden of Divine Songs and Collected Poetry of Hryhory Skovoroda*
- *Adventures in the Slavic Kitchen: A Book of Essays with Recipes* by Igor Klekh
- *Seven Signs of the Lion* by Michael M. Naydan

- *Forefathers' Eve* by Adam Mickiewicz
- *One-Two* by Igor Eliseev
- *Girls, be Good* by Bojan Babić
- *Time of the Octopus* by Anatoly Kucherena
- *The Grand Harmony* by Bohdan Ihor Antonych
- *The Selected Lyric Poetry Of Maksym Rylsky*
- *The Shining Light* by Galymkair Mutanov
- *The Frontier: 28 Contemporary Ukrainian Poets - An Anthology*
- *Acropolis: The Wawel Plays* by Stanisław Wyspiański
- *Contours of the City* by Attyla Mohylny
- *Conversations Before Silence: The Selected Poetry of Oles Ilchenko*
- *The Secret History of my Sojourn in Russia* by Jaroslav Hašek
- *Mirror Sand: An Anthology of Russian Short Poems*
- *Maybe We're Leaving* by Jan Balaban
- *Death of the Snake Catcher* by Ak Welsapar
- *A Brown Man in Russia* by Vijay Menon
- *Hard Times* by Ostap Vyshnia
- *The Flying Dutchman* by Anatoly Kudryavitsky
- *Nikolai Gumilev's Africa* by Nikolai Gumilev
- *Combustions* by Srđan Srdić
- *The Sonnets* by Adam Mickiewicz
- *Dramatic Works* by Zygmunt Krasiński
- *Four Plays* by Juliusz Słowacki
- *Little Zinnobers* by Elena Chizhova
- *We Are Building Capitalism! Moscow in Transition 1992-1997* by Robert Stephenson
- *The Nuremberg Trials* by Alexander Zvyagintsev
- *The Hemingway Game* by Evgeni Grishkovets
- *A Flame Out at Sea* by Dmitry Novikov
- *Jesus' Cat* by Grig
- *Want a Baby and Other Plays* by Sergei Tretyakov
- *Mikhail Bulgakov: The Life and Times* by Marietta Chudakova
- *Leonardo's Handwriting* by Dina Rubina
- *A Burglar of the Better Sort* by Tytus Czyżewski
- *The Mouseiad and other Mock Epics* by Ignacy Krasicki
- *Ravens before Noah* by Susanna Harutyunyan

- *An English Queen and Stalingrad* by Natalia Kulishenko
- *Point Zero* by Narek Malian
- *Absolute Zero* by Artem Chekh
- *Olanda* by Rafał Wojasiński
- *Robinsons* by Aram Pachyan
- *The Monastery* by Zakhar Prilepin
- *The Selected Poetry of Bohdan Rubchak: Songs of Love, Songs of Death, Songs of the Moon*
- *Mebet* by Alexander Grigorenko
- *The Orchestra* by Vladimir Gonik
- *Everyday Stories* by Mima Mihajlović
- *Slavdom* by Ľudovít Štúr
- *The Code of Civilization* by Vyacheslav Nikonov
- *Where Was the Angel Going?* by Jan Balaban
- *De Zwarte Kip* (Dutch Edition) by Antoni Pogorelski
- *Głosy / Voices* by Jan Polkowski
- *Sergei Tretyakov: A Revolutionary Writer in Stalin's Russia* by Robert Leach
- *Opstand* (Dutch Edition) by Władysław Reymont
- *Dramatic Works* by Cyprian Kamil Norwid
- *Children's First Book of Chess* by Natalie Shevando and Matthew McMillion
- *Precursor* by Vasyl Shevchuk
- *The Vow: A Requiem for the Fifties* by Jiří Kratochvil
- *De Bibliothecaris* (Dutch edition) by Mikhail Jelizarov
- *Subterranean Fire* by Natalka Bilotserkivets
- *Vladimir Vysotsky: Selected Works*
- *Behind the Silk Curtain* by Gulistan Khamzayeva
- *The Village Teacher and Other Stories* by Theodore Odrach
- *Duel* by Borys Antonenko-Davydovych
- *War Poems* by Alexander Korotko
- *Ballads and Romances* by Adam Mickiewicz
- *The Revolt of the Animals* by Wladyslaw Reymont
- *Poems about my Psychiatrist* by Andrzej Kotański
- *Someone Else's Life* by Elena Dolgopyat
- *Liza's Waterfall: The hidden story of a Russian feminist* by Pavel Basinsky
- *Biography of Sergei Prokofiev* by Igor Vishnevetsky

More coming . . .

GLAGOSLAV PUBLICATIONS
www.glagoslav.com

Milton Keynes UK
Ingram Content Group UK Ltd.
UKHW012142041223
433798UK00003B/84